HOT KEYS

HOT KEYS

by

R.E. Ward

2022

This Trade Paperback Original Is Published By
Bold Strokes Books, Inc.
P.O. Box 249
Valley Falls, NY 12185

First Edition: November 2022

CREDITS

Editors: Jenny Harmon and Cindy Cresap
Production Design: Susan Ramundo
Cover Design By Tammy Seidick

Acknowledgments

Firstly, I want to thank my parents. Mom and Dad, you always believe in me and it makes such a difference. I love you both.

I also want to thank the whole crew at BSB for guiding me through this process and for all their hard work. Special thanks to Jennifer Harmon for taking a rough novel and wrangling it into shape with me.

And finally, thank you, Elizabeth, for listening to me talk incessantly about this novel and for being by my side the entire way. I love you.

Dedication

To Liz, my love and the light of my life.

Chapter One

Singing was all about breath control. Betty May knew this intimately. As a singer, she needed to take deep breaths, from the diaphragm. Shoulders back and relaxed. Stand up straight, and let your voice project out to the world. New York City was, to Betty, a living, breathing entity. A set of lungs inhaling deeply. In her mind, the automobiles and horses and chatter of people walking the streets were the city's voice. New York singing its heart out. Sometimes it felt like it was singing just for her.

Tonight, she was exhausted. Her boss had kept her late typing up some boring document, but she wouldn't let it get her down. The city's song breathed life back into her. Made her itch to sing along. If only she had someplace to do it besides her little apartment.

Moving to New York from Wisconsin had been her dream since she was a little girl. She and her best friend, Jack, would take over the city as famous musicians. In her mind's eye it was glorious, a life of glitz and glamour and joy. It was a far cry from the empty belly life she was living at the moment, but she wouldn't give up. Her New York dreams were too big to ever give up on.

Betty hummed to herself as she walked home. Her office job as a secretary was boring. Soul sucking. The kind of thing she wasn't suited for at all. She was too saucy by half to be any good at talking with the men who visited her office. They were all stuffy and uptight businessmen who couldn't take a joke. Or worse, lecherous pigs who looked at her like they owned her. Betty May belonged to no one.

The sound of bright, cheerful laughter snapped Betty out of her morose musings. Across the street she saw a group of three women giggling as they stumbled their way into an alley. They were gorgeous. All three of them wore beaded dresses that barely skimmed the bottom of their knees, showing off their shapely legs. Feathers adorned their bobbed hair, and rouge painted their cheeks. They were a vision. She knew immediately that wherever these women were headed was where she wanted to be.

She darted across the street, abandoning her walk home for the promise of adventure.

Betty watched quietly from the mouth of the alley as the girls flung open a nondescript-looking door and wobbled their way inside. She crept after them, peeking around the door. One of the girls knocked three times, then once more after a pause. Huh. Now what was that about?

"Was that the right password?" another girl asked.

Before anyone could answer, the door swung open, revealing a large man. Music filled the air, along with the sound of chattering voices. Of course! This had to be one of those speakeasies she'd heard rumor of. The girls tumbled through the door, and then it was closed firmly behind them, leaving her in silence. Well. Silence just wouldn't do. Not while there was the tantalizing promise of something exciting just beyond the door in front of her.

She wasn't exactly dressed properly, wearing a sensible belted navy blouse and a white pleated skirt that brushed her ankles, but she strode forward with confidence nonetheless and knocked the secret knock. The huge man opened the door, and Betty May found herself curtseying with a saucy little wink. "Hello! I'm Betty May, how do you do?" The man just looked at her, before stepping aside to gesture her in.

Entering the room beyond was like stepping into another world.

There was a haze over the whole place that made it seem all the more mysterious, as the smoke from the patron's cigarettes wafted playfully through the air.

And the outfits! Girls in knee-length dresses, draped in beads and sparkling shawls with their hair coiffed and decorated with feathers and glittering jewels that caught the light. Compared to them she felt like a wren in the presence of a room full of peacocks. How was it possible for so many beautiful women to be in one space?

Not to be outdone, the men wore dashing suits, some of them having already sloughed off their jackets, revealing suspenders and crisp white shirts.

Shadowy corners lurked at the edges of a dance floor, dark and inviting. And off to the side was a bar. If the dance floor had been a sight to behold, the bar was on a whole new level of bedazzlement, with electric lighting illuminating it like a beacon of hope for the weary soul in need of a drink. Promising liquid salvation on its sawdust-covered floors.

She wandered along the edge of the dance floor in awe. Bodies swayed and jumped, and Betty was sorely tempted to join them.

But then she saw it.

Up at the front of the room was an empty stage, with a baby grand piano covered in cloth sitting woefully silent. And a lonely microphone that called to her like a lover from across the room. Betty smiled as an idea crystalized in her mind. With newly found determination, she marched her way over to the bar.

Yes, this was going to change their lives. She just knew it.

❖

Rain was a musical instrument that few men could rival. Not that Jack Norval would ever try to. Why try to outshine greatness when you could play along with it? After all, a piano on its own was no band.

So, on days when the sky opened up and the thought of venturing outside made him shiver, he could often be found at the bench of his old piano. His fingers mirroring the pitter-patter of the rain as they flew over the keys as if under a spell, he'd let the staccato rhythm of the drops be his metronome. Let the gentle sound of it conduct a song all its own, with him to play along.

It was one of the reasons he loved rainy days so much. Of course, he was never so jovial when he had to go out and get wet, but he'd be lying if he said that the mere sound of a shower didn't make his fingers itch to press against ivory, no matter where he was or how sodden his clothes might get. Today, drops of rain beat out a jaunty tune against the windowpanes, but for once, Jack wasn't inclined to play along. In fact, his well-worn piano stood quiet in the corner as he waited anxiously for his housemate to emerge from her room.

He shuffled his feet along the crack formed by the floorboards shifting over time. It was a dangerous little thing, the kind that could catch a toe easily if you weren't paying attention. They'd asked the landlady if she would fix it a while ago and had only gotten an unimpressed grunt in response. She hadn't even looked up from her newspaper. It didn't seem too promising, but Jack had a good feeling about it. She'd be sending a handyman up any day now…probably.

"Hey, maybe we should call this off," he said. He toed at the spot where the crack ended, before turning to follow it all the way back, his hands firmly in his pockets. "I mean, it's raining pitchforks out there. We should probably just stick to home for today. Wouldn't wanna catch a cold, especially you, Bets. Gotta keep those pipes in good, working condition, right?"

"Jack Edward Norval, if you think a little rain can stop me from getting us this gig, you're screwier than I thought." Her lilting voice came from the bedroom, clear as day through her half-opened door. It was downright indecent how little shame

Betty had about getting changed with her door open. "This place is right on the outskirts of Tin Pan Alley. Come on, Jacky boy, this is our dream!"

"No! Our dream is to be real artists, not some low-life criminals playing at a juice joint!"

The click-click-click of Betty's heels was all the warning he got before he was faced with an eyeful of his annoyed roommate. She was hardly dressed, wearing a red drop waist dress that barely amounted to a shift in Jack's eyes. It barely covered her knees! And her arms were practically bare, with only a black beaded shawl to cover them. Though the ridiculous amount of makeup on her face almost made up for it with its coverage. Still, despite the impropriety of her standing there like that, he couldn't help but feel a warm rush of affection for her. She was gorgeous, petite with long legs, shiny brown hair cut in a short bob, and big beautiful green eyes—the kind of girl any Tom, Dick, or Harry would go wild for.

"Bets!" he protested. "You're hardly dressed."

She huffed a laugh at him and cocked her hip. "I'm positive I don't need to worry about that." She winked, and he had to look away as his face warmed. "Look, Jack, we haven't eaten anything but potatoes and hotdogs for a week now. If we don't get work soon, we're going to starve," she continued, serious as a funeral. "I know you're too straitlaced for this kind of work, but you gotta trust me. All you have to do is play. And I know you can play, right?"

Jack nodded, fingers toying with the strap of the bag on his shoulder. She was right, as always. No matter how in his own head he got, she always had a way of bringing him back down to earth. There was no other girl in the world like her. Shame hit him like a baseball bat to the gut. She deserved better than this life. She deserved the Ritz, and here he was offering her nothing but a tiny New York apartment.

Some friend he was.

"Yeah, you know I can," he sighed. "I'm sorry, Bets, it's just...I don't like it. Places like that are filled with cons and gangsters, and I don't want us caught up in that kind of business," he said, frowning.

Betty tapped her chunky heel against the worn-out floor, making it clear by her expression that she wasn't impressed one bit by his impression of the place. He was right though.

According to her, they needed money from a drunken and rowdy group who tipped as big as they lived. She'd smelled of gin and smoke when she'd staggered in that night, elated at finding this place. The smell had been strong enough that he'd have believed she was on a bender if he hadn't known better. She wasn't that keen on drinking, and he could count on one hand the number of times he'd seen her drunk. And she always told him that smoking was bad for her voice.

Personally, Jack found it all a bit nerve-wracking. "But we need the money," he relented.

"We sure do, baby boy." She grinned at him, punching his shoulder harder than one would expect from a skinny bird like Betty May. "Don't worry so much. And fetch the umbrella. We don't need to show up all wet for our audition."

"Don't you need to get dressed?"

She looked at him unimpressed. "Don't be stupid, sweetie, I am dressed! Come on." She grabbed his hand and aggressively towed him toward the door before he could protest. He hurriedly grabbed ahold of the polished wooden handle of his umbrella, half convinced she might tear his arm off at the delay.

"Betty..." He stopped himself, stamping down his old Midwestern sensibilities. For having hated the stuffiness of his hometown so much, he sure did find himself clinging to those very same values he'd scoffed at.

Thankfully, Betty was too excited to have even heard him and she let the sound of her name pass by like an automobile down the sodden streets.

The rain-slick sidewalks did little to improve Jack's nerves or the grim mood that settled on him like a damp blanket. Despite taking to life in New York like an admittedly clumsy fish to the water, there was nothing good that could possibly happen at a veritable den of sin to the likes of which they were heading. Of that he was certain. The laid-back attitude of the city had been a breath of not-so-fresh air at first. But now, three years into living here, he was starting to realize that a loosening of morals wasn't always the best thing.

"Relax," Betty chided him. "You're so stiff. You gotta have loose fingers for tonight."

Jack blinked, flabbergasted. "You can't be suggesting that I'll…That I'm going to…"

Betty's raucous disbelieving laughter was sort of insulting, and louder than it needed to be. "You dumb lug, I meant for the piano! Christ, Jack, I'm going to smear my damn makeup, I'm tearing up."

"Well, it's not *that* unbelievable." Jack made a displeased sound, face reddening. Betty was still giggling, dabbing delicately at her face with a handkerchief. "Of course not, sweetie. Especially at a place like this. They have all sorts of people there." She paused, elbowing him in the side a bit harder than Jack thought necessary. "You know, at a place like this I betcha there'll be a lot of other—"

"What's this place called again?" he interrupted, a tad desperately. Betty gave him a far-too-knowing look, but let him get away with it anyway.

"The Trespass Inn," she said, grinning brightly at him. "Cute, right? And close by too. It's like a dream come true." Jack bit his tongue. If it was a dream, he thought it far more likely to be the kind where you were being chased by vicious old women with teeth like bears, or the ones where you've just fallen asleep only to be jarred awake by the sensation of falling. But Betty was happy. Happier than he'd seen her in a long while. And her dresses had been fitting far more loosely than they ever had before. So, he smiled wanly, and let her warm up her voice as they walked side by side, snapping his fingers every once in a while like a metronome to keep her in time.

"We're here," she said, nodding to a line of shops across the street from them.

Jack scanned the line of old storefronts, but all he could see was a butcher's shop, a fabric store, an Italian restaurant called Gino's, and a sign proclaiming there to be a psychic named Madame La Utirips in one of the apartment spaces above the stores.

"Are you sure? Where's the sign?"

Betty patted his arm. "It's a juice joint, Jacky. There is no sign. C'mon."

She led him around to a small alley between two shops, all the way up to another door. The curling edges of the same Psychic Medium poster that was around front mirrored Jack's urge to curl in on himself as Betty yanked open the door without so much as a knock.

Beyond the door, looming in the narrow entryway were two staircases, one leading up into darkness and one leading down into more darkness. Neither way seemed all that appealing. Grasping his elbow, Betty marched him down the rickety stairs, past slightly damp barren walls, down to yet another door. This one, complete with peeling paint and a missing doorknob was chained shut with a peephole that was currently closed.

There was muffled music playing from behind the door, the familiar strains of Leo Reisman that Jack would recognize anywhere. Taking a breath, Betty raised her hand and knocked, three quick raps in a row followed by a pause and one more rap.

The peephole slid open and a large man looked out at them. He had the type of face that communicated without words that no nonsense would be suffered. Jack was pretty sure this guy could snap them both in half at the same time without a second thought and probably without much provocation.

Automatic words of an apology were on the tip of his tongue when Betty beamed at the man and said, "Hiya! Remember me? We're here to audition."

The man looked silently between the two of them, as if sizing them up. Jack was just about to turn tail and flee when the door swung open. He was bigger than Jack had guessed, but instead of moving toward them threateningly, he nodded sternly and moved aside to let them in.

They stepped through the door and Jack could barely believe his eyes. The space was a wide-open boxy room, with a smattering of seating off to the right and an enormous bar made of dark wood to the left. But the main attraction was the wide-open space between the door and the slightly raised stage at the other end of the room. Jack could only assume that it was meant to be a dance floor, as the few people who had arrived by this time were flocking to it, dancing with a wild abandon that had Jack floored. He'd never seen dancing like this. Not since he'd arrived in the city, and *certainly* not back in his stuffy old Midwestern town.

Smoke swirled through the air in lazy spirals, wrapping the sparse crowd in a haze as it rose from a dozen or so cigarettes. It twirled like one of the dancers, caressing the glitz of the patrons' outfits and the smooth stretches of skin on display.

Jack promptly began hacking up a lung, deep phlegmy sounds wracking themselves from his chest.

"Jack?" Betty asked, concern clear in her voice.

"I'm fine, I'm fine," he spluttered, waving her off. "It's just...just *hazy* in here."

Betty rolled her eyes at him, but her hand was still in his. Anchoring him to her, and the comfort of her presence. "Come on, you big lug," she said, pulling him along behind her. "They told me last night that we gotta talk to whoever's at the bar."

A group of drunk women laughed and staggered past them, one of them knocking against him without even realizing it. They smelled strongly of alcohol and perfume, and they could barely walk straight. Part of him, the part that grew up amid cornfields in Wisconsin, was horrified at this display, while another part, buried deep and quieter, was glad that they were having fun. That secret part of him desperately wanted to feel as free as they seemed to be.

The man behind the illegal bar who was pouring drinks looked to be no older than his mid-thirties, with dirty blond hair cut short and styled back with grease. It was a style that Jack wasn't sure he could ever pull off, making him look like a man about town while toeing the line of how Jack expected a gangster to look. He had pale white skin and the sort of serene look on his face of someone who was at peace with his lot in life. His hat was tossed onto a bottle on the shelf behind the bar. The bar that was chock-full of liquor. Jack had never seen so much booze all in one place before. It glimmered under the bare bulb lighting, a rainbow hue of bottles with mysterious liquids held in their depths.

It was wild. It was terrifying.

If they were caught here, who knew what would happen. Never mind that neither of them had even touched a drop of liquor, Jack had heard that the police came down hard on anyone who even spent time at an illegal bar like this.

He could imagine what Betty's mother would say if she got arrested for patronizing a *juice joint*. God, she'd never forgive him, never mind that it was Betty's idea to be here in the first place, and he was the tagalong. He could practically feel her disapproving glare from a thousand miles away.

"Hi there." Betty greeted the bartender with a brilliant smile, trying to look like she didn't have a care in the world. "I'm Betty May Dewitt, and this here is Jack Norval. We're here to audition."

The man eyed Jack with interest, an appraising glance over. "You sure you two can play the kind of music we need?" he asked, and though his tone was not unkind, the question set Jack on edge.

Lord, it was strange, hearing those words here in a dingy juice joint when all his life they'd been uttered by fancy, city music academy staff. Though for them, he'd been too rough-and-tumble. A dirty country boy who could probably only play chopsticks on his mama's old worn-out piano.

And now here he was, being judged by this man for no doubt being *too* straitlaced to play at his rundown bar. A flush suffused his neck, for once born from pride and not self-consciousness, and before Betty could answer for them, he blurted out, "If it's music, I can play it. As long as your piano works, of course."

The man's eyebrows climbed up toward his hairline, but he was smiling, an impressed little smirk. "All right. I'm Charlie. Why don't you follow me and we'll see what you've got," he said, and finally offered his hand to shake. Handshakes completed, Charlie turned, leading them toward the stage, and Betty cozied up beside Jack, buzzing with excitement.

"Jacky boy! Look at you being all assertive," she crooned.

Jack huffed in response. "Yes, well. I'm getting real tired of people assuming."

Betty's eyes were blazing when he glanced at her. But then they were at the stage stairs, and Jack saw a beautifully maintained baby grand, the likes of which stood out like a sore thumb amidst the rundown interior of the bar.

"Oh," he said softly. He approached the piano as though she were a wild mare, skittish and shy, and grazed his hand over her polished black top. She was gorgeous. He was already in love.

"Ready to wow 'em, Jacky?" Betty asked. When he looked over to her, she was already cradling the mic stand like a lover between her hands.

"Sure thing, Bets," he said, certain that he was. He'd brought his own sheet music in his bag, but he didn't need it. He had their songs by heart, and if he got the chance, he knew he could improvise something so lively that even *this* crowd would have to exhaust themselves to keep up.

Charlie turned the gramophone off, grinning when the crowd erupted into complaints and boos. "Come on now, folks,"

Charlie said, using the second microphone to address the crowd. "Wouldn't you all prefer some live music to dance to?"

"You know we would, Charlie," someone yelled from the crowd. Jack felt the familiar thrill of being in front of an audience, a perfect combination of confidence and nerves. He glanced up at Betty, who shot him a wide smile and a small wink, confidence practically pouring from her.

"Then pipe down and let me introduce our entertainment for tonight," Charlie continued. Just like that the buzz of annoyance changed to one of mounting excitement. Charlie had a natural way with the crowd, something about the way he spoke made it feel like he was a close friend in on a joke. He spoke to the quickly growing crowd like pals, as patrons in the back booths abandoned their posts and crept closer to the stage, enticed by the promise of music.

"And now, presenting for the very first time at the Trespass Inn, Mr. Jack Norval on keys, and Miss Betty May Dewitt," Charlie roared over the hubbub of the crowd, who welcomed them with a swell of loud and slightly wobbly cheers and whistles.

Elation buzzed through Jack's veins now. No matter where they were, a crowd was a crowd, and Jack lived for the moment when the sound of clapping matched the wildly racing rhythm of his heartbeat. "It's pronounced Betty May Do-it," Betty purred into the microphone, causing an even more uproarious swell of clapping, cheering, and hoots and hollers. Jack barely held back a laugh at that. Her last name wasn't even Dewitt, it was Felton. But she loved the drama, and the titillating appeal that came from the double entendre.

"Thank you for the introduction, Charlie boy," she continued, then turned to him and winked. "Hit it, Jack!" So, Jack did. He played hot and fast, delighting in the way Betty kept with him every step of the way. He played like a man on fire, and Betty sang her heart out, and song after song the crowd screamed and hollered and cheered like they were Cole Porter and Bessie Smith up on the stage. Jack felt the music through his fingertips all the way up to the roots of his hair, and he went wild with his improvisation, making the piano soar with jazz tunes that had the whole speakeasy dancing with abandon.

By the time they finished their set, the crowds were screaming for more, and with a nod from Charlie, Jack and Betty were happy to oblige them. This was where they both felt most alive. Jack with his fingers blurring along ivory keys and Betty dancing and singing and riling the crowd up higher and higher into a frenzy. When they finally did have to stop, or risk exhaustion, the whole speakeasy gave them a rafter shaking round of applause.

"Jacky, that was the cat's meow! My God, I thought your fingers were gonna burn up!" Betty thrilled, grabbing onto his arm as they waved and bowed before making their way off stage as the gramophone started back up.

"I thought the angels had come down, Bets," he said back, smile wide and just as thrilled. "You sang your heart out!"

Betty bounced on her heels, and then let go of his arm to do a little twirl. "Ahh, Jack! Honey, there's no way he can say no to us now! I'm going over there to talk to Charlie. You coming with me?"

Suddenly it was like the room snapped back into focus, and Jack remembered where they were and why they were there. God, they were in an illegal juice joint. How could he have ever forgotten that, music or no? "I think I'll stay here for a bit," he said weakly, staring at the dance floor teeming with skin and glitter between them and the bar. "Meet me back here?"

"Will do, Jacky boy!" she sang out, and kissed his cheek before weaving expertly through the dancers.

"Woo! That canary sure has some pipes," a man said almost the moment she was gone, sidling up beside Jack. "She's quite a Sheba, ain't she? Is she your gal?"

Jack glared at him. Betty didn't need his protection, but that didn't mean that he didn't feel protective nonetheless. "No," he replied tersely. "She doesn't *belong* to anyone."

This new interloper didn't seem to catch his drift though, because all he did was smile in delight and ask, "So you think I got a chance with her?"

"No," Jack answered again, looking the man up and down. He was shorter than Jack by about a head, but for all that, he still seemed far more confident than Jack had ever felt in his life. His brown hair was a mess, as though he'd been running his hands through it all night, and it was long enough that it nearly reached his large deep brown eyes. His grin was crooked and he looked far too nice under the seating area lighting.

"Aw damn," he said, though he didn't seem too put out by it. "Dunno why. I'm a real catch." He smiled that crooked smile right at Jack, like he thought he'd agree. "Name's Sammy, by the way." He threw his arm around Jack's shoulder rather than shaking his hand. He smelled of liquor so strong that Jack half expected to feel wetness between them from a spill. But his side remained surprisingly dry.

"I'm Jack," he replied as kindly as he could manage while trying to shake himself loose from the vice grip of the rum-soaked fool.

"Jack," Sam said, rolling the name around on his tongue like he was trying to get a feel for it. "Jaaaack. All right. Like a big ol' wad of cash," he giggled, apparently not noticing Jack's feverish attempts to shake him off.

"Get off of me," he finally said, and was surprised when Sam did.

"S'okay, Money. You don't gotta shout," Sam shouted, right as the gramophone went silent between songs.

"Christ. Go drink some water," Jack snapped. He was certain that Sam was moments away from dying of alcohol poisoning. He felt like he was getting drunk just by proximity to him and his fumes.

"M'kay. I'm gonna go upchuck first though," Sam said, patting Jack's shoulder dismissively. He wandered drunkenly away toward the exit rather than the washroom that was right next to them.

"My God," Jack muttered to himself, watching him go. "This place is full of fools." Before he could spiral too much into the depths of anxiety where he found himself, Betty was bouncing back over to him. The smile on her face was like the sun, and Jack knew with a sinking certainty that he wasn't going to like what she was about to say.

"We're hired, Jacky boy! We are now officially night owls employed by the Trespass Inn!" she said, doing a little twirl to the music. Over her shoulder he could see Sam (he refused to call him Sammy) vomiting all over the stairs right before the door swung closed again.

"This place is…" Jack paused, trying to think up a phrase that encapsulated just how repulsive it was. "A hotbed of sin," he settled on, cringing even as he said it. He sounded like Mrs. Brant, his old devoutly Christian music teacher back in Wisconsin.

Betty giggled, slapping his arm. "My God, Jack. You sound stuffy as all get-out," she said, laughing even harder as a man tumbled to the floor in front of them, then looked around in confusion, as though he wasn't quite sure how he got there. His laughing companion stooped down to help him to his feet, swaying as she did, her crouch revealing the lacey top of her stocking. It was an absolute spectacle of debauchery.

"You better get used to it, honey," Betty added, kissing his cheek. "This place is our new home."

❖

They returned the next day, this time during the daylight hours. Betty felt almost bad for Jack. The poor guy was clearly a nervous wreck, with his hands shoved into his pockets and his teeth gnawing away at his lower lip.

"We don't *have* to do this, Bets," he said for what seemed like the thousandth time, hesitating outside of the door to the stairway. "I could get another job. Three jobs wouldn't be so bad."

"Jack," she said sternly. "You won't even need *two* jobs if this pans out. I promise you, there's good money in this. Plus, Charlie said we get to keep all of our tips!" Betty anticipated getting a truly large number of tips. After all, she knew exactly how good she and Jack were, and how much they deserved. Now if only she could get *Jack* to see it.

"All right," he said reluctantly, as he let her lead him down the rickety old stairs. "But I like my job teaching kids piano," he added sullenly. "I'm not quitting that."

"Yes, honey, I know," she replied gaily as she opened the door. He really was such a sweetheart.

The speakeasy was empty this time except for a small group of men standing at the bar. There was Charlie, who she recognized, standing next to an incredibly muscular Black man. He was taller than Charlie by about an inch and had been smiling right up until he saw them, at which point his expression shifted into something tough and closed off. A mean expression that made him look less handsome than he had when he'd been smiling.

Off to the side there was a smaller man, who looked all the smaller by his loose-fitting clothes. His hair was a dark brown and styled messily, and he was leaning against the bar with a wide grin and a look of mischief in his expression. He was Italian, with dark hair and eyes.

Sitting beside the Italian man was the hulking white man with sandy hair who'd manned the doors the previous night. She knew from her chat with Charlie after their performance that his name was George.

"Hello there," Betty said cheerfully, towing a hesitant Jack along behind her. "Charlie boy, it's good to see you!" she cooed, with a hint of a suggestive lilt to her voice. He was quite the looker, and Betty would be lying if she said she wasn't interested in him as a fling. She liked to have fun, but falling in love wasn't her style.

"I'm Betty May, and this here is Jack," she said, holding out her hand for the Black man to shake. He seemed surprised by the gesture, but took her hand, nonetheless.

"The name's Leroy," he said, shaking her hand firmly. "I'm part owner here with Charlie. He's been telling us good things about you. And this over here is Sammy Esposito." He pointed a thumb toward the man at the other end of the bar, who perked up like a dog at the sound of his name.

"Hey, Money! Good to see ya again," he said to Jack, who looked like he'd rather swallow a raw fish whole than be there at the moment. "And it's a pleasure to meet you, Miss Betty." He held out his hand and shook hers with much more enthusiasm than Leroy had, with a firm grasp and an enthusiastic up-down pump.

"Leroy and Sammy," she said, smiling her most winning smile. "I'll be sure to remember the names. And George! It's lovely to see you again, big guy!" she added, getting a quiet smile in response.

"Good to meet you," Jack mumbled, shaking Leroy's hand. To anyone else Betty was sure he must look stuffy as all get-out, but she could tell that it was entirely nerves. He was eyeing their surroundings with trepidation, as though he was going to need an escape and was already plotting their route, his normally friendly smile tight with anxiety.

He looked so out of place here among these men.

He wasn't weak by any stretch of the imagination. He couldn't have been what with having had to work the cornfields back home. But he didn't look nearly as…scrappy as these fellas did. It was clear to see that any one of these other men were ready for a fight at the drop of a hat.

Jack's muscle definition was already starting to disappear from their cushy New York life, not to mention their lack of good food lately. And Jack, unlike the others, needed something worth fighting for to ever turn to violence. He'd only once punched anyone at all, and it was the man who'd tried to kiss her without her consent at a party. So really, the guy had had it coming. But of course, being around all of these men was making him, quite reasonably, anxious.

Betty, on the other hand, wasn't all that nervous. She had a good feeling about these men, and she was confident that she'd already started to charm them. It wasn't all that hard to charm a man, really. A few smiles, a lingering touch, and for those who weren't interested, a sunny disposition was all it took to wrap a man around your finger.

"Now, if you're going to work here, you need to know the rules," Leroy said menacingly, getting right into it. "And here's the first one. Our business *stays* our business, you understand me?" Jack nodded so quickly it was almost funny, clearly intimidated. Hell, to be fair Betty was too. But she wasn't going to let it show.

"A lot of things happen here," Charlie picked up for Leroy, much less aggressively. "And we don't go blabbing about those things to anyone but our own. Not even patrons."

"Of course," Jack said immediately.

"Understood," Betty said, serious as a funeral. She'd figured as much, considering the whole damn place was illegal as it could get. She just hoped they weren't into anything too sinister, like what the mobsters they talked about in the papers were getting up to. She'd never forgive herself if she got Jack caught up in something like that.

"We run a relatively clean establishment here, so no funny business. We catch you trying to sell your own alcohol or anything like that, you're out, got it?" Charlie told them seriously.

"Right, because a juice joint is such a fine upstanding business," Jack laughed in disbelief. No one seemed to mind, thank God, except for Sammy. He perked up like a dog who'd spotted a squirrel, the urge to fight practically radiating from him.

"All right, you don't have to be such an upstage asshole," Sammy said defiantly. He leaned forward like he wanted to get into Jack's face, but wasn't quite ready to give up his comfortable lean. It was almost cute, like when a little dog got feisty and nipped at your fingers, except that she was certain Sammy could do *a lot* more damage to Jack than a little dog could.

But Jack just glared right back at him, jaw clenched. "I'm just telling the truth. I don't know if you realize, but your work here is *illegal*," he said. "Not that I'd go blabbing your business," he clarified quickly to Leroy and Charlie.

"Whoo boy, Charlie, you sure did hire a fire extinguisher, didn't you?" Sammy said, rolling his eyes. "This guy's probably never had fun in his whole life."

"Pipe down, Sammy," Leroy admonished him, though it sounded less like a demand and more like a well-worn catchphrase. Charlie rolled his eyes behind both of their backs as Leroy went on. "You're gonna scare him away, talking like that. And from what I hear he's got a way with playing the keys that we haven't had around here in a while."

Charlie nodded. "Sure does. And Miss Betty here can sing like the sweetest canary. We sure lucked out with these two," he said, tipping his hat to them both in turn.

"Why, Mister Charlie, you're quite a flatterer," Betty giggled, her face warming slightly. Then she smacked Jack in the side, projecting *thank him, you dummy* so hard that she was surprised she hadn't said it out loud.

"Right. Yeah, thank you," he said after a moment, still occupied with glaring daggers at Sammy. Those two were very clearly going to be trouble, though what type of trouble was yet to be seen.

"So, what else do they need to know, Leroy?" Charlie asked, clearly thinking it over.

"Right. I guess we could give them the tour in a bit. But first let's finish with the rules. We have a room in the back where the production side of our business is. You're welcome to dip in on the house, but don't go messing with the setup, and don't go getting messy before you're up on stage. Bottles with the stuff we don't water down are under the bar or on the left side of the shelf if you're looking to get blotto. The right side we give to guests."

"Your rum is homemade? And watered down?" Betty asked. That seemed a little *too* dishonest for her liking, but then again, this *was* a speakeasy and she'd heard enough buzz about the type of drinks some places served, the kind that you'd be lucky enough to wake up at all after drinking.

"Some of it is homemade. Some of it we get from our suppliers. Sammy handles that end of the business" Leroy said, nodding to the man in question. "You don't survive in this line of work if you aren't selling people some watered down jag most of the time."

"Our rum is top quality knockoff swill though," Charlie boasted, grabbing a bottle from the right side and pouring some of the dark liquid into a slightly greasy looking glass. "We don't water it down nearly as much as most places."

"Yeah!" Sammy agreed emphatically. "S'better than the panther piss they serve down at the Cherry, that's for sure. Though the Queen's sells some good stuff." Charlie handed Jack the glass of rum, and Betty nearly laughed at the look on his face and the gingerly way he held it as though it were a snake about to bite him. He quickly passed it over to Betty, and she laughingly passed it to Sammy, certain that he'd drink it for them. It wasn't that she *didn't* drink, but she figured Jack could use some solidarity right now. At least it might keep the boys from hassling him about not drinking.

Sam tossed it back and grinned as he passed it back to her to pass to Jack. Jack made a face, and placed it back on the bar empty, with Leroy and Charlie none the wiser.

"Are those other speakeasies?" Jack asked.

"Sure are," Leroy replied. "The Cherry is the worst. It's a clip joint run by some nasty people. They hijack our liquor shipments as much as they can and then try to offer us protection, so it won't happen again."

"We were close to going out of business at one point," Charlie said, pouring more rum into the now empty glass. "Dealing with not only them, but the KKK too, when they come in to stir up trouble. It was a rough time. But then we found Sammy. He's vicious enough that most gangsters know better than to try anything with us."

"Damn right I am," Sam said, snatching the glass of rum before Charlie could pass it to anyone else. He downed it in one go and slammed it back down onto the bar hard enough that Betty was surprised it didn't shatter. "They know from experience."

"Wow, you're a hard-boiled fella ain't you?" Betty teased him sarcastically.

"Sure am. Here." Sammy handed his glass back to Charlie. "You're both going to want to take a drink. We gotta make sure you aren't dry agents, though honestly with all that this-is-illegal talk, you'd have to be the worst dry agents in the world. No offence."

"Offence taken," Jack said, but he took the glass and took a sip regardless. He made a face that most definitely wasn't helping his case, and then passed it to Betty.

She drank the rest of it and grinned. "There you go, Sammy. You need anything else?"

"How about a kiss?" Sammy crooned, with no real malice. It was funny, for all he acted so hard-boiled he wasn't the vilest man Betty had ever had to deal with. She got the feeling he was eighty percent bravado and just enough bite to back it up.

"Darling, I'd sooner clock you in the kisser than actually kiss you," she said sweetly, much to the vocal delight of Leroy and Charlie. "What about you, Jack?"

"I'm not kissing anyone!" he yelped.

"Whoo boy, Sammy, she's not gonna take none of your shit!" Leroy laughed, slapping Sam on the back.

Sammy shrugged. "Can't blame a guy for trying."

"She can," Jack informed him. "And she will."

They carried on talking for a while, then Charlie and Leroy took them on a very short tour. The speakeasy was mostly a wide-open space, with seating on one side, the low bar on the other, and a dance floor in between. There was a back room to put your things in that doubled as a storage room and optimistically served as the break room, with a single rickety chair. Behind a second door, barely noticeable under the peeling posters and bubbled up paint was the small room where they brewed their juice, two large copper stills bubbling away that took up almost the entire space. The heat and the smell of cooking grain was heavy in the air, and the walls were shiny with condensation thrown off from the pots.

In all honesty, the place was much more impressive at night, when it was filled with handsome men and beautiful women in glittering dresses with feathers in their hair. In the light of day, the grime and smoke-stained walls seemed less glamourous and decidedly more run-down.

"So, you still want to work for us?" Leroy asked, once the tour was over. They moved to sit with Sammy and George who had migrated over to the seating area.

"'Course we do!" Betty said before Jack could open his mouth. "We'd be posi-tutely delighted to work here."

"You sure are chipper, ain't ya?" Sammy said with that shit-eating grin back on his face.

It was true, she did tend to be pretty darn upbeat. Most folks seemed to think she was naive. Or that she was constantly drunk, or on drugs. But she barely touched alcohol, and she'd only ever tried weed once back in Wisconsin. It made her feel far too floaty for her liking, and she hadn't touched it since.

No, her secret to happiness was far simpler. Betty May was of the opinion that every moment of life was worth living. She'd spent enough time feeling down and out that she sometimes felt that was the only thing keeping her alive. So even in her darkest hours, Betty pushed that thought forward. There was always a strong feeling, deep in her gut, that things could and would get better. That once the hardship had passed, every moment that brought her to that sunshine would be worth living. Even if it was sometimes hell to get through.

"I sure am," she laughed, giving Sammy a slap on the back as well. "And you are too."

Sammy beamed at that, all puffed-chested and proud of himself.

She paused, tapping her chin as though she were thinking hard. "I think I like you," she said finally. "You're good for a laugh."

"Hey!" Sam hooted, a wide smile crinkling the skin around his eyes as he gestured in mock offense.

"He is," Charlie agreed as Leroy doubled over with laughter. Jack looked smug as a bug, and Betty felt her heart warm.

This was going to be good for them. She could already tell.

CHAPTER TWO

It was another night of singing and watching the drunken crowds revel in the music, but Betty was feeling too jittery to enjoy any of the energy which usually kept her floating through the long nights. She kept smiling, sure. She was, after all, a damn professional. The roof could be caving in around her and she would still put on a hell of a show, but tonight her heart wasn't in it. Not even the energy of the crowd and Jack's white-hot playing was enough to raise the cloud of gloom that had settled over her as soon as she opened her eyes this morning.

Maybe it was the weather—the sun had hardly risen this morning and the city was cloaked in a dense cloud cover that promised rain. Or perhaps it was just one of those far-too-common days where melancholy was her trusted companion.

She threw herself down into a chair with a bone deep sigh. She was exhausted, the kind of tiredness that seeped into your bones and made every movement feel about ten times harder than it should, and she was feeling a little bit irritated on top of that. Safe to say she was ready to head home and try again tomorrow for a better day. What she absolutely didn't need at the moment was Sammy to come swaggering over, drunk as a skunk, to try to talk to her.

"Hiya, Bets," he said, making his wobbly way toward the chair beside her and placing his drink down. He stunk like gin tonight but looked as dapper as ever. "Whatcha doing?"

"Having a drink," she said, a grin tugging at the corner of her mouth when Sam scanned the empty table for a glass. She picked up his half full cocktail and cheers'd him with it cheekily.

"Aww c'mon, no fair!" he laughed as she sipped at it. It was sweet and cold, tasting like honey and lemon, with the slightest abrasive edge of alcohol.

"I need it. I'm exhausted," she said, taking another sip.

"You're exhausted? I've been out all-night making door-to-door deliveries," Sammy complained. He looked put out about it too, but it was possible he was just upset that she'd taken his alcohol.

"Does that get you a good amount of money?" Betty asked, genuinely interested. The world of bootlegging was so strange and mysterious to her. Sometimes she felt like the Trespass was a world of its own, and that she was an explorer discovering it for the first time every night she came in. It was like Sammy was from a whole different world than the one she'd come from.

Sammy nodded. "Two dollars a bottle," he said cheerfully. "You can make a good amount of money on it, since it's risky business for the poor suckers like me delivering the hooch. Only other bad part about it besides the risk of getting caught is that you gotta beat up the customers who try to take the bottles and close the door, but that's not so bad."

Personally, Betty found the thought of that quite stressful, but she supposed Sammy had been at it long enough that it was old hat to him by now. "Well," she said, "Maybe that's the business I should be getting into."

Sammy howled with laughter, which was both flattering in that she was hilarious, and annoying at the same time. Betty thought that was Sammy in a nutshell. Sweet and a pain in the ass all at once. "Sure. You can be my partner" he joked. "We'll split the profits sixty-thirty."

"Sixty-forty," she corrected him automatically.

Sam tapped his chin in thought. "All right," he said after a moment. "You drive a hard bargain, but deal," he said putting out his hand to shake.

Betty giggled, delighted. "Oh, Sammy," she said. "You and I are going to get along just fine."

Sammy grinned back at her; his handsome face lit up with a shared joke. Raising a hand to the bar, he soon had another cocktail in his hand. "To getting along just fine," he said with a dramatic wink as they clinked glasses.

And they *did*. Betty enjoyed his company. He was brash and foul-mouthed, and violent, but he was *fun*. She liked fun.

Unfortunately, Jack didn't seem to feel the same way.

"He's infuriating! I can't work with him always around," Jack was saying. It was a Saturday evening about a month after they'd started, before the crowds started to trickle in, and Betty had heard this complaint so many times that she could practically say it along with him.

So, she hadn't exactly been listening attentively to Jack's complaints, but she'd at least been trying. That was, right up until the most gorgeous woman she had ever seen entered the speakeasy, sauntering her way over to the bar. Betty's breath caught as though the air inside the bar had shifted and thinned. Jack was still complaining, but suddenly his Sammy complaint of the hour seemed muffled and far away.

Holy hell, but who was *that*?

"Betty? Are you listening to me?" Jack asked, the slightly put-out whine in his voice enough to drag her back to the present. She realized she was gripping the edge of the table and made a point to relax her fingers one by one.

"Yes, sweetie. Sammy is the worst, I hear you," she said, not taking her eyes off of the woman for one second.

She was a Black woman around the same age as Betty, with her black hair mostly hidden under a silk scarf wrapped around her head in the style of a turban. Her face was kind and open, with beautiful eyes and a half smile gracing her full lips. And the way she *walked*, the way her hips swayed, had Betty mesmerized. It wasn't like the lithe stride of a dancer, no. She moved heavier on her feet than that. But with such a grace and fluidity, despite her solid steps, that it almost seemed like every movement she made was part of a dance. She wasn't dressed like a flapper, but she wasn't in street clothes either. At least no street clothes Betty was used to seeing. Instead, she was wearing a long flowing red robe-like dress with art-deco silver embellishments down to her waist and picking back up on her bottom hem. Her sleeves hung down to her knees, and scarves and bangles and jewels dripped from her like raindrops. A warm curl of interest had risen in Betty's belly, and she felt a faint flush begin to rise in in her cheeks as she took in the ample curves highlighted by the dress.

Leroy greeted the mystery woman with a warm embrace, and Betty had a moment of absolute dread, thinking that this must be Mary, his wife. It was a cold rush that felt like someone had breathed ice directly into her chest. But no, they didn't kiss. Surely he would have greeted his wife with a kiss? Leroy held up a finger to the woman, gesturing her to wait a moment then moved toward the shelves of giggle juice. He scanned them for a second before grabbing a bottle to present to her, mockingly bending a half bow like a waiter in a fancy restaurant. She took a bottle with a laugh that had her throwing back her head, like her whole body was too full of mirth to laugh just with her mouth.

And then she left.

The door had barely closed behind her before Betty was across the room, a bewildered Jack in tow. "Who was that?" she demanded of Leroy, who looked just as startled as Jack.

"Hello to you too, Bets," he said, grinning fondly when she gestured at him impatiently. "That was Madame La Utirips. The very one on the advertisements. Her real name's Eva," he told her.

Betty blinked. "Oh. I thought those were just a cover for the Trespass," she said. She'd always assumed that the psychic upstairs was invented specifically to explain why so many people were always coming and going from the alleyway. After all, a seance required quite a few people from what she'd heard.

"Nah, she's a smart girl. She's cashing in on all that psychic spirit mumbojumbo," Leroy explained with a laugh. "Does a damn good job of it too. Lotta folks claim she's the real deal."

"But you don't think so?" Betty asked.

Leroy chuckled. "I don't believe in that kinda thing. It's all kindsa make-believe with knocking and tea and candles and all of that nonsense. I don't believe you can talk to any kind of spirit until the good Lord takes you. Or you lie in the ground. Either way is just as well for me. I'd rather live my life than spend my time thinking about what's gonna happen after it."

Betty nodded. That seemed sensible to her. She'd heard about the spiritualism craze of course; it seemed like you couldn't walk down a street without seeing a lunch counter offering tea readings with a lunch purchase. But she'd never been compelled to investigate it for herself. She tried to avoid thinking about that sort of thing, just in case she tempted fate.

But it sometimes seemed like everyone else in the world was swept up in spiritual madness. Seances were a regular weekly event for some of her friends and getting one's palm or tea leaves read could be done at almost any place on any given street. But if this Eva woman was a psychic, Betty would consider that just maybe she had been missing out.

"She can learn a lot about you from looking at you and talking to you for a few minutes. I don't begrudge it. I figure if the woman has a knack for figuring people out, why not use it to make some jack by telling people what they need to hear. Or want to hear."

"I think she's genuine," Charlie said, beaming beatifically from across the bar as he poured a tumbler of whiskey. "She's got that something, you know?"

"Oh, I know," Betty said emphatically, thinking of her gorgeous face and the way her dress had hugged her curves just right. "You think I should get a reading?"

"It's your money," Leroy said with a shrug.

Charlie shook his head at his friend's pessimism. "Go for it, Bets," he said at the same time that Jack said, "No!"

"Oh come on, Jacky." Betty laughed. "It's one reading, it's not like I'm dropping some heavy sugar for it. Plus, it's payday soon, isn't it, Leroy? And we're owed a raise I think."

Leroy laughed at that. "What a gold digger you are," he said with no malice. "Yeah, all right. You've been bringing in the crowds better than anyone we've ever had playing here before. I guess I could cough up a few more bills per pay."

"Starting now?" Betty asked sweetly, raising her eyebrows expectantly.

Leroy chuckled, shaking his head as he rummaged around in the cash box and pulled out a few crumpled bills to hand to her.

"You are pos-i-lutely my favorite person in the whole world," Betty cheered, tucking the cash into her bra, making a point to bat her caked up lashes sweetly at him.

"I thought I was your favorite," Jack said with a much put-upon fake pout. But it was less than a second before he cracked and smiled at her antics. Betty took a moment to feel all warm and fuzzy at that. Jack was really warming up the more they spent time here. It was nice to see him smile so freely again. She wasn't sure that the city was the right place for a boy like Jack, but she also knew damn well that a cornfield wasn't the right place either.

"'Course you are, sweetie," she said, patting his cheek. "You're all my favorites. Even Sammy."

Jack looked like she'd just insulted his mother. "How dare you, Bets! Sam? He's a lounge lizard, a ragamuffin, a—"

"Real big shot bootlegger who could snap a rube like you in half?" Sammy finished for him, coming up behind him and slinging an arm around his shoulder.

Good timing.

Betty giggled, not only at the poleaxed expression on Jack's face, but also at the way Sammy had to stand up taller to manage the gesture, the height difference made up for by the sheer force of personality Sammy projected.

"Betty. Why? Why betray me like this?" Jack asked, expression pained as he tried to shift Sam's arm off his shoulders to no avail.

"Why, Jack, I have to keep things interesting around here, don't I?" she asked with a sly look.

"As if you need to add any excitement to *this* place," Jack said with a snort. He was all talk though. He'd started to like it at the Trespass Inn, Betty could tell.

"What's that supposed to mean, Money?" Sammy asked, razzing him. "You got a problem with this place?"

Betty giggled. "Well, as lovely as it is to watch you boys fight, I gotta go! I have a palm reading with my name on it," she said, waving good-bye with a little flick of her dress, the beads on the hem clinking merrily behind her.

"Don't take any wooden nickels, Bets," Jack called after her. "And don't do anything Sam would do—ow!" Betty didn't have to look back to know Sammy had probably pinched him.

Betty's brisk pace slowed as she began to ascend the rickety old stairs, her heart in her throat. She hadn't felt this nervous since that first night she'd worked up the nerve to walk into the Trespass to check things out.

But this was even higher stakes, at least for her. She knew how to perform for a crowd. How to woo and flirt and make herself a star who was hard to refuse. But this would just be her and Madame La Utirips. A one-person audience who held both mystery and potential in a crystal ball.

Since she was going so slowly, she took some time to look at the stairwell that she normally ignored. The walls of the little stairwell were covered in strange little charms and herbs, and in between them were all sorts of advertisements for Madame La Utirips's services. Palm readings, rune casting, love potions, and crystal ball sessions. She even offered seances and magical charms to take home. It was quite a business.

As Betty got closer and closer to the door at the top of the stairs, the air began to grow heavier with a thick perfume and the smell of smoke. It wasn't the acrid tang of tobacco smoke, but something warm and fragrant that she couldn't identify as anything she had smelled before.

The door was painted with peeling blue paint, with a purple eye painted right in the center of it. The eye seemed to survey her somehow as she looked at it, despite it being nothing but paint and wood. It was like a warning. Enter here only if you are ready to be seen. Betty took a deep breath and reached out to run her fingertips across the pupil. She was *always* ready to be seen. So why was she hesitating?

Before her courage could fail her, she rapped her knuckles against the door.

"Come in," a voice called, clear as a bell even through the wooden door. "Come in, my child, and catch a glimpse of what lies beyond the veil."

As a performer, Betty appreciated the drama of the greeting. She also appreciated the drama of the room she walked into. Silk scarves were draped across nearly every surface, and a beaded curtain separated the room from what appeared to be the rest of the apartment. Candles dripped their wax onto nearly every flat surface in the room, and incense burned merrily away in a holder, sending thin plumes of smoke spiraling into the air. So *that* was what the unidentified smell had been, although she still couldn't match the scent to anything in her memory.

At one end of the room there was a large round table with a rich black tablecloth draped over it, and many rather ornate chairs sat empty, gathered around it. But none of that was what interested Betty. No, what caught her attention was Madam Utiri—no, *Eva*, Betty thought with a secret thrill at the intimacy of knowing her name before Eva knew hers. She sat at a smaller table opposite, her skin glowing beatifically in the candlelight. In front of her sat a large crystal ball, with a deck of large cards just to the left of it which seemed to beckon for Betty to reach out and shuffle them.

"Hello," Betty said, her voice soft and breathier than she'd expected it to come out. "I saw you downstairs." God, she sounded so stupid. Like a brainless flapper drunk on spirits and dancing. Even though she hadn't done either of those things this evening.

"Hello. Would you like a sandwich and a palm reading, my dear?" Eva asked, her eyes sharp enough to pierce Betty right through. She felt as though Eva was amused at her, although her expression remained serene. It was suddenly so much harder to breathe, and the smoke and perfume seemed to choke her as her face warmed under Eva's unwavering gaze. Her cheeks flushed with a combination of embarrassment and something else, that hot curl in her belly returning.

"Perhaps just the reading," she said, eyes locked onto Eva's as if in a trance.

Eva laughed, and gestured at her to come deeper into the room. "I do wish I could, but it's illegal, my darling girl. I haven't been able to sell just a reading for a while now. Come in, I'll get you a snack and we can begin."

Betty made herself comfortable, or as comfortable as she could on the stiff-backed old chair opposite from where Eva had been sitting, while Eva disappeared behind the curtain to fetch her a drink and snack. The smell of incense was strong here, but Betty didn't mind. It felt right. She wondered if the scent clung to Eva's clothes even when she wasn't here. If this was what she smelled like even out in the real world, away from this dimly lit paradise.

Eva returned with a plate and a cup of tea and placed them both on the table in front of Betty. The tea was steaming, and the little sandwich looked surprisingly delicious. It reminded her that she hadn't eaten since the afternoon before. "Thank you," she said, digging in immediately. Eva settled across from her with a little smile on her face and a twinkle in her eye.

"Of course," she said graciously.

"Why's it illegal?" Betty asked when her mouth was no longer full.

Eva laughed. "Fortune-telling is illegal, but entertaining while someone has lunch isn't," she said, tapping her nose cheekily. Lord, she was cute.

"Clever," Betty responded, taking another bite of her sandwich. She was so nervous. Conversation usually came easily to

Betty, but with this mystic it was hard to even get two words out without freezing up.

"Do you know what kind of reading you'd like, Little Nightingale?"

Betty's heart did a little somersault at the nickname. Did that mean that Eva had seen her singing at the speakeasy? Or was that simply something she called every woman who came for a reading? "What do you think would be best?" she asked, genuinely at a loss. She knew some of the things that she offered from the posters in the stairwell, but she didn't know what some of them even were. Runes? Tarot cards she'd heard of sort of sideways, but she had no idea what exactly they did. Scrying? She was lost, though secretly she hoped that whatever method was best would involve Eva touching her, in any way she saw fit.

"I think a tea leaf reading," Eva said. "I've poured the tea without straining the leaves already."

Huh. Had she known that Betty wouldn't know what she wanted? Or was she just as good at guessing as Leroy thought she was? "Thank you," she said, taking a sip. She got some leaves in her mouth, which wasn't the most pleasant feeling, but the strangeness of this was softened by Eva leaving momentarily, only to return with her own cup.

"Half of the delight of a tea leaf reading is the ceremony of drinking together with someone," Eva told her, like they were sharing some secret together, a warm smile curving the edges of her lush lips. "You have to be connected to give someone a reading that's worth anything."

"So you sit and chat with everyone who comes in for this?" Betty asked, a small thread of disappointment tugging in her chest. Of course, someone like Eva would give personal attention to all her clients. God, she was so stupid, expecting something, or, well, anything from this woman. What the hell had she even been expecting? She didn't know Eva at all, didn't know if she was even like that.

Eva laughed, a sound that sent shivers through Betty, cutting off her internal recriminations. Again, Betty was struck with how she laughed with her whole body. Like the joy she felt came from deep inside and swelled so big and bright that she couldn't keep it in.

"No, Songbird. Only the special ones," she said. The corners of her eyes creased with her smile, and Betty suddenly desperately wanted to kiss those lines.

"Oh," she said softly, her whole body glowing with the words. "Well then, I'm honored."

Eva nodded, and a little bit of the majesty and mystery of her softened around the edges with her newly shy smile. "Now, let's read your future." Betty nodded and passed her the china cup. Their fingers brushed and something in Betty thrilled at that little bit of contact.

"I see love in your near future," Eva said confidently, staring at the inside of the cup like it was a novel to be read. "With someone unexpected. See the heart here, with the anchor beside it? Near the castle." Eva tilted the cup toward her, but all Betty saw were muddy looking leaves. If she squinted, she could sort of make out a heart. But she certainly didn't see whatever Eva was seeing.

"You are filled with a great sadness, aren't you, Nightingale? I see sadness, not in your future, but in your past. And a nightingale with broken wings trying, but failing, to fly. A betrayal. Your heart breaking." Betty felt herself holding her breath and released it deliberately. How could Eva possibly see that? How could she know about the things she'd been through? Or was she just guessing, like Leroy had said?

"As for your future, be careful who you trust. There is a fox, a knife. Signs of fighting and hatred." Eva had such a commanding tone that it was hard not to get swept away in what she was saying.

"I'll be on the lookout, then," she said, heart fluttering when Eva smiled warmly at her.

"Good. You deserve to be safe and happy."

Betty blushed. "Thank you."

"Don't be afraid, Nightingale. You have better things waiting for you in the far future. A swan, which means good luck in love. And a ship for success."

"Well, I look forward to that." Betty giggled. "As long as the fox doesn't get me."

Eva placed her hand on Betty's wrist, stealing the air from her lungs. "I'll make you a charm bag. Free of charge, dear. You will be safe." Betty was sure she must be imagining the way Eva's hand lingered upon her wrist before she pulled away.

"A charm bag?" Betty asked.

"Filled with herbs and stones meant to protect you," Eva explained. "It will warn you of danger."

"Thank you," she said gratefully. Eva smiled that beautiful smile at her and set to gathering ingredients to place in a little cloth bag on a string. She handed it to Betty, and several little stones clinked together within the bag as Betty took it.

"Keep that with you. It will help when you need it most," Eva said. "And take care, Nightingale, until we meet again."

Betty blinked. Oh, of course. The reading was over.

"Thank you ever so much," Betty said as she paid Eva for her services. "For the fortune, and for the sandwich."

Eva grinned at her, and Betty had to turn away hurriedly before Eva could catch sight of her blush.

CHAPTER THREE

It came as quite a surprise to Jack that he didn't hate working at a speakeasy. Sure, it took some adjusting to, especially as far as his sleep schedule went. Having to go from a normal citizen to a night owl was rough. He'd had a hell of a time with it at first, but he was starting to get into the swing of things now. He'd only fallen asleep teaching piano two or three times so far.

The booze and debauchery also took some getting used to. Jack couldn't even count the number of times he'd come across a couple in some dark corner getting more intimate than was entirely appropriate for a public place. It always made him blush to the roots of his hair and sputter apologetically, as though *he* was the one in the wrong for walking up on their *very public* rendezvous.

He'd seen more body parts working here than he'd ever seen in his life and he was becoming more acquainted with feminine underclothing than the time he'd snuck into his mother's drawers as a child to see what treasures they contained.

Surprisingly, the people who worked there weren't the low down, rough types he had feared. Charlie and Leroy felt like they were his older brothers, or what he imagined having two boisterous, booze slinging older brothers would be like. They'd razz you within an inch of your life, sure, but they were also always there with an open ear and a comforting word. It almost made Jack miss his brother Edwin, although they had never really been all that close. And Edwin certainly would never greet Jack with a friendly shoulder punch and the ever-open invitation of a cocktail. Nor would he likely go the extra mile for him like Charlie and Leroy did. Although Jack still wasn't certain how he felt about their methods.

It had been about their fourth or fifth week working there when Jack realized that working three jobs was a hell he could no longer manage. Given that his *one* factory job was hellish enough on its own, he decided he had no choice but to quit. With the amount of tips that were flowing in from the drunk revelers he was pretty sure he could afford it. Heck, he was hopeful that he could even slow down to only a few students in his piano teaching endeavors.

The only problem with that was that the factory he worked for didn't exactly run a clean business. It made him nervous about trying to leave, to say the least. "I'm quitting," he'd said when he'd finally gathered his courage to talk to his bulldog of a foreman. "And I'd like to be paid what I'm due before I go." He figured it was a reasonable enough request.

Unfortunately, his foreman wasn't a reasonable man.

All he did was laugh in Jack's face. "You aren't quitting," he snarled. "And you sure as hell aren't getting whatever you think you're owed."

Jack stood there, feeling completely out of his depth. He'd expected pushback on the money, but he'd never imagined that his foreman would try to keep him from quitting.

"I'm not coming back. Where's my money?" Was all he could say, flabbergasted at how things were going.

His foreman spat on the ground, face red now, as though he hadn't expected Jack to try again. "You're not going anywhere. We need workers. More like you. Spineless. You'll be back in here tomorrow, or you'll never be getting that money," he shouted, jowls quivering. The man was large enough to crush Jack if he tried to fight him, and no amount of protesting or threatening to go above his head would change his mind.

Jack had headed home, disheartened.

What had finally changed his foreman's mind was Leroy. Jack had casually complained about the whole situation to him and Charlie, hoping for some sympathy at most; what he got instead was Leroy handing him a huge stack of bills the very next night, a shit-eating smirk curling across his face.

"Your old foreman says hello, and to never come back," he'd said simply. Jack had been too scared to ask for more details. Jack was also too scared to point out that there was more money there than he'd been owed.

Later, Jack overheard Leroy and Charlie laughing over the expression on *that boob's* face when they'd shown up, and had quietly promised himself never to piss the two of them off.

The irony of his illegal job having honest bosses wasn't lost on him, and it was nice to have the money he was owed. So, Jack became a part-time pianist at a speakeasy, and part-time music teacher on the side. It was an exhausting life, sure, but in a far different and far more thrilling way than the backbreaking work at the factory had been.

"Hello, George," Jack greeted him as he came in. They weren't yet open for the night, but he and Betty liked to come in early to get warmed up. George nodded to him, a friendly gesture despite his lack of verbal response. Jack would almost have thought he was mute if he hadn't heard him talk a handful of times. George was a kind man, but Jack had also watched him break a man's arm without any hesitation. Though in all fairness, the fella had it coming—it was only after the man had gotten rowdy and started touching the girls on the dance floor, grabbing at their behinds, that George had stepped in to make sure he wouldn't be grabbing anything else anytime soon.

But either way, George was an interesting character. Silent and strong and hard to get a read on. The perfect bouncer, Jack figured.

The actual work Jack and Betty did at the Trespass was worth putting up with all of the shady business. Charlie and Leroy allowed them to play whatever kind of music they wanted, as long as it kept the people dancing, which meant they had the kind of freedom that they'd never had before at any paying job.

Jack used it as an opportunity to play all the songs that challenged and delighted him most. And Betty did about the same, picking songs that let her show off her impressive range and her vocal chops, much to the delight of the crowd. And of course, they were both able to pick things that were *fun* to perform. It was a great change of pace from listening to seven-year-olds plunk away at "Twinkle, Twinkle, Little Star" during the day.

If there was one downside, beyond the illegality of the whole business, it was Sam. Sam who cornered him as soon as he and Betty were off stage one evening, with a broad smile on his face.

"Money! My old buddy, my pal, my top fellow," Sam greeted him, throwing his arm around Jack's shoulder, the ever-present stink of booze wafting off of him. He did that a lot, touching Jack. Although Jack managed to shrug him off nearly as often. "How's things?"

"Better before you showed up," Jack said, without *too* much malice. Sam was probably the most annoying human being he had ever met, but it was strangely hard to stay mad at him. Probably because he seemed to flit through emotions like they were nothing but gusts of wind. Jack found it hard to stay mad at someone who went from cheerful to grim at the drop of a hat.

"Aww, you don't mean that," Sam said, elbowing him in the arm. "You just need a drink."

Jack laughed. "No, thank you. I think I'm drunk just from proximity to you," he said, grinning when Sam frowned at that.

"I don't think that's how that works," he said muzzily. "But I'm too zozzified to be sure."

Jack hummed his agreement and tried to walk away, but Sam was like a little leech attached to him at the hip.

"So, Money," he started.

"Jack."

"Huh?"

Jack sighed. "My *name* is Jack."

Sam cackled like the little devil that he was. "Yeah, Money. Congrats. You know your own name. Very impressive."

"Oh, for crying out loud, of course I know my—" Jack stopped, pinching the bridge of his nose between his fingers and taking a deep breath. "What do you *want* Sam?"

"Can't I just hang out with my new pal without getting the shakedown?" Sam whined. He truly was drunk, based on the slight slur of his words, but otherwise Jack wasn't sure he'd have been able to tell. He was good at faking sober, simply by virtue of always acting a little bit drunk, even before he'd started drinking. Though Jack was starting to wonder if he was ever truly sober or if he'd really only ever seen him fried.

"Hmmm." Jack pretended to think about it. "Nope. You're after something, aren't you?"

"Whaaaat?" Sam asked, drawing out the vowel in the most annoying way possible. "Me? No way! I'm just tryna talk to you!"

Jack peered at him suspiciously. That didn't really fit with what he knew of Sam. They weren't on the best terms really, and Sam could usually be found hanging around anybody *but* Jack when given the option. He'd called him a milquetoast enough times that Jack didn't have any illusions as to what Sam thought about him. To him he was a boring old killjoy who wasn't worth a second glance. "Why don't I believe you?"

"Because you're a strange, stuffy fella," Sam said authoritatively, nodding his head. It was almost cute, if you forgot that it was *Sam* making the gesture. "But that's okay. I'll still hang around you."

"Gee, thanks. Just what I wanted." Jack sighed, resigning himself to a very long night. If Sam caught the sarcasm, he gave no sign of it. Instead, he hooked his bony fingers into the crook of Jack's arm and leaned in close to whisper. "Hey, so I have a proposition for you." His breath smelled of booze and a little bit like honey, and despite it not being that unpleasant, Jack couldn't help the shiver that worked its way down his spine at Sam's moist breath in his ear.

"Christ, just say it at a normal tone," Jack demanded, shoving at him. Sam's claws clung to his jacket, but he swayed back, laughing like he'd just pulled one over on Jack.

"Okay," he said, then belched. "Okay, look. There's this Sheba who comes in every night," Sam started, only to have Jack put up his hand to stop him.

"No," he said firmly. "I can already tell you that whatever it is, it's a no."

"Aww come on, you didn't even listen! I just need someone for her friend to dance with for a little bit. We won't be long, only fifteen minutes, I swear! She doesn't want to leave her friend alone for too long." Sam looked so put out about it that Jack almost felt bad.

Almost.

"Ask Leroy," he said, still trying with limited success to free himself from Sam's clutches. God, he had a strong grip.

"Leroy's got a wife, and a kid on the way," Sam said, like Leroy having a family was getting in his way. "He's not going to dance with another bird."

"Then Charlie," Jack tried again. There had to be *someone* who could do this instead of him.

"Charlie doesn't dance!"

Jack knew this. Betty had complained about as much a few times before, before eventually giving up on him as a chronic bore.

"Neither do I. Ask literally anyone else but me," Jack plead.

"Please, Money? I'll owe you one! I swear, it'll just be for a few minutes. Fifteen minutes tops, like I said, and she's a real doll, I promise ya, I wouldn't leave you with some canceled stamp, swear on my life." Sam promised, giving Jack what looked to be his damn best puppy dog eyes.

It wasn't all that effective. Sam could go without. It wouldn't kill him. He was absolutely not going to give in, no matter how Sam begged.

"Ughh," he groaned after about two seconds of the puppy dog treatment. "Fine. You owe me two whole hours without you in them. Tomorrow night."

"Deal," Sam said quickly, sticking out his hand to shake on it. Well, at least he had let go of Jack's sleeve.

He shook Sam's hand with trepidation, then wiped it off on his pant leg just in case. He couldn't be certain where those hands had been. Sam practically bounced them over to the edge of the dance floor, where he was quick to point out two girls dancing together wildly.

"The one in the pink dress is yours. She's not bad, right?" he said, as though Jack should want to dance with some stranger just because she was pretty.

"Sure, Sam. Fifteen minutes," he reminded him. "Then you come back and I'm free."

"Of course, of course," Sam said, pulling him onto the dance floor by the hand. "Twenty minutes tops, then you're back to being boring."

"You said fiftee—" Jack was cut off as Sam practically flung him into the girl's arms.

"Why hello there, I'm Jean," the girl purred, batting her heavily mascaraed eyelashes and looking Jack over like he was a piece of meat. He could already tell she was a real bearcat.

"Um, Jack," he said nervously, already having to drag her hands up from his buttocks to his back. They slid right back down again, like they were magnetized. Caught up in trying to protect his rear from her wandering hands, he almost missed her knee slyly bumping between his legs as she pressed the warm length of her body against him.

"How about we, um, dance like this," he suggested nervously, pulling back and guiding her arms up around his neck.

"Sure," she said easily, and promptly leaned in for a kiss that only narrowly missed Jack's lips, leaving a sloppy trail of lipstick on the edge of his jaw. Thank God he had fast reflexes.

Jack ended up dancing with her (by which he meant stepping on her toes an inordinate number of times while she wound herself sensually against him, occasionally trying her luck for another pat of his rear) until close, at which point Sam *still* hadn't returned.

"I hate him so much," he griped to Jean, both of them sitting at a table while they waited.

"Join the club," she muttered, her head resting in her hands, feathered band lying on the table beside her. "I'm exhausted, my head is pounding from these goddamn cocktails and my feet hurt like the devil. I just want to go home."

"I could leave you alone," Jack said hopefully. "Let you rest and all."

Jean popped up and grabbed his arm faster than a rattlesnake strike. "No way! I don't want to be alone here!" Jean protested "Don't you dare leave me! This is the kinda place where *gangsters* go! Why, Zanetti could be right around the corner!"

She clawed at him just like Sam had earlier, only *she* actually had nails.

"Okay," he said quickly, before she dug her talons into his actual flesh. He truly doubted any big crime bosses like Zanetti would be at the Trespass, but it wasn't worth fighting with her. "I'll stay, I'll stay!"

"Good," she said.

They sat there in silence for a moment or two, until she roused herself a bit and shifted, pressing up against him. Her bosom was especially tight against his body, and he had to squirm away as best as he could or risk feeling utterly indecent. "Do you want to neck a bit?" she asked him, her expression hopeful.

"No!" Jack said immediately, blushing. She glared at him, clearly offended. "I uh, I mean no thank you," he said, trying to wipe the offended look off of her face. "I'm just, I'm far too tired. Uh. Thank you, though. For the offer?"

Before things could devolve and Jack ended up getting smacked, Sam finally showed back up with the other girl in tow, both looking thoroughly disheveled.

"Jeanie!" she crowed, looking sheepish. "I've been looking all over for you!"

"Sure you have," Jean muttered, then shot a glare Jack's way as she stood. "Well, good night. You've been quite a *gentleman*," she accused him, grabbing her friend's hand and leading her to the door.

"Where *were* you?" Jack said as soon as they were far enough away. "You said you wouldn't be gone long!"

"We weren't, were we?" Sam asked, looking dazed. He had lipstick on his collar, and bruises darkening on his neck. Jack couldn't look at him. Partially out of disgust and partially due to the twist of attraction that made its unwelcome home in his gut. It was unfair how damn attractive Sam was.

"I hate you," Jack said huffily, grabbing his jacket. "Ugh. Where's Betty? I'm going home." But Betty was all the way across the room, and Sam, of course, didn't let him be.

"Seriously, Money. I owe you one," Sam said, slapping him too hard on the back. "That was some good time."

"Oh, I'm *so* glad you had fun," Jack said sarcastically. "Meanwhile I was stuck dancing with this woman I don't know. And I can't even dance! I just sort of shuffled until we both got tired. Then we had to try to have a *conversation*! She wanted to *neck* with me, Sam!"

Sam looked at him like he had six heads. "And that's a bad thing?" he clarified. "Because it sounds to me like you had a chance to have some fun for once."

"You little—" Jack bit back on all the words he could use to describe Sam. All of them were too vile to say. "I don't want to neck with some random girl! I don't want to...ugh. Never mind—" Jack cut himself off. He didn't need to go letting some gangster know that he wasn't interested in broads like that.

"Hey, don't blame me! It's not my fault you're such a Mrs. Grundy," Sam said. "The way I see it, I did you a favor, leaving you with a choice bit of calico like that."

"Absolutely not," Jack said. "But speaking of favors, you owe me more now. Instead of two hours of no Sam, I want a full night of silence whenever I'm around," Jack demanded.

"What? No way, that's nuts," Sam replied, his eyes wide. "I can't be quiet for the whole night!"

"You're going to have to," Jack said, moving toward the bar where Betty was chatting with Charlie. "You owe me." Unfortunately, Sammy decided to follow him.

"Come on," he whined. "What about money? I could give you some jack, if you want."

Jack glared at him, reminded of the stupid nickname Sam had for him. "No. You shut up for the whole night, or I let people know you go back on your word," he said menacingly.

"Who goes back on their word?" Betty asked, as they arrived at the bar. "Surely it's not Sammy?"

"Of course not!" Sam protested, then cringed. "Aw shit. Fine. You win, Money. I'll shut up tomorrow night, every time you're near me. It's a deal," he said sulkily.

"Whoo boy, now that's something I want to see," Charlie guffawed, leaning forward over the bar. "Hey, Jack, you want to spend your whole night at the bar? I'd love some peace and quiet for once."

Sam made an obscene gesture toward him, but Jack laughed. "Sure. Anytime I'm not playing I'll hang around here."

"It'll be difficult, won't it?" Betty mused thoughtfully. "For you to order a drink if you aren't allowed to speak."

"Money!" Sam yelped in alarm, whipping around to face Jack. "You can't do that to me! Come on, I got you a dance with that girl! I don't deserve this."

"More like you *forced* me to dance with her," Jack muttered sourly. "You can go one night without a drink."

"And you can order them when Jack's on stage," Charlie reminded him.

Sam didn't seem soothed.

"Last time I ever ask you for a favor," he grumbled, flopping himself dramatically over the bar. "I'm going to die tomorrow night."

"Good," Jack said vindictively, not bothering to specify which of those statements he was responding to.

As they left the bar, Betty giggled, clinging to Jack's already much abused arm. "How long do you think it'll take him," she asked, "to figure out that he can just get the booze himself?"

"Probably until he sobers up," Jack said.

"So never, then?"

Jack laughed. "Sure. That sounds about right."

Chapter Four

"Where's Sammy this evening?" Betty asked. There had been a distinct lack of fighting and posturing so far tonight. She was certain something was up.

"He's out on a run," Leroy said.

"A run? He doesn't seem the athletic type to me," Jack replied. That got a laugh out of Leroy.

"Of course not. He's on a rum run."

Oh. Sometimes amidst the glamour of being a singer at a speakeasy Betty forgot that the whole place was illegal. And that Sammy really *was* a criminal. "What's that like?" she asked. Leroy shrugged.

"Rough business. We're expecting a shipment of Canadian whiskey coming in from Detroit. Whiskey from Walkerville Distillery smuggled down the Detroit-Windsor funnel, then brought down to New York by the bootleggers. We're paying a pretty penny for this stuff, too, but legal hooch sells for almost double, even when watered down. But the boys who bring us the whiskey aren't the friendliest types. Mark my words, he'll come back here roughed up."

Only an hour later Leroy's prediction came true. The gramophone was playing as Sam sauntered down the stairs, looking like he didn't have a care in the world. But Betty spotted blood soaking through what looked to be a scrap of Sam's shirt that he'd turned into a bandage.

"Sammy! What happened to you?" she asked. Charlie poured him a drink, calm as can be, as though he saw his colleague bleeding out every day.

"They tried to up the price on us," Sam said. "Thirty more dollars. I couldn't let that slide."

Charlie sighed and handed him his drink.

"I don't suppose you could have talked it out?" Betty asked.

"Nah," Sam said with a nasty grin. "They had a new guy there, and he was getting on my nerves. And anyways, he said something about a change in power in New York. Vitale is out, and I guess the Purple Gang's taken over."

"But you got the whiskey?" Charlie asked.

"Of course I got the whiskey. Who do you think you're talking to?"

"Well, what happened?" Betty asked. She was intrigued to say the least. She knew almost nothing about this aspect of the business, and as scary as it was, it also seemed exhilarating.

Sammy grinned and started in on the tale. "So, the guy hops out of the car, heater in hand, and he shoots right at me. If I wasn't so fast, I'd have been a goner. I rolled outta the way, but he clipped my arm. Guy was a good shot, lemme tell ya. Then George pulled out his heater and—" Sam stopped abruptly. Betty turned to see what he was looking at and spotted Jack making his way over to the bar. Right, Sam had promised to be silent tonight whenever Jack was close by.

"Dammit. Meant to spend more time out bootlegging," Sammy whispered as Jack closed in.

"You've been avoiding me," Jack said, a smile on his face. "It's been kind of nice."

Betty laughed at the putout scowl on Sammy's face. Poor little bunny.

"So, Sam," Jack continued. "How's your night been?"

Sam made a rude gesture at him, then flinched as the movement irritated his wound.

"Come now, Jack. Be nice," Betty said, taking pity. "He's hurt."

Jack's eyes flicked to the gunshot wound quicker than a jackrabbit. "What happened to your arm?" Jack exclaimed, staring bug-eyed at the bright red spot of blood that had leaked through Sam's makeshift bandage.

Sam went to answer, but caught himself at the last second, shaking his head.

"Oh, for heaven's sake, you can talk! You're bleeding!" Jack told him.

Sam shrugged and mimed zipping his lips, much to Jack's chagrin. "Come on, Sam! This isn't funny, you're hurt!" Sam shrugged again.

But now it was Betty's turn to frown. In all the excitement she had forgotten that Sam's injury was probably quite serious.

"You little—" Jack glared at him, then turned and marched away with a determined look on his face. The moment he was gone, Sam let out a sigh. "Not talking is horrible," he whined, "Charlie, I need a drink. I'm in pain here."

"I'll bet," Charlie said, moving to pour Sam another rum.

"You have to take care of that wound, before you do something stupid like get an infection," Betty warned him.

Sam frowned. "I won't get an—" he stopped abruptly again at the sight of Jack returning with bandages in his hands.

Bless Jack. She knew he'd never have abandoned someone in need. It was clear from Sam's expression though that he'd assumed Jack was storming off in a huff, not going to grab supplies. He probably didn't think an injury from a fight with a bunch of bootleggers over a case of illegal hooch would gain him much, if any sympathy from Jack. But that just proved to Betty how little Sam knew them both.

"Charlie, I need a glass of alcohol for Sam's arm, something clear, and not watered down." Jack said, staring at Sam as though daring him to protest. But Sammy stayed quiet. "And you," Jack continued to Sam. "Sit down. If you're going to insist on being an fool, the least you can do is let me bandage up that arm."

Sam hesitated a second longer, but the stern look on Jack's face, and a sharp nudge from Betty prompted him to sit.

Jack was careful as he poured alcohol over the wound. Betty watched like a hawk as Jack slowly and patiently began to clean the wound.

Sam hissed quietly at the sting, and Jack muttered a low "Sorry," at him. Sweetly too, not sarcastic. Betty could just hear Sammy razzing him about being a good moll or something like that, but he stayed silent. And his shoulders relaxed like he was sinking into a hot bath. How interesting. She'd never seen Sammy look so calm before.

"There," Jack said when he was satisfied with his work, giving the crisp white bandage a final tug "That should just about do it."

"Why Jack, you're practically a doctor," Betty said. She inspected Sammy's bandaged arm and deemed it a better job than even she could have done.

Sammy nodded and grinned at Jack, a silent thank you.

"Yeah yeah, you're welcome," Jack said, rolling his eyes. "I can't believe you got injured and decided to dillydally by the bar instead of patching yourself up. How in the world do you survive?"

Sam shrugged, his grin never wavering. "Thank you," he finally said, with feeling.

Jack blinked, then grinned at him, deep crinkles forming around his eyes. "No problem, Sam."

Betty recognized that smile. *Oh, Jack. What are you getting yourself into?*

"But you're not supposed to talk," Jack continued. "I think you owe me at least an hour tomorrow for going back on your word."

The indignant noise Sam made at that was loud enough that a few guests turned to look at him. Betty giggled behind her hand.

So, Sam scowled at him and shook his head.

"Sorry? I can't hear you. You'll have to speak up." Jack laughed. Sam grumbled, his hands clenched into fists by his sides.

"What was that?" Jack said again, then yelped as Sam finally snapped and smacked him in the arm. But true to his word, Sam managed to stay quiet the rest of the night.

❖

Betty went back to Eva the very moment she got paid again. Eva didn't seem surprised to see her, but then again, she *was* supposed to be psychic. Maybe she'd seen her return in her crystal ball. Whether or not she was psychic didn't bother Betty. Eva was magical in and of herself. Gorgeous, well possessed, and mysterious. She was, as far as Betty was concerned, the perfect woman. Which made her a dangerous woman. She'd have to guard her heart while she was with Eva.

But Betty was, in a word, smitten.

Eva's parlor was just as mystical as Betty remembered. They sat with their steaming cups of tea, cozy as they drank it unhurriedly. "Shall I look into my crystal ball while we drink our tea, Nightingale?"

Betty's whole body lit up at the nickname. She loved the way Eva said it, like it was special. Like the nickname was only for her and could only ever be for her. "Please," she said.

Eva nodded and gazed into the glass. It was strange, she didn't do any theatrical hand waving, or act as though she was possessed by spirits, or do any other thing Betty would have expected of a psychic.

Instead, she simply stared intently at the crystal ball, silent and serious. Betty expected to be bored, her restless spirit causing her to tap her fingers or move her legs, but instead she found herself falling into the same gentle pattern of breathing as Eva, a soft sense of calm wrapping around her like a coat on a cool day.

"Give me your hands," Eva said after a while, startling Betty with the sudden intrusion into the silence.

"All right," she said.

Eva's hands were warm and soft, and Betty couldn't help but run her thumbs across the backs of them to feel her skin. Her face heated at having done something so bold, but Eva's smile was the only thing that gave away that she'd noticed. And she didn't say anything, just continued to focus entirely on the ball in front of her.

Betty didn't mind. Sometimes the best things in life came after a long wait. And she was content to sit and hold this beautiful woman's hands. To watch her eyes track along the crystal ball as though she was reading words that only she could see. Eventually, she hummed thoughtfully, and Betty perked up.

"So, what do you see in my future?" Betty asked sweetly, batting her eyes a bit. Hoping beyond hope that Eva would understand what she was looking for.

Eva laughed, a beautiful deep sound that sent little shivers through Betty. "I see a nightingale," she began, her eyes trained less on the crystal ball and more on Betty. "I see shattered glass and whiskey," she continued. "These images are for someone you care for, I believe. And…" she paused here. She looked up fully at Betty now and maintained eye contact. "I see your dress on a bedroom floor."

Betty's breath caught, a shiver running through her. "Whose floor? Do you recognize it?" she asked. Her voice was soft and breathy, and she kept her hands soft and still in Eva's strong grip. Eva's eyes never left her for a moment, and Betty found herself unable to look away. Not that she wanted to. She thought she might be content to drown in Eva's presence for the rest of her life.

"Yes, Princess Girl. I know it very well," Eva answered. The atmosphere in the room had changed, the cool calm from earlier fading away to a sultry heat. Betty felt the hairs on the back of her neck prickle as warmth began to rise in her, her hands still clasped in Eva's.

Betty leaned across the table, watching for any sign that she'd gotten it wrong. That there was some other way to explain the electricity between them. But all that happened was a press of lips, soft and sweet and deep, followed by another, and *another*. There was a small clatter as Betty tumbled forward over the table, her body moving without command, desperate to touch Eva as much as she could. Eva laughed again, but it had gained a husky, hot quality to it that warmed her from inside better than a shot of whiskey ever could. She pulled Betty around the table and into her lap, leaning in to touch their lips together again.

"I think I like the future you see," Betty finally said, when she needed to pause for air. The cards were scattered across the table and her lip paint was smeared enticingly over Eva's gorgeous mouth.

"And so do I," Eva said, then eased Betty to her feet and stood to lead Betty by the hand deeper into the apartment.

Their tea sat forgotten on the table for the rest of the night.

❖

"You look happy," Jack accused Betty.

She had been smiling and singing and carrying on around their apartment for a week or two now, her happiness practically radiating off her, but every time Jack asked what she was so pleased about she'd told him it was too soon to say.

He hated that phrase more than anything now. "Too soon to say why, I guess?" he checked in, perhaps with a little too much snark.

Betty had the good grace to look guilty about it at least. "Jack…" she trailed off, her eyes pleading.

"It's fine," Jack said huffily. "You used to tell me everything, back before we started our life of crime, but I guess being a criminal has changed you." Betty laughed at him for his dramatics but did move over to flop down with him onto the old threadbare couch. She settled in so that she was leaning against him with her head on his shoulder.

"I'm sorry, Jack," she said sincerely. "I really want to tell you, but I'm nervous."

Jack blew a breath out his nose. "You never used to be nervous to tell me *anything*," he said. It wasn't entirely fair of him, but he'd been feeling put out by all the secrecy. Even at work, she would disappear for a while, and Jack was starting to get a nasty suspicion. Taking a breath, he decided he had to get confirmation if the worst was really happening. "Is it Sam?"

Betty blinked. "Is what Sam?"

Jack's face heated. "Is it Sam that you're, you know." He waved his hands vaguely in front of him in the hopes that she would somehow understand what he meant without him having to say it. Though he wasn't exactly sure how to express *fooling around* without doing something downright lewd either. Unfortunately, his impromptu hand puppet show only left her more confused. "You know," he tried to clarify. "Are you...together."

Betty laughed so hard at that that Jack was afraid they'd be getting noise complaints. She was doubled over with it and was slapping his leg much harder than he really thought she needed to as she cackled. "Jack, oh my *God,*" she finally managed, wiping the tears from her eyes. "You oughta be a comedian. Christ, can you *imagine?*"

Jack could. He had been, in fact, and it had been downright awful. He breathed out a sigh of relief before pouting at her as she just *kept on* laughing at him. "Okay, okay. So it's not Sam," he said.

"No, Jack. I can't believe you'd think I was going around with him," she said, though she was still laughing.

"Well, you won't tell me anything! I figured it had to be the worst thing possible!"

Betty looked contrite at that, her laughter dying, a familiar guilty expression coming across her face. He wasn't just being overdramatic when he said that they told each other *everything.* So, to have her hide something from him felt like a slap in the face. It felt like he was losing her. Like they were drifting apart now, carried further from each other by a world of booze and sin. Who better for her to be with than Sam, who embodied that world so perfectly? It would have made so much sense.

He was relieved as all get-out that it wasn't him.

"Oh, honey, you must be going wild about this," she said. "Especially if you thought I was interested in *Sammy*." She snuggled back up into him, putting her arms around his waist. "I'm sorry, Jack. I just wasn't sure how you'd take it. But I'm seeing Eva."

"Eva?" Jack asked, trying to figure out who had stolen his best friend's heart.

"The psychic," Betty said. She sounded so nervous, and Jack had no idea why.

"But, Bets, that's great! Why in the world would I have minded that?"

There was no reason for him to be upset over it. Some people would have gotten their noses out of joint about that kind of thing, especially back in their hometown, but Betty knew for a fact that Jack wasn't one of them.

"It's just...after what happened with you and James," she said, and Jack's whole body went hot, and then cold. He hadn't heard James's name in what felt like a long, long time. He hadn't wanted to hear it. He didn't want to think about him.

"Oh," he cut her off. "That's...that's not...that has nothing to do with you being happy now," he managed, only noticing how stiff he'd gone when Betty squeezed him tightly.

"I'm sorry, Jacky. I shouldn't have brought it up. I don't want you thinking that I kept Eva a secret from you for any other reason than why I did."

Jack blew out a shaky breath. "Thanks, Bets," he said, consciously unclenching his fist. "I'm not mad. I'm really happy for you." He made sure to let it show in his voice how genuine that was. He really was beyond thrilled. Betty was so sweet, and so lovely, but she never stayed in a relationship for long. Not since what had happened with her old boyfriend Richard. But that lead right back to thinking about James, and Jack didn't want to think about that. He shook his head, dispelling the doom and gloom as best he could.

"So, when do I get to meet her?" he demanded, squishing Betty to his side so that she couldn't escape the conversation.

Betty swallowed dramatically and pretended to try to wriggle away. "No! No way, Jack. You better not tell her any dumb stories about me!" she said. "I swear!" she added when all he did was laugh at her.

"Okay, okay!" he said, letting her go. "I'll only tell her the minor ones, like when you got stuck up in the hayloft without your clothes after that girl ran out on you after you drank a whole bottle of wine on New Year's."

She shrieked and slapped his arm as he laughed at her. "What about the time you lost your trousers in front of dang near the whole town during the spelling bee?" Betty shot back.

"Betty! I was eight!"

"And you just stood there, bare-legged and blushing while the teacher was having a tizzy."

"I suppose the moral is that we both have a truly endless well of humiliating stories to tease each other with." Jack laughed.

"Anyways, it's not serious. Just a bit of fun," Betty said. Jack frowned but let it go. If Betty said it wasn't serious, he'd have to believe her. He managed a sigh of relief after a few moments, a glow of laughter and warmth wrapped around them both. He felt rather silly now that he knew what Betty had been hiding. He hadn't *really* wanted to pry; he'd just been so anxious about it all. But he should have known that Betty would always be his north star, whether in the cornfields of Wisconsin or the bustling streets of New York City.

"Betty May, you're the absolute bee's knees, you know that right?"

She smiled and moved back in to settle her head against his shoulder. "So are you, Jack. You silly old fool."

Chapter Five

True to his word, Jack told Eva the worst stories about Betty. He'd told her about the time Betty had declared herself the "Corn Princess" when she was six, and about the embarrassing time with the girl on New Year's. But Betty also suspected that he'd also told Eva some of why they'd come to New York. Maybe not all of it. Probably not about what her boyfriend Richard had helped James do to him. About the loss of trust, the loss of any semblance Betty had left of stability and hope for love. No. He wouldn't have told her that.

But no matter. It was better to focus on the fun stories. The ones that she was happy for Eva to know. And of course, she responded in kind by telling Sammy that Jack wanted to spend more time with him.

"You're evil," Jack told her, coming over to stand at the table where she and Eva were sitting. "What did you tell Sam? He won't leave me alone. He's been stuck to my side like glue all day long. I only managed to shake him off when he went to grab a drink."

"I don't know what you mean," Betty replied, as Eva laughed behind her hand.

Jack pointed at her, though the gesture was rather less threatening than he likely thought it was. "You did something. I'm sure of it."

Before Betty could respond, Eva chimed in. "I think the Corn Princess is getting back at you," she said, smiling at Betty with fiendish delight.

"I was six years old!" she nearly shouted.

Eva giggled, and it was so darn cute that Betty thought it might be worth the mortification of Jack having told that stupid story.

"I think the corncob skirt sounds impressive," Eva told her, reaching out to take her hand.

Jack looked between them and smiled, a look so soft on his face that it made Betty's heart ache. But the look didn't last. The sound of a familiar voice made Jack frown and sigh through his nose in exasperation.

"Hey, Money! Where'd ya go?" Sam asked, coming up beside Jack with a drink in his hand and a grin on his face. Betty had the feeling he knew exactly what he was doing to annoy Jack, and that he wouldn't have needed her fake story about him wanting to spend time with him in order to be in on the plan. "I turned around and you were gone."

"Yes," Jack said, through gritted teeth. "That was the point."

"Come on and dance with me, Money," he said, then laughed at the look on Jack's face. "Oh, come on, it ain't that bad."

"It is," he assured him. "I'm all left feet. Besides, I don't want to dance with *you*."

Sam laughed again. "Okay, then we bring the ladies out on the floor! Eva, Bets, you two want to dance?"

Betty wasn't sure what Eva would answer, but of course she laughed her beautiful deep laugh and said, "Well, if it's the only way to get Jack out there, then I guess we'll have to, right, Betty?" Jack gave her his very best pleading puppy dog look, but she had absolutely no sympathy for him.

"Let's dance," Betty said gaily. She never missed the chance to move to the music, especially now when it meant touching Eva. And with Sammy on one side and Betty on the other, they dragged poor Jack over to the dance floor. He looked at it as though it were a minefield.

"Come on, Money, you danced with that girl before. Show us what you've got," Sam said, already moving his body to the music. He danced with a sort of chaotic energy that Betty figured made sense. He was, after all, a bit crackers. What other kind of man would choose to be a bootlegger?

Jack, bless his soul, showed them what he had. It wasn't much. Mostly he just frowned and stepped on a lot of feet. But even *he* was laughing by the third song, losing some of the stiffness in his body as Betty and Eva held his arms and Sam danced up to complete their little circle.

And when Eva and Betty shouted their excuses, Jack may have given her that pleading look again, but he stayed on the dance floor regardless. Though that may have had more to do with Sam grabbing him and bodily confining him to the dance floor than his own willingness to keep on dancing.

Giggling like schoolgirls, they made their way up to Eva's apartment and fell into bed together.

Eva's body was soft under her hands, sensual in a way that she'd never experienced with her hard muscled boyfriend back home. Her only other experience with a woman had been on New Year's, and all they'd done was kiss and undress before the other girl had gotten spooked and run out on Betty.

But with Eva, they did far more than simply kiss and take off their clothes. Eva's mouth was warm on Betty's naked breasts, then lower on her stomach as she pressed kisses down her front. Then finally it was warm between her legs, Eva's tongue drawing a symphony of moans from Betty's lips. And when she shuddered apart, it was Eva's name she moaned, as shivers of pleasure juddered their way through her.

A while later, Betty woke to find Eva gone. The sound of someone in the front room where Eva did her readings prompted her up, wrapping a blanket around herself to stave off the chill. Eva was there, setting up what looked to be a bowl of water on the table where she usually did her other magical readings.

"Sweetheart, why don't you come back to bed?" Betty said, hoping that she would make an appealing enough picture to tempt her. Eva looked up and reached out her hand. And like a magnet, Betty moved forward to hold it.

Eva squeezed her hand and shook her head. "I feel called to scry. I'll come back soon, little Nightingale. You should go back, stay warm." Betty frowned at the thought of going back to the bed cold and alone. It didn't seem even half as appealing as staying right there where Eva was.

"Can I watch?"

Eva laughed, a deep warm rumble. "If you'd like. I'm afraid it's quite boring. Unless you like watching me silently stare at a bowl."

Betty shrugged. What Eva wasn't aware of was that Betty would watch her do anything, no matter how mundane, just to see the way her expression shifted and her chest rose and fell. How watching the glow of firelight from the candles dance upon her dark cheek would be enough to keep her enraptured for the whole evening.

But that was dangerous thinking. She had started to like Eva so much. Too much maybe. It was starting to feel frightening. Intoxicating. Like the alcohol they served at the Trespass, but twice as dangerous for Betty. She didn't know what she'd do if she fell in love. Love left you open and raw and ready to be hurt. Love got taken away, by fate or by choice. She didn't want to be in love. And so she wouldn't be. She'd spend this time with Eva like she would with any other fling, and when it was over, she would move on.

But for now, she could bask in the warmth of Eva's presence, as long as she kept enough distance to avoid being burned by her flame. "I don't mind," she said, sitting down across from Eva at the small table. "I'll be quiet as a mouse."

Eva gave her that warm, indulgent smile. The one that made Betty's heart flutter in her chest.

She stayed silent, watching as Eva's breathing slowed into a gentle, meditative lull. She stayed silent and tried not to even breathe as she watched Eva watch the bowl And soon enough the soft sounds of Eva's breathing and the warm darkness had lulled her to sleep, right there at the table.

❖

Rum-running was a dangerous business, or so Sam always said. Jack had seen him injured enough times to believe that.

"Most days I feel like everyone's out to get me," Sam told him. He took a healthy gulp of his drink, the smallest grimace betraying the fact that his drink had nothing to cut the sting of the gin. Jack figured that you couldn't exactly call that paranoia when it was true. There were the coppers eager for arrests, other speakeasies out to get them, and hell, even the other runners who wanted to raise the price of liquor. It seemed like everyone wanted a piece of Sam.

"I gotta look out every day. You see a guy off the street as just another man. I see him as someone I might need to punch, you see?" Sam said. "For example..." Sam paused and looked toward the door where a six-foot stack of muscle was walking in. When Jack looked back to Sam he looked ill. "Shit."

Sam clambered out of the booth he was sharing with Jack and made his way over to the bar. Jack followed silently, dread coiling in his stomach.

"Hey, Charlie," Sam said, quiet as a mouse despite the cover of the music. "You invite him? The big Bruno looking fella, over by the door?"

Charlie looked up, his expression shifting from friendly to serious just like that. "Nope. You recognize him?"

"I think it might be...but no. Fella I'm thinking of had hair. And he wasn't as big."

Jack looked back to the hulking man. From the way he was scanning the place, it was obvious he was looking for someone in particular. So not here for pleasure then.

"Leroy isn't back yet," Charlie said. Both he and Sam turned just far enough that they wouldn't be recognized, but could still see the man skulking around the edge of the dance floor. "You think there'll be trouble?

Sam snorted a laugh. "'Course there will. When is there ever not? Specially with a goon like that packing heat."

Jack blinked. Heat? He looked back and scanned his belt line. Well shit, he really did have a gun.

"All right, then what's the plan?" Charlie asked.

"I can try to avoid him as long as I can. You wanna close up shop early? Get all these folks out of here so we don't go losing too much business?"

"Too late," Charlie said, looking over to where the man was staring straight back at them.

"Aw shit," Sam said. Jack winced, stepping off to the side, in case the man decided to put that gun to use. But the guy didn't take out his heater. He walked over, grinning from ear to ear.

"Split Lip Sammy," he said

"Baby Grand," Sam said, his voice steady and light, as though he was greeting a long-lost relative. The only thing that gave him away was the flat look in his eyes, and his hands which flexed and curled by his sides. "You look different. You get a new haircut?"

"Still a wise guy I see," Baby Grand said.

"And you still have no sense of humor. Good to see some things never change."

"There's someone who wants to see you," Baby Grand snarled at him. "He's been missing you something fierce ever since you came to this hole." Beside him, Jack watched Charlie moving away in what to a casual observer would look to be fear. But Jack figured he was heading to fetch Leroy and George. The only two who had much of a chance against this guy. What a night for them to be off running errands. Jack prayed they'd get back in time.

"Tell him where he can shove it for me," Sam answered.

Whoever this Baby Grand guy was, he didn't like that much. He threw a punch, hitting Sam square in the jaw.

Someone screamed as Sam kicked Baby Grand's legs out from under him. As Sam tried to get himself back onto his feet, Jack realized that someone in the crowd must have noticed that Baby Grand had a gun. Because patrons were suddenly rushing to the exit like the hounds of hell were chasing them out.

Sam rolled as Baby Grand tried to slam him down, then scrambled to his feet. He wiped the blood from his lip with his shirtsleeve and spat. "Fuck you."

Jack figured Sam's one advantage here was that he was smaller and faster, but there was no way he could beat Baby Grand as far as muscle on muscle went. Sam aimed a kick at his gut, but it turned out Baby Grand was faster than he looked. He grabbed Sam's leg and tossed him to the ground with a sickening thud.

Jack had to bite back on a yell. What could he do? He couldn't help here. He was a musician, not a brawler.

The wind knocked out of him, Sam tried to roll, wheezing as Baby Grand landed another solid kick to his gut. Everyone was gone now, which meant if Leroy and Charlie didn't get back fast, Sam was toast.

"Hey! Leave him alone, you ugly mug," Jack shouted. Brawler he may not be, but he couldn't just stand there and watch Sam get beat into a pulp. Gathering his courage, Jack leapt right up onto Baby Grand's back like a lemur, arms tight around his neck and legs kicking furiously.

Sam looked shocked. Jack figured that out of all of the people he'd have expected to stay back and help, Jack wouldn't have been high up on that list. Heck, even Betty would have been higher. But Jack was who he'd gotten.

Baby Grand threw him off like a sack of potatoes, and Jack hit the ground hard and heavy. He landed on his arm too, but he didn't make a sound. Just sat back up and glared. He wasn't going to give up that easily.

Sam had used Baby Grand's moment of distraction to climb back up to his feet. Jack followed suit, ready to attack him again. But then Baby Grand pressed the muzzle of a gun against Sam's head, and everything went still and silent the moment it touched him.

Christ. This was it, then. Sam was going to die. Jack stood frozen, not willing to move a muscle, just in case it made Baby Grand shoot.

"I'm gonna take your sorry body back to Zanetti to use as a bearskin rug," Baby Grand rumbled. "I'd ask if you had any last words, but you don't deserve 'em."

"Fuck you," Sam spat. It seemed he was unwilling to die without having the last word. Jack felt strangely proud of him. Sam kept his eyes open and looked right at Jack. It was almost like he was willing him to run. And Jack understood why. There was no way this guy would let him get out of here alive, not after witnessing a murder. But in some stupid show of solidarity, Jack refused to move. God, Betty was going to be so pissed. So heartbroken.

The last thing Sam saw before Baby Grand pulled the trigger was going to be Jack's wide, terrified eyes.

Chapter Six

Blood and glass. For a moment in time, that's all that Jack's senses could process. Blood and glass and the thud of a body hitting the floor.

Sam.

Sam was on the ground, his eyes wide, breath ragged. And right in front of him, Baby Grand, with his gun.

Only the gun wasn't in his hand anymore.

Sam moved, lightning fast, and grabbed it, leveling the barrel at the gangster as he waited for him to rise from the floor. There was blood on the fallen man's head, and Jack realized distantly that there was also blood on what was left of the gin bottle clenched tightly in his fist.

"I um…" He stared, uncomprehending as Sam kicked at the thug on the ground, nodding satisfied when he found him to be unconscious. He still had the gun pointed at him, and Jack noticed now that his hand was shaking. And the look on his face was something dark and dangerous that Jack had never seen before.

"Sam," he said, then tried again when he didn't react. "Sam. He's down. I…I knocked him out," he said in utter shock and disbelief. The arm that he'd been thrown onto ached, but he was pretty sure it wasn't broken or even fractured. "Sam," he said again.

That seemed to snap Sam out of it, and he lowered the gun. He did take a moment to give him a rather nasty looking kick to the head, and Jack flinched at the cavaliere show of violence. But then again, there was a bullet hole in the wall only a few inches away and up from where Sam's head had been, so he couldn't exactly blame him for being a little bit rough.

"Nice job, Money," Sam finally said, impressed and disbelieving all at once. Weirdly, through the fog of confusion about what on earth he'd just done, Jack managed to find it in himself to feel almost touched by the admiration on Sam's face. "Didn't think a milquetoast like you would have such a strong arm on him," he continued, unceremoniously shattering any good regard Jack might have momentarily been shocked enough to feel toward him.

"You—" he said, brandishing the shattered remains of the bottle at him. It was once again gratifying to see the slightly startled respect on Sam's face. "Should razz me less, thank me more."

To his surprise, Sam did.

"Yeah. Thanks, Money. I owe ya one," he said, then added with a wry smile, "again." Jack blinked, unable to think of anything to say to respond to the genuine tone and the way Sam's eyes went soft with gratitude.

"Don't look so shocked." Sam laughed like Jack was both the funniest and most puzzling person he'd ever met. "You just dry-gulched a guy for me. Least I can do is thank you."

"Right," Jack said, already certain that another night of silence from Sam was in order. But the blessed relief of that could wait. Right now, Jack *wanted* Sam to talk. "Who the hell was that guy anyways? And why was he gunning for you?"

Sam snorted. "His name's Baby Grand Bianchi. He's a real asshole, works for Dimitri Zanetti."

A shiver worked his way through Jack. The name was familiar, but only because it was in the papers so often. Dimitri "the Barber" Zanetti. A mob boss so foul that the whole city knew him by name, and by his pictures that were always appearing in the paper. He looked like what anyone might guess a mobster would look like, tall with dark hair and always wearing a well-tailored suit.

He looked nothing like Sam, a scrappy, short guy who was always laughing and carrying on around the bar. Who wore shirts two sizes too big from the Salvation Army, and who more often than not had a smattering of bruises across his body.

"Why in God's name is *he* sending goons here?" Jack asked, his voice shaking. He'd just attacked a mob member. Sent by the biggest mobster this side of the country.

It didn't feel real. But it was. He'd done that, and now for all he knew he was a target. He hoped that Sam's kick to Bianchi's head had jumbled up his brains, and maybe he wouldn't remember that Jack had even been there. He held his aching arm, amazed he'd escaped so relatively unscathed.

Sam shrugged like this was no big deal. "I used to work for him. He doesn't take well to being betrayed, and leaving the Family is the ultimate betrayal in his eyes. It's even worse that I switched sides. He don't have any hold here at the Trespass and he hates that."

"You...worked," Jack managed, suddenly seeing Sam in a whole new light. He'd known that he was a gangster. That much had been obvious. But he hadn't realized he'd belonged to the *mob* at some point. He swallowed slightly, pushing away the stray thought about exactly what Sam had done in the mob, how much blood he had on his hands. The shock of the encounter was starting to sink in, and he realized he felt slightly weightless, as though his head was floating a few inches above his neck.

"Yeah. I used to work at the Cherry, before I got respectable."

Jack laughed at that, a tad hysterically. "You? Respectable?"

Sam glared at him, a stupidly adorable pout on his lips. Gangsters shouldn't be able to look *cute*, in Jack's opinion. It was just wrong. Though maybe it was also wrong for Jack to be focusing on the curve of Sam's lips, and not that fact that he had knocked out (maybe almost killed, a thought that didn't bear dwelling on right now) a genuine mob thug.

"Fine, *more* respectable." Sam produced some cuffs from what seemed like nowhere, but must have been from the pocket of his oversized pants, and set to making sure the big guy wasn't going to get up anytime soon. "Anyways, they picked me up off the streets. They were a rough crowd. Way rougher than any Tom, Dick, or Harry you'll meet here. Used to have me doing all kinds of bad things for 'em," he admitted, like the words pained him to say. "Mostly worked as a grifter and a goon for them, but occasionally they had me working as a can opener. Did a couple of soup jobs stealing things from safes, you know? Beat in a lot of faces like I do now, that kinda thing."

Sam paused, scratching the back of his neck. "But I also had to clip a few people for them," Sam said, his expression more heartbroken than Jack had ever seen it. "Didn't like to do that, but once you're in with that crowd, you don't say no when they tell you to get something done."

"Yeah," Jack agreed helplessly. The adrenaline rush was starting to subside now, leaving him feeling shaky and a little bit like he might laugh—or cry—at any moment. He'd figured that Sam might have killed before, based on how damn violent he was when he fought. But mob hits. Actual contract killings. He'd never have guessed. Not with how sweet he could be sometimes, and the way he smiled so carefree.

No wonder he drank so much.

Sam sighed, a deep and *tired* sound. "Then one day I'm running some gin for them, normal day and all, and when I hop in the automobile, I find out they're taking me for a ride."

Jack wasn't entirely sure what that meant, but it didn't sound good. "Oh" he said. "Is that…bad?"

Sam snorted. "Yeah, Money. It means they were trying to bump me off."

"Oh," Jack said again, feeling cold all over. They had tried to kill him. Sam had been on a hit list. No, scratch that. Sam was *still* on a hit list. Christ.

"So, I fought back. They were trying to get me to some other location so I popped off and, well, the driver was the only other guy to get outta that automobile in one piece." Jack processed this. Lord, he'd never known the extent of what Sam had himself into, but he'd known it was bad. Just not this bad. He could imagine Sam, drunk and happy-go-lucky like he was every night at the Trespass, climbing into an automobile full of people who wanted him dead with a smile on his face and whiskey on his breath. It was a wonder he was still alive, and relatively in one piece.

"I'd been looking for a way out though, so I guess it wasn't all bad," Sam said with a shrug. "I didn't like the way they did business there. They started giving people wood alcohol, you know? The stuff that makes you go blind. And I guess I was getting a little too vocal about it."

Blind? Christ, Jack had heard stories about that kind of thing, but it was hard to believe it was true. Still, he trusted Sam. If he said they were selling liquor that hurt people, he was certain they were.

"So, you probably think I'm some no-good gangster now, huh?" Sam asked him, his grin wry and almost sheepish. Like he cared what Jack thought about him. And wasn't that a strange thought. Sam, caring what a corn-fed Midwestern boy thought about his life of crime.

But oddly enough, Jack didn't think he was a no-good gangster. He'd lived in this city long enough to know how down on their luck a person could get, and how quickly it could happen. And with someone like Sam, who didn't have a lick of sense, and who had such a hard start in life…it was no wonder he got into rum-running. Just with the wrong speakeasy it seemed.

But Sam had got out of that motorcar, and he'd gotten out of the Cherry. He'd found the Trespass, and he was here now, doing his best to only brutally maim the other thugs who got in his way. Not ideal, to be frank, but still. He was trying. Sometimes that's all a fella could do in this city.

"Sam, I've always thought you were a no-good gangster," Jack said, but the words carried no weight. And he slung an arm around Sam's shoulder for good measure. Ostensibly to help support him, but in reality, he just wanted to. He'd noticed that it seemed to settle something in Sam, being touched casually. He'd seen him melt under the hands of damn near every dame who'd ever given him the time of day, but it wasn't only that. Even Charlie and Leroy seemed to make him melt with nothing but a hand on the shoulder. It was like he was starved for any physical affection he could get. And without fail, Sam seemed to sink into the touch like a man climbing into a warm bath.

"Hah. Damn right you did." Sam laughed. "So anyways, that's why they're after me. But they've had a problem with the Trespass for longer than I've worked here. Rumrunners always want to be the only ones in town. Booze makes men crazy in more ways than one." Jack hummed. It made sense really. He'd heard Charlie and Leroy talking about the Cherry enough times to know that there was no love lost between the two juice joints.

"Anyways, whadda'ya say we give this guy the bum's rush?"

Jack looked to the absolutely enormous man, then back at Sam. "Really? He's huge!"

Sam cackled at him and slapped his good arm in a way that was likely meant to be friendly, but mostly just stung. "You just knocked him out, Strong Arm. We can do it if we both work on it, yeah?"

Jack eyed Bianchi up skeptically. "Well, okay. If you say so. But you'll have to do most of the work. He really messed up my arm."

"Oh damn! I forgot," Sam said, moving forward to grab Jack's forearm. "He threw you pretty damn hard, Money. Are you all right?" He moved Jack's arm gently, back and forth then up and down. Jack wasn't sure that it was entirely medically sound to do so, but Sam had been injured enough times before and he seemed to heal just fine without a doctor's help.

"I'm okay," Jack said, but he stood and let Sam examine him without protest. "I, um, I can probably even help lift him."

Sam nodded, giving his arm a little squeeze. "All right. If it hurts, let me know. We can take a break if we need. I don't need your arm popping outta the socket or something." Jack didn't think that was likely, but it was sweet that Sam cared.

They did manage to move Bianchi, though the dead weight had them both struggling. But by half dragging him they maneuvered him to the back door that had a shorter staircase up to the street level, thanking the Lord the whole way that the front stairs weren't the only entrance. Otherwise, they'd have had to carry him out in pieces, and Jack wasn't quite comfortable enough in his new life of crime for that yet.

"Whoo boy, he needs to lose a few pounds. And some muscle," Sam said once they'd thrown him out into the alley. Jack was a little bit concerned at how out cold he was, but despite it feeling like hours, he was reasonably sure he'd only been out for a few minutes at this point.

Surely he'd be fine.

"Sure. Tell him that to his face," Jack replied. He wiped at the sweat beaded on his brow and looked Bianchi over. "You gonna leave him in those cuffs?"

Sam grinned, wide and sort of evil looking. "Sure am. Let him go back to the Barber in bracelets, see how he takes it."

Jack frowned but didn't comment. It seemed cruel, but then again it didn't get much more cruel than trying to murder them both in cold blood, so who was he to complain?

"Hey," Sam said once they were back inside with the door locked as he poured himself a drink. "Thanks again. Anytime you need anything I'm your guy, okay?" Before Jack could respond and likely embarrass himself by being overly sentimental, Leroy and Charlie came tearing through the front door like bats out of hell, only to come up short at the sight of Sam and Jack lounging at the bar.

"What happened?" Charlie asked, leaning over with his hands on his knees and breathing heavily.

"What took you so long?" Sam fired back, then laughed and raised his glass. "Money here coldcocked Bianchi in the back of the head with a bottle of gin. And don't worry about it, Leroy, it was a bottle of the watered down stuff."

Leroy and Charlie both looked at Jack like they were reassessing him. "Damn. Thanks, Jack," Leroy said. "I'd say we owe you a drink, but it looks like you already took a whole bottle."

Jack laughed, relieved that it was said with no malice. "I sure did. Didn't do me any harm, but from the way Bianchi fell I'd say that stuff must be bad for you." That had everyone cracking up, and Jack glowed with pride, not only at the joke but at the realization that this was real. He'd gone up against a member of the mob and won. He was really there, standing in an illegal speakeasy, being congratulated by these gangsters he'd learned to call friends.

Sam retold their story, with some notable embellishments, but Jack didn't bother correcting him. The story was far more fun the way Sam told it anyway.

❖

"Jack, you brave old fool," Betty said, throwing her arms around him. He'd just finished telling her the story of how he'd knocked out a literal mobster, and Betty was beyond impressed. "I almost wish I'd have been there, just to see it all happen!"

"No, you don't," Jack assured her.

Betty rolled her eyes. "I know, I know. But it sounds like quite the show."

She wondered if this was the trouble Eva had foretold. If it was, she was sure glad it had ended how it did.

Jack and Betty performed for the first half of the night, until it was finally time for their break. Jack seemed glad for it. He'd complained that his arm was still hurting from where he'd landed on it. But Betty felt like she could stay there singing for the rest of her life. The joy on the faces of the dancers made her glow bright as a star.

But if Jack wasn't playing, she couldn't very well sing acapella. So, she went to sit at a table on the edge of the dance floor, smiling to herself as she watched flappers and their fellas dance.

"Here you go," Charlie said, placing a drink in front of Betty with a sly smile.

Betty looked at it in confusion. "Why, Charlie, you didn't have to get me a drink."

"I didn't," he said with a shrug. "It's from our favorite psychic over there." He nodded to the bar where Eva was leaning, looking as beautiful as ever in a long green dress. Betty felt her heartbeat pick up and her face heat. "Thank you, Charlie boy. I'll take it from here," she said, gesturing Eva over.

Charlie nodded and headed back to the bar, passing Eva as she came over to Betty's table.

"Hello, Nightingale," Eva said, gracefully lowering herself into the chair beside Betty.

"You didn't have to buy me a drink," Betty said, running her hand down Eva's arm. "The band drinks for free."

"A beautiful girl deserves to have her drinks bought for her," Eva said. She was smiling that mysterious smile that had Betty entranced.

"Well, thank you," Betty replied. She felt suddenly shy, like this was the first time she'd ever flirted. Which was ridiculous. She was Betty May Dewitt. She was practically born to flirt. Betty toyed with her long string of pearls, smiling the smile that had won her the affection of many different people over the years. "You aren't working tonight?"

"I'm taking a break," she said. "I like to come down and watch you sing."

Betty blinked. She'd never noticed Eva, though she supposed she tended to watch the dance floor while she was on stage. "Oh.

Did I do a good job tonight?" She took a sip of her drink, finding it sweet on her tongue.

"You know you did." Eva laughed. "I like watching you down here, in your element. You look like you were born to be on stage, Nightingale. I like the way everyone's eyes are glued to you. I like knowing that it's *me* you'll be coming home with tonight."

Betty's face heated so hot she felt like she could fry an egg on her cheek. "Oh? And what makes you think I'll be coming home with you?"

Eva smirked. "Maybe I saw it in my crystal ball."

Betty swatted her playfully, giggling. "Well…" she said, eying Eva up and down. "Who am I to argue with fate?"

Eva stood then, holding out her hand to help Betty up.

"Tell Jack to play without me," she told Charlie as she walked hand in hand with Eva toward the stairs. "I'll be busy for an hour or so."

Betty flopped down on the bed about forty-five minutes later, breathless and satisfied.

"Lord," she said. "You sure know how to have a good time."

Eva laughed. "You too."

They lay in silence for a moment, catching their breath, before Betty turned over onto her side so that she was looking at Eva's silhouette in the dim lighting.

"How'd you end up in New York?" Betty asked, trailing her fingers along Eva's naked skin.

"I was born here. My mother was a medium and did laundry, and my father was a barber," Eva told her.

"So medium is a family profession, then," Betty said.

Eva nodded. "For as far back as my mother can remember on her mother's side. We've been seeing the future for a long time in our family." She laughed. "Though I expect our gift won't be passed on unless by some miracle I have a child."

Betty hummed. So, Eva wasn't interested in men then. "Who knows, maybe you'll fall for a fella someday," she said, torn by the implications.

"I doubt it," Eva said, shrugging. "I don't want a child anytime soon, but who knows what the future holds."

"Besides you." Betty giggled.

"Besides me," Eva agreed.

They lapsed into comfortable silence. Betty basked in Eva's warmth, thinking about her as a child. Wondering if she could really see the future or if it was some kind of con. She really couldn't see Eva conning people like that though. She was so sweet and kind. And she'd just spoken about her gift as though she believed it was real.

"My parents are good people, but they didn't understand why I couldn't get myself a man," Eva said eventually. "I moved out soon as I had the money. Not a lot of money mind you. It was a rough few years. Until I found this apartment, and the Trespass Inn. It was like finding a whole new family. That first night I heard music coming from downstairs I came down. George almost didn't let me in, since I wasn't dressed right. But he's sweet and he let me in when I explained I lived upstairs."

Betty remembered her first night at the Trespass, dressed in her office clothes. She wondered if George just had a sense for women he ought to let in, no matter what they were wearing.

"It must have been something, finding out you lived over a speakeasy," Betty said.

Eva nodded, some of her long black tresses falling into her face. She tucked them back behind her ear. "It was. The landlord told me it was a factory down there. I was a little nervous at first about it all, but then I met the boys. You know good people when you meet them, and they're good people. Even Sammy."

Betty giggled. Poor Sammy got razzed more than anyone else. But it was true. He was a good egg.

"They got me customers," Eva continued. "Helped me find my way in this part of town. They were friends to me when I needed some most. All my other friends well, they find the fact that I'm a psychic a little bit off-putting. I find it hard to maintain relationships with most folks."

Betty frowned. Eva was such a sparkling person; she couldn't imagine anyone meeting her and not gravitating toward her. Even if she was a bit odd with her psychic practice, that only made her all the more interesting. All the more fascinating.

"Jack tells me you came to New York to be musicians," Eva said eventually.

Betty hummed in agreement. "We had a couple of hard years back home, Jack and I. It was time for us to move out of our old town. And look at us now, playing for a living!" She wanted to share more. Tell Eva about Richard and James. Share like she'd been shared with. But that seemed too much. Maybe some other time.

Eva nuzzled her nose against Betty's shoulder. "You sure are. You sing so beautifully, Nightingale. Whatever you left behind, I hope you like this life better."

Betty thought about her life back in Wisconsin. About the people she'd left behind. People who'd done nothing but hurt and disappoint her.

"I do," she said solemnly. "I really do."

CHAPTER SEVEN

Gaining Sam's respect came with the downside of Sam deciding that he and Jack were now good friends. Jack still wasn't quite certain he wanted or needed that kind of friend in his life, but it seemed that it was too late. From the moment he'd clocked Bianchi, Sam had started spending more and more time with him, to the point where weeks later, he was practically a staple by Jack's side.

Sam was loud, and rude, and disgusting. He was always drinking, belching, and farting like it was his favorite sport, and bleeding and throwing up on various surfaces. Most notably including Jack's pants, his shirt, and once directly in his hair. Didn't matter that he was loyal as a dog, and could, upon the rare occasion, be even more precious than one. He was a goof, and Jack stood by that opinion.

"I'm just saying, it wouldn't hurt for you to take a girl into the back room once in a while," Sam was saying, raising and lowering his eyebrows in a way that would almost be comical if it wasn't so vile.

"I'm perfectly fine," Jack protested, for the hundredth time. "I don't want to take anyone to the back room, now that I know what goes on in there." He wrinkled his nose, gently trying to shake his arm free of Sam's iron grip. He didn't even remember Sam grabbing him, but it sure was happening. "It's not sanitary."

Sam howled like this was the best joke he'd ever heard. "Nookie ain't supposed to be sanitary," he said. The look on his face was something Jack had never seen before. Almost sultry, if Sam could achieve such a thing. "It's supposed to be messy. Wild." Jack was suddenly almost *too* aware of how tightly Sam was gripping him. Of how close their bodies were. "It's supposed to be...well...sticky." Sam cackled, and just like that, any glimmer of appeal he might have had went out the window.

"You disgust me," Jack said, finally managing to free himself from Sam's gremlin grip. "I don't know how in the world you get women to go with you."

"It's because I got charisma," he said, puffing out his chest. "Unlike *some* people here. And I know how to have a good time."

Jack frowned. For all that Sam hung around him, he certainly wasn't shy about letting Jack know just how boring he found him. It was starting to become a bit of a sore spot. "Oh, go dry up," he said, having had enough of Sam for the night.

"How 'bout you loosen up instead, Money," Sam said, like the little monster he was. "Here. Have some gin. See what that does for you." He slapped his half empty glass down onto the table in front of Jack, somehow still managing to spill some onto the table with the splash despite the liquid being down so low.

Then he sauntered away, leaving Jack alone and irritated. "That stupid, horrible little...ugh." Jack glared at the liquor as though it was Sam himself. It wasn't like he'd never had a drink before. He'd had a sip of whiskey from his father's bottle when he was around twelve or so, and he could still remember the burn of it, and the confusion as to why the heck his father drank it if it tasted so vile. Then there had been the time when he and Betty had shared a third of a bottle of rum once, when they'd both been feeling down and out. Jack had vomited on his new slacks, and Betty had ended up with a terrible headache the next morning, making the experience entirely worthless. What was the point of drinking when you were down when all it did was make you feel that much worse in the morning? He'd sworn off drinking since then, beyond a glass or two when social pressure made it necessary. Social pressure like proving he wasn't a dry agent.

But that had mostly been when he was younger. He'd grown since then. He could handle a little bit of alcohol. "I'll show him hard-boiled," he said aloud to himself, grabbing the glass and staring it down. He took a deep breath, steeling himself for the unpleasant taste, and took a swig. He spluttered at the sharp taste, and practically gulped down his mouthful. It stung his throat on the way down, making him cough and choke, and kept right on burning all the way down to his stomach. God, how could Sam stand this stuff?

"Whoa, hey. Are you okay?" a man's voice asked, startling Jack into a further coughing fit. A gentle hand rested against his shoulder, and he looked up ready to defend himself, only to see a kind expression and piercing blue eyes.

"I'm—" Jack choked. "I'm all right. Just went down the wrong pipe."

The man smiled, showing perfectly straight teeth. A smile that belonged in a magazine, or maybe even in a film. Even the little crow's feet crinkled up near his eyes only served to make him seem all the more handsome. Jack suddenly found it hard to breathe for a whole new reason.

"Glad to hear it," he said cheerfully. "The name's Billy. Nice to meet you." He held out his hand and Jack shook it. His grip was firm and his palm was warm against Jack's own.

"I'm Jack, nice to meet you too," he managed to say, surprised to find that it was. This was probably the first civil introduction he'd had since he'd started working here. At the very least it was the most sober introduction. It was marred slightly by the fact that he was still coughing a little, sure, but it was still nice.

"I heard you play earlier," Billy said, his charmingly eager expression warming Jack far better than even the gulp of gin had. "You were fantastic. I've never heard someone lay on the keys like that before. You sure are something, Jack."

Didn't that just light him up from the inside out. He found himself smiling shyly, but proud enough to burst as he thanked him. "That's kind of you. I'm happy to have had such a good audience tonight."

"You know, I was hoping to talk to you. I was wondering how you got a gig at a place like this," Billy said. "I'm outta work right now and I'm something of a horn player. Thought maybe, if you were looking…"

"We are!" Jack said, too eager. God, one handsome face and he was acting like an overeager kid. He cleared his throat again. "I mean, we'd love to have someone on trumpet. I'll talk to Charlie about getting you an audition."

"Charlie, huh? Is he the owner?"

Jack nodded. "Him and Leroy. They've been so great, you'll love working for them." Jack paused. Funny, how much his opinion of his bosses had changed from when he'd first met them. He'd thought of them only as low-life criminals before, but now they were something like trusted friends. Brothers even. "That is, if you can swing it," he added with a laugh.

"Oh, I can blow." Billy laughed, clearly confident in his ability. "I've never worked for a juice joint before though. It seems a little risky, don't you think?"

Jack nodded. "Sure. But like I said, Charlie and Leroy are great." He bit back on all of the stories he wanted to tell about gangsters and guns, and rum-soaked patrons' antics. He couldn't go blabbing speakeasy secrets to just anyone. Sam had said as much the first time they'd come in for work. "They take care of their employees. It's a good job, if you don't mind all the fools." Speaking of Sam, the fool in question was causing a stir on the dance floor, trying to pummel a guy about twice his size, and doing a damned good job of it. Jack laughed as Sam dragged him toward the door, and with George, gave the guy the bum's rush.

"That dolt. He'll fight anything that moves. Probably attack his own reflection like a dang canary," Jack muttered. It was true too. Sam was so hungry for a fight that Jack was surprised he hadn't gotten punched himself.

Billy laughed. "So, is he the rumrunner for this joint?" he asked, leaning in against Jack's side to be heard above the gramophone. He smelled of cigarettes and cologne, and Jack found it suddenly much more difficult to breathe. "He seems the type."

"Who, Sam?" he breathed. He had to be careful here, he knew, but all he wanted to do was tell this man anything he wanted to hear, just to keep him close. But no. He had to keep a clear head. "He struts around here like a peacock but he's all show," he said, wary of saying too much. Billy seemed like a great guy, but Jack still remembered the solemnly serious way that Leroy and Charlie had warned him our business stays our business. "You can ignore most of what he says. He's mostly talk."

"Ah, gotcha." Billy nodded, letting Jack's vague answer go easily enough. "Seems like you two are real good friends," he said. "Given the way he's liquored you up."

Jack's face warmed. So Billy had seen Sam give him the gin. He'd been taking notice of Jack, he'd said. Ever since he heard him play. It was flattering. It was exhilarating. It was embarrassing as all hell, since he'd just coughed like a kid having his first drink.

"What? Him? And *me*?" Jack exclaimed, a bit over-the-top, trying to make Billy laugh again. The way Betty May always did when she wanted to grab a fella's attention. "Nah. No way. He's just a lounge lizard who thinks he's the berries." They watched together in amusement as Sam tried and utterly failed to flirt with a beautiful brown-haired girl in a black dress. She smacked him and stomped away, and Billy leaned heavily against Jack as they laughed together.

"I can see that. So, you and him, you aren't..." Billy trailed off, and though Jack wasn't entirely sure what he meant, he felt compelled to answer rather than ask for clarification.

"No, we aren't friends. We aren't close," he said, barely stopping himself from saying *we aren't anything* bitterly. He didn't even know why he felt bitter. Anyway, it was best not to let this stranger know he felt anything at all about Sam.

"Right. Well, I'm hoping you and I can be friends," Billy said.

"Sure! I'd like that," Jack said, smiling. Finally, someone nice in this place where a new acquaintance was more than likely to vomit on you, or greet you with drunken shouts and grabbing hands. He was over the moon at the novelty of such a civil guy wanting not only to make his acquaintance, but possibly work with him too. "Why don't you come on with me, I'll introduce you to Charlie," Jack said, turning away before Billy could catch his blush. The man was going to think Jack was drunk as a skunk from how rosy his cheeks were. "He's over at the bar, that's where you'll find him most of the time."

Billy followed him over, weaving through the pressing crowd of dancers with a graceful ease to where Charlie was serving out drinks. "Hey, Charlie, I'd like you to meet Billy. Billy…" Jack trailed off, realizing that he hadn't even gotten his last name.

"Billy Lindh," he said, holding out his hand. "Pleasure to meet you."

Charlie eyed his hand suspiciously before reaching out and shaking it. "Name's Charlie," he said. Jack grinned, remembering the first time he'd met Charlie. It was validating to know that he was withholding of handshakes with everyone, not just him and Betty.

"I was wondering if you had any openings for a horn player," Billy said, getting straight to the point. It was clear to see that Charlie wasn't as charmed as Jack felt, but he did give him an appraising look.

"That depends," Charlie said finally. "On how well you play."

Billy gave Jack a sidelong glance and grinned. Like they were in on this together. "How about I bring my trumpet tomorrow night then?" he said, turning back to Charlie with a wink.

"Sure," Charlie agreed easily. "Leroy'll be around all night tomorrow. We'll check you out, see how good you are."

Billy nodded, grinning. "Who knows," he told Jack as they walked away from the bar. "If I'm lucky, I just might be spending a lot more time around this joint."

❖

Billy's audition went well enough that Charlie and Leroy hired him on the spot. He wasn't the best horn player that Jack had ever heard, but he had talent. And he made up for his lack of technical skill with passion. He quickly became a fixture around the bar. And even more quickly, became a fixture with Jack.

He was kind, and funny. Fun, in a less wild and dangerous way than everyone else who worked at the Trespass was. Jack didn't feel like chatting with him was as fraught with the danger of getting punched as it was with someone like Sam, for example. Billy was more civil than the whole lot of them too.

Jack liked him a lot.

Whenever they weren't on stage together, they were spending time with each other in the seating area, watching the antics of the various patrons and staff members at the bar. Tonight, Sam was one table over, sitting with Charlie and talking about getting a few bottles of bathtub gin from one of their suppliers. "I'm just telling you, I think they're gonna try something. I heard from that Louis fella that Two Tone and Brandon *both* tried to raise the price on him last minute the last few times he's gone to get his supply."

"That's all right," Charlie said, as unshakable as ever. "That's why I bring you along. I'd like to see them dare raise the price with you glaring at them like you're out for blood."

"They will," Sam informed him. "Two Tone especially. The fella's dumber than a wooden post. And he don't mind getting confrontational."

"Sounds like someone I know," Billy said, having been listening in for a while now. Jack hid his laugh behind his hand at the look Sam sent him for that.

"Hey," he said, then looked between Billy and Jack like a man betrayed. "Really, Money? You think *he's* funny? *Him?*"

Jack shrugged, unable to wipe the smile off his face. "What can I say. I have a weak spot for jokes that you're the butt of."

Sam grumbled, but he looked like he was thinking something through. "Hey, Charlie. Why don't we bring Billy along with us tonight?" Sam said, trying and failing to look innocent. "I'm sure he'd be more than happy to help out. We could use an extra hand carrying the liquor back."

Charlie looked at him, and something passed between them that Jack couldn't quite read. "All right. He'll have to be blindfolded at least half the way though. You okay with that, Billy?"

Billy frowned, looking between them like he was expecting some kind of trap. "I suppose," he said after a moment.

Jack frowned. "How come you've never invited me out rum-running before?" he asked, sounding more put out about it than he'd meant to. It wasn't like he was dying to go out and become a bootlegger, but it'd be nice to be asked. Especially if Sam was willing to take Billy.

"Your initiation was different," Sam said, waving his hand. Initiation. Huh. So that's what this was? Billy seemed to breathe again at that, like he'd thought they were planning on bumping him off or something. "We knew we could trust you almost soon as we met you. You acted so much like a dry agent that there was no way you actually were one."

Jack was about to protest, on Billy's behalf and his own, but it seemed he didn't need to. At least on Billy's part. "I understand," Billy said, nodding. "I can't promise I'll be much help if it comes to a fight, but I don't mind getting my hands dirty if it'll help you trust me."

"Don't worry about that. If there's a fight *I'll* be taking care of it," Sam said, puffing his chest out. Proud as a peacock. Behind his back, Charlie rolled his eyes with a fond little smile.

"I want to come with you," Jack said, ignoring Sam's boast. Both Charlie and Sam laughed, but Billy looked concerned. Jack frowned. It was rude of them, really. He could hold his own. He'd proved himself with Bianchi, hadn't he? "I'm serious. You didn't take me out rum-running when I started here. It's only fair."

"It could be dangerous," Billy said, his brow furrowed. "Are you sure you want to do this?"

Sam snorted derisively. "It's not so dangerous. We're taking *you* aren't we?" He looked at Jack, grinning lopsidedly. "Anyways, Money here is more hard-boiled than you'd think."

Oh. Well, that was nice at least.

"Is he?" Billy said, looking almost angry about something. But just as quickly as it came, his expression eased back out into something fond, directed at Jack. "Well, if you're sure, I'd definitely feel a sight better having you along with me on this little adventure."

"Of course, Bill," Jack said warmly. Billy was always so kind to him, and it felt good to know that he was happy to spend time with him, even if what they were doing wasn't exactly the nicest thing in the world.

"Fine. Great. Everyone's coming. Then let's get going," Sam growled, clearly grumpy now. Though why, Jack had no idea. He'd been perfectly cheerful before.

Jack blinked. "What, right now?" he asked, startled. He'd figured this little venture would be at the very least a night or two away.

"Yeah, Money. We have an appointment," Sam said. "We have some bottles to pick up from a supplier. Bathtub gin. One of the bestsellers here."

Right. Jack knew that the Trespass made their own rum, but he'd never really wondered where they got their gin from until now. Seemed like it was homemade too. He was starting to wonder if all speakeasy booze was homemade. Seemed like it could be, given how blotto it got their guests. If you were making your own booze it was hard to regulate how strong it was.

"Get your coats, boys," Charlie said. "I'll let Betty know where you'll be, Jack."

"Thanks, Charlie," he said, as he walked toward the coat room. Anticipation was coiling in his gut, and Jack was surprised to find that it wasn't anxiety. No, he was strangely excited for what was to come.

"I didn't sound like a dry agent," Jack whispered to Billy a little while later as they headed toward the door. He'd been thinking about what Sam had said the whole time. "Just because I don't like to drink—"

Billy laughed and patted him on the back. "I'm sure you didn't, old pal," he said as they stepped out into the coolness of the night air.

"If you think for one minute that I'm going to let you boys have all the fun," Betty was snapping at Charlie and Sam. "You've got another think coming!"

"Bets, it's dangerous," Sam tried to tell her, earning himself a mighty glare. Betty pursed her red painted lips and put her hands on her hips.

"You're bringing Jack and Billy. Why not me?" Betty demanded. "I'm just as hard-boiled as them."

"She's right, you know," Jack chipped in. "She could probably beat Charlie in a fight. Maybe even Sam."

Sam looked between Jack and Betty, and in a rare moment of smarts, kept his mouth shut.

"All right," Charlie said. "You can come. Just make sure you're ready for if things get rough."

"Of course," Betty said. "I'm wearing a red dress anyways, so a little blood won't bother me much."

"Let's hope it doesn't come to blood," Billy said. "Especially not with a lady along. Are you certain you should be joining us, doll? It's dangerous for a woman."

Betty scoffed and marched ahead, following close behind Charlie who was leading the way. "I'll be just fine," she called back to him. Billy frowned, and Jack wondered what he was thinking. "You can't seriously be all right with her coming along?" he said after a moment.

"Betty does what she wants," Jack replied. It was what he loved about her.

Billy gave him a look, but then he shrugged and nodded to Jack. "Let's go catch up."

Charlie and Sam actually did blindfold them about halfway through the walk. Jack hadn't really thought they would. He'd sort of assumed Charlie had been joking. Sam had claimed that Jack and Betty didn't need to put one on since they were already trusted employees, but it was only fair. If Billy wasn't able to see, then neither would Jack.

"You're an odd egg," Sam had said, shaking his head as he moved to cover Jack's eyes. His fingers were deft as they tied the knot, and Jack could feel the warmth of his body as he stood close behind him to put the blindfold on. "You could skip this part, but you're still doing it."

"It's only fair, if Billy has to do it," he repeated, shivering when Sam finally stepped back, feeling all the more cold now as the brisk night air rushed back in.

"That's...honorable, I guess," Sam said, patting his back, before taking his arm. Charlie had done much the same to Billy and would be guiding him the rest of the way. Betty had declined the blindfold with an incredulous snort as she gestured at her heavily made-up eyes "You think I'm going to risk wrecking this for some errand? I don't think so," she'd said.

It felt silly, walking down the street in a blindfold, arm in arm with Sam. Childish, like they were playing some strange game of hide-and-seek as adults. But the realization that what they were about to do was anything but a game became a lot clearer now that he couldn't see. He was suddenly starkly aware that his coworkers, whom he trusted deeply, were criminals. That he and Billy, and Betty were essentially at their mercy, being taken to a strange location where they had no way of knowing what would happen. Mostly he was worried over Betty. But she'd likely give him a piece of her mind if he ever admitted he was fretting about her.

But despite his misgivings, he trusted Charlie and Sam. No, if there was going to be a problem wherever they were going, it wouldn't be because of them. It'd be the other criminals they were going to meet. Finally, after what seemed like hours, but was likely only fifteen to twenty minutes, they arrived. Sam had been surprisingly good at leading him, keeping his arm held tight in his grip, making sure that he hadn't tripped, and warning him when the terrain had been uneven.

"You can take off the blindfolds," Charlie said from somewhere to his left.

Charlie, Betty, and Billy had chatted almost the whole time they'd been walking. Jack didn't know how they managed. He could barely speak from the knots tying up his stomach.

"Let's just hope it isn't Two Tone Tommy at the house tonight," Sam said in disgust, as he led them up to a small, old house.

"He whistles two tones when there's coppers, is that it?" Billy asked, sounding sure of himself.

"Nah," Charlie said, "He sure tries though."

"Ol' Two Tone can't carry even *one* tone in a bucket," Sam said, rolling his eyes. "But he still insists on trying to whistle. It's like listening to a wet breeze."

"I think it's sweet that he tries." Charlie laughed. "He means well."

"He sounds like a fun fella," Betty said.

"He's a bum," Sam groused. "I'd rather deal with someone who won't preach Jesus to me the whole damn time I'm trying to buy some illegal bathtub gin."

Billy laughed, which only seemed to make Sam even more annoyed.

They knocked on the door four times in a row, then waited. From the other side of the door came what Jack could only call... hell, he didn't even know what to call it. It was like someone trying to imitate a whistle with their voice. Perhaps someone who had never actually heard a whistle. It sounded...rather wet. Then Sammy knocked again twice, and the door swung open.

"Lads! C'mon in," the man in the doorway said, stepping back to allow them to file in. His accent was strongly Irish, so much so that Jack had to shake his head a little to focus. "And oh, who's this breath o' fresh air? I didn't know yous were bringing a gal along!"

"Betty May, pleasure to meet you," Betty said, curtseying to him with a wink.

"You aren't sleeping with any o' these here men are ya?" he asked bluntly. "Unless yer married that's one hell of a sin, if you don't mind me saying."

Betty barked out a laugh at that. "These fellas? No way," she said.

"Hey!" Sam cried out indignantly. Betty looked at him, at once pitying and indulgent—the way one might look at a younger sibling who insisted they could climb the same tree.

"Oh, honey," she said. "You know what I like about you, Sammy? You dream big."

Sam grumbled as the other men laughed at his plight.

"I like you," Tommy said to her. "Come on in."

The apartment they entered was fairly regular, though it looked rather beat up compared to most liveable places Jack had seen. The wallpaper was yellowed and peeling, with smoke and water stains near the ceiling, giving the whole place a rather jaundiced feel. It smelled of smoke and men's sweat.

Two Tone Tommy was a man in his late forties, whose face was craggy and whose skin was nearly as papery as the peeling walls. He spoke with a thick Irish accent, which meant that Jack could hardly understand a word he was saying. He seemed jolly enough, though prone to shouting.

For all his protesting, Sam and Two Tone seemed to get along just fine.

"Y'look like the devil's gotten into ya," Tommy said, greeting Sam with a clap on the back. "You haven't read that Bible I gave you yet, have ya?"

"Haven't had the time," Sam said in a way that suggested he wouldn't be making the time any time soon. "How's your sister been? I haven't seen her in a while."

Two Tone grimaced, smacking Sam's arm hard. "Colleen's a married woman now, you hear me? Keep your grubby hands off her." But for all he was protesting, he went ahead and poured Sam a heaping glass of gin all the same. They were both already a little bit drunk, and by the time they'd been there a couple of minutes, Jack could tell that they'd be completely blotto by the time this meeting was through.

"Gotta sample the wares," Charlie supplied, as Two Tone placed glasses of gin in front of everyone. Though Jack noticed that he wasn't touching the gin himself. It seemed like no one was, except for Two Tone, Sam, and Betty. Jack felt better about ignoring his glass. "At least that's what he tells us."

"Jesus help us, mercy," Two Tone said after pounding back his drink, his accent thick around the words. "Already drunk off o' this batch. It's a strong one I tell ya."

"No stronger than the price we already worked out though," Sam said, his tone warning.

Two Tone put his hand to his heart. "Surely you aren't suggesting I'd try to swindle ya! A good Catholic boy like me."

"That's exactly what I'm suggesting," Sam shot back. Jack had seen him stand like that before. Leaning in like he wanted to start something and was waiting for the slightest excuse to pounce. It usually preceded Sam beating the lights out of whoever had dared confront him. If someone didn't jump in, Jack had no doubt that there was going to be a fight.

"It ain't unfair of me to ask for more money for better quality gin, is all I'm saying," Two Tone said, either oblivious to Sam's unspoken threat, or else just not bothered by the thought of a fight. "The price has to be fair, you know."

Billy stepped forward before Sam could answer that, grinning his endearing grin. "How about we all have a drink and talk it over," he said. Sammy spun, all that simmering anger directed at Billy now. But Two Tone was clearly interested in the idea.

"Who's this fella?" Two Tone asked. "I like him. He has good ideas."

Sam grumbled out something that sounded less than charitable, but his rage subsided somewhat as Billy stuck out his hand to Tommy, ignoring him. "The name's Billy Lindh. Good to meet you."

Jack looked between Sam and Billy, still not positive there *wouldn't* be a fight. Sam still looked like he wanted to coldcock Billy. But when Jack caught his eye, Sam must have seen the worry in Jack's expression, because he took a deep breath and nodded stiffly. "Sure. Let's go *talk* about it."

They sat at an antique table covered in scratches and water stains that had clearly seen better days. The whole house, or at least what Jack could see of it, was filled with trash, and this extended to the table as well. Two Tone simply swept his arm across it, sending it all scattering onto the floor. "Rare to have a dame here with us drinking," Two Tone said.

"Don't worry," Betty replied primly. "I'll try not to drink your whole supply." That got her a hearty laugh and an extra slosh of gin into her cup.

They drank gin from glasses that were too large to be for straight alcohol. Two Tone didn't have anything to offer them to sweeten the taste, so all except for Sam's and Betty's glasses continued to sit mostly untouched. The taste of the gin was so vile that Jack had taken a single sip and almost spat it out all over the table. Not that it would have made much of a difference in the cleanliness of the place.

Betty was taking the occasional sip from her cup, but Jack could tell by the way she straightened her shoulders before each mouthful that she was bracing herself for the taste. It was a bit like horse piss, if he was being honest.

Billy poured Two Tone another drink, from his own glass. He'd stopped drinking almost immediately, but Two Tone hadn't yet noticed. "Jus' telling you," he slurred, tilting sideways in his seat. "Jus' saying, Ireland. There ain't no place more beautiful on God's green earth."

"It does sound beautiful," Billy agreed with him, for the third time. He didn't sound a bit drunk, probably because he'd had less than one-quarter of his glass of gin.

"It really does," Betty added, her words a little bit slurred as well. Jack was certain that she was only drinking so much to prove a point, but he wasn't about to say anything about it in front of all these men. He'd be a fool to think she'd let him get away with that.

Jack had long since stopped trying to agree with Two Tone on anything. It was obvious that old Tommy wasn't holding up too well, and he seemed to take even agreement as a challenge when he was this bent. "You're damn right it is," he shouted. Then slipped from his chair to the floor. "Jus' beautiful."

And then he started to snore.

"Poor hoary-eyed old rummy," Billy said, shaking his head. "Seems like with him asleep you'll have to just leave the money on the table for him. The amount he asked for at first, I think."

Billy grinned, and Charlie and Betty hooted with laughter. "Real clever, Bill," Betty said.

"We ought to take you out on all of our calls," Charlie said. "Bet we'd save some money."

"I coulda fought him," Sam grumbled unhappily. "We'd have paid the first price after I was done with him."

Billy nodded. "Sure. But this way we saved you both some black eyes."

Sam huffed, grabbing some bottles and shoving them into Billy's arms. "Fine. Here, make yourself useful." Jack shook his head. He wasn't sure exactly why Sam seemed to have it out for Billy, but it was obvious he didn't like him one bit. Jack personally thought Billy had already been plenty useful. Just because Sam liked to fight, didn't mean Jack liked to watch it.

"Here," Jack said, grabbing a few more bottles from Sam and putting them in his bag. "I'll carry them. As long as they don't break and get all over my sheet music."

Sam glared at him, then shook his head as though trying to dispel his annoyance. "Money, who the hell brings sheet music on a run like this?"

"I do," Jack said, confrontationally. But unlike his confrontational attitude with Two Tone, Sam laughed, seeming to appreciate Jack's answer.

"All right, Money. You do." He slung his arm over Jack's shoulder. "Now what do you say we get out of here before he wakes up," he said, nodding to the heavily snoring Two Tone on the ground. Betty nudged Two Tone with the tip of her shoe to encourage him to roll over onto his side. Jack raised an eyebrow at her, and she shrugged "I don't think we want a source to choke on his own vomit, Jack" she said.

Charlie placed the money on the table, and they left quietly, though Jack was certain it'd take nothing less than a herd of elephants to wake Two Tone up.

The blindfolds went back on for the trip back, although Betty declined again with an, "after all the gin I've had I won't recall the trip anyways!"

"You're quite a bearcat, Betty May," Sam said. "I oughta teach you somethin' about fighting."

"I'd be tickled pink," Betty said. "You can start right now!"

"All right," Sam said. "First things first, you gotta stay calm. The moment you panic is the moment you've lost."

They chatted like that the whole way back. By the time they reached the point where they'd put the blindfolds the first time on, Jack was almost hoping to keep his on. The night air was freezing, and having Sam hold onto him was about the only thing keeping him the slightest bit warm.

"Thank you for bringing me along tonight," Billy said when they arrived back at the Trespass, shaking Charlie's hand. He turned to shake Sam's, but Sam refused to move an inch. Billy shrugged and moved over to Jack's side. "It was interesting."

"It was good to have you there," Charlie said. "Maybe we'll bring you along again sometime."

"Oh, I don't know," Billy said, slipping his arm around Jack's shoulders. He was warm and smelled good, like cologne. A shiver worked its way through Jack, a remnant of the cold that still lingered on his skin. "I think that was more than enough excitement for three musicians, wouldn't you say, Jack?"

Jack wasn't entirely sure what he meant. Hell, as far as illegal speakeasy activity went, that trip had been damn near tame. But he nodded anyway. "Sure," he said, not really meaning it. "That was good enough for me."

"I'd go again," Betty said, swaying on her feet. "It was fun."

"Right. Well, I'd better get going," Billy said, removing his arm from Jack's shoulder and leaving him cold again. "Good night, gentlemen, Betty." He tipped his hat to them and took his leave.

"Night, Billy."

"See you tomorrow."

Sam frowned silently, watching Billy leave. "I don't like that guy," he said darkly. "There's something off about him."

"Like what?" Betty asked.

"He's a grifter. I'm sure of it," Sam told her.

Jack shrugged. "I think he's pretty nice. I'm glad he's working with us now."

"You would be," Sam growled, then stomped away to the bar.

"Well, good night to you too," Jack huffed. Fine. Time to go home, he guessed.

Betty swayed into Jack, slinging her arm around his shoulder. "Oh, honey, don't take him too seriously," she said. "He's just mad he didn't get to fight."

Jack figured that was probably true, but Sam didn't have to be so rude. At least Billy was more polite than Sam. Jack had a feeling he was going to like working with him just fine.

CHAPTER EIGHT

Betty hummed as she walked down the street with Jack, both of their hands full with groceries.

"I just hope that we can get home in time, before the rain stops, so I can play along," Jack said. It was hard to hear above the roar of engines and the clip-clopping of hooves, but if you listened close enough, you could hear the rain. The soft tap-tap-tapping of it against the windows of the shops along their way home had Betty damn near ready to dance, which was fitting since they were nearing the Trespass.

Hah. Maybe she should drop in and say hi. Maybe even sneak up to Eva's apartment and pay her a visit. "Do you think we ought to stop in at the Trespass?" Betty asked, trying to sound innocent. "You could play on the baby grand." Jack gave her a look, not convinced by her feigned altruism.

"Well…" he said, then paused, eyes growing wide as he looked just beyond her shoulder at the busy sidewalk across the street. "Betty May," he whispered. He grabbed her arm, a little too tight., "Over there. That's Bianchi!"

Bianchi. The man who'd tried to kill Sam. Betty looked over, and sure enough, there was a hulking man with a bald head under his hat and a mean look in his eye. He was standing with a group of three other trouble boys, something in their demeanor just threatening enough to suggest you better skitter past without saying hello. Bianchi was a striking presence out there on the street, to the point where the other three were barely noticeable. Except for the one taller man who had a nasty-looking scar stretched all the way across his left cheek. But there was no doubt that they were all with him. And they were whispering among themselves.

What were they doing there, so close to the speakeasy?

"Come on," Betty said, pulling Jack forward before they drew attention to themselves by standing there frozen in the street. "Pull your hat down, hide your face as much as possible. We can double back around through the alley. Go in the back door and warn them." Then she'd run upstairs and warn Eva. Just in case they decided to go up the stairs instead of down into the speakeasy. Betty and Jack walked their way around the block, passing the speakeasy, only to double back and slide down into the alleyway behind the Trespass. The door tended to be left unlocked, and thankfully today was no exception. Betty towed Jack down the stairs at full speed, her heart beating wildly in her chest.

"Hello," she called out, praying that someone was there.

"Betty! And Jack! What are you doing here this early?" Leroy asked, though he sounded genuinely glad to see them. Leroy always was a nice guy.

"They brought us lunch, looks like," Sam said, nodding toward the bags in Betty's and Jack's hands.

As warm as it made her feel to be greeted like this, there wasn't time for banter. "We were heading home, and Jack spotted Bianchi and three other men snooping around here," she said hurriedly. Jack was breathing heavily beside her, and Betty suspected it wasn't entirely because he'd rushed in. She still remembered how frightened he'd been telling her about his first contact with Baby Grand.

Her words snapped Leroy and Sam to attention real quick.

"What'd they look like?" Sam asked, serious as a house on fire. "The other guys with him."

"One was tall, sort of squished face, and skinny," Jack said, trying his best to remember the details. "Other two were more round, I guess? I can't be sure. I was more focused on Bianchi than anything."

"Skinny guy have a scar?" Sam asked urgently.

"Yeah, right across his cheek," Betty said.

Sam swore vehemently under his breath. "They brought Matchbox. You thinking what I'm thinking?" he asked Leroy. Betty had never seen him look so serious before. Not even right before a fight. It made her shiver, a cold fear worming its way through her.

"Yeah. I think I am," Leroy agreed gravely. "Betty, Jack, you better get on outta here. Things are about to get hot."

Sam was already moving with the speed of a man on a mission, grabbing something from behind the bar. Betty frowned, looking at Jack. Back when they'd first started working here she was sure he would have taken the opportunity to leave. But now…

"We're not going anywhere. If they're coming for you, it's not going to be four against two," Jack said firmly. "We can at least help even out the odds a bit."

Leroy looked impressed, but not necessarily surprised. More proud than anything. Like he'd figured as much, and was pleased at being right. "I 'preciate that, Jack," he said. "But, Betty, you should head out. This is too dangerous for a bird."

"No way am I leaving you boys to deal with this on your own," Betty protested. "And anyways, you haven't even told us what's going on."

Sam came back around, carrying two fire extinguishers. "Matchbox likes to light places up. And he's awfully fond of a pipe bomb too. When Leroy said it was about to get hot, he meant it."

Jesus. They were going to burn down the Trespass? Or bomb it? But what would happen to Eva? Her heart began to beat urgently in her chest. Betty had to warn her before the building began to burn.

"I have to find Eva," Betty said. Whatever expression she had on her face, it must have been enough to convince them that she wasn't going to be persuaded to go home.

"Okay. You go warn her what's coming. Jacky, there's more of those in the back room," Leroy said, nodding toward the extinguisher in Sam's hands. "Run and grab some for us. Should be about five more. Six if we're lucky." For a moment, Betty was going to ask why in the world they had so many fire extinguishers, before he remembered that Sam *knew* this Matchbox fella. So, that answered that question. Jack got to work grabbing fire extinguishers. Leroy ran over to the back door, locking the bolt and setting two of the fire extinguishers near the wall there.

Betty ran to the stairs, her heart in her throat. If they lit the place on fire, there would be no way for Eva to get out. Her window was too high up. She reached the door and was about to yank it open when she heard it. The quiet murmur of voices, and a low laugh. And then the smell of gasoline wafting in from just outside of the door.

She was too late.

The only thing she could do for Eva now was fight the fire.

There was the sound of someone trying the door to the alley, before the dull thud of metal hitting brick, and muttered curses. Then a few seconds later an explosion shook the bar.

And just like that, someone threw a lit match onto the gasoline at the front door, and both ends of the speakeasy were on fire.

"Oh God," Betty said, already feeling the heat flooding into the room. They were lucky both doors were fortified. Or maybe not so lucky. The place was a fortress, yes, but what good was being locked in a fortress on fire?

"Hurry," Sam said, already fighting against the flames licking up under the door.

Betty had never used a fire extinguisher before, but she watched Sam and picked it up easily enough. She sprayed it in a sweeping motion, just like Sam was doing, aiming low toward the ground. All she could think of was Eva upstairs, unaware of what was going on. Could she smell the smoke yet? Was she choking on it? She couldn't help but imagine the fire creeping up the stairs, catching on the peeling paper like kindling, creeping closer and closer to Eva's home.

"We'll keep the back door closed, but this one we might need to open," Sam shouted over to Leroy. "Don't want to give this fire any air, but we can't let it go burning up the stairs to Eva's place."

"Right," Jack said, sounding surprised. Betty hadn't known that either, not really. Her mother had always told her to leave the door closed if there was ever a fire, but she'd never known the why of it. She certainly hadn't expected Sammy to know. Not with how dumb he played and how often he got knocked around the head.

"Be ready," Sam told Betty and Jack, looping his jacket over his hand. "Stand back and start spraying the second this opens up, got it?" Betty nodded, holding the extinguisher at the ready. Her heart was pounding hard in her chest, but she felt strangely serene. Like time had slowed itself down around her, and even seconds were drawn out long enough that she knew she'd be ready when Sam threw the door open. She had to be. She needed to keep Eva safe. She *would* keep Eva safe.

The fire roared when Sam opened the door, leaping up with a blast of heat that almost sent both Betty and Jack backward with its intensity. The violent crackle was loud in her ears, and a burst of black smoke began to fill the air, making her eyes burn. But she managed to stay put, shrinking in on herself as she pointed the spray of foam toward the bottom of the flames in a steady back and forth line.

Sam and Jack joined her, and soon the flames began to dwindle, amid their triumphant shouts. Leroy was already moving to help them, having dealt with the relatively minor fire that had crept under the back door, but hadn't gotten past the stairs. They'd deal with the alley later, Betty assumed. Right now they needed all hands on deck for the fire that was *in* the building.

Mercifully, it seemed Eva hadn't decided to leave her apartment, and they managed to fight back the flames until all that was left was a blackened mark on the floor and walls of the stairwell. Still, Eva could have been affected by the smoke. Betty couldn't breathe easy yet.

"It's not so bad," she heard Sam reassuring Leroy, as she placed her fire extinguisher down with trembling hands.

"Right," Jack said. "It makes it look even more dark and mysterious in here. And it didn't get the stairs at all!"

Betty ran then, up the stairs two by two, ignoring the calls of her name that came from the men downstairs. "Eva," she yelled, almost tripping as she reached Eva's door. "Eva, darling!"

She flung the door open, breathing heavily. It smelled strongly of smoke in her apartment.

"Nightingale?" Eva said, her voice rough with sleep. Betty burst into her bedroom, flinging herself onto the bed before Eva could even stand.

"Oh, you're okay! You're okay, oh my God, Eva," Betty said. She was breathless with relief.

Eva squinted up at her. "Were you smoking in here?" she asked.

Betty barked out a laugh, relief suffusing her body in a sudden rush that made her go limp, muscles turning to liquid. Every ache in her body became apparent. She let out a high-pitched laugh that sounded frantic, even to her "No, you know I don't smoke. There was a fire downstairs."

"A fire? Is everyone all right?" Eva asked. The news looked like it had woken her up quicker than a splash of water to the face could have. Betty pressed a kiss to her cheek. "They're okay," she said.

Eva threw on a robe and they headed downstairs to check on the boys. They were gathered up the stairs at the back door, gloriously cool and damp air blowing in from the outside. The stink of the alley and the wet smell of rain smelled like perfume in that moment, like safety. Leroy was swearing darkly under his breath, leaning into the alley to survey the damage. "Those motherfuckers are going to pay for this," he said, his fists clenched tightly at his sides.

Betty squeezed Eva's hand, then climbed the stairs, peeking curiously out from behind Leroy to find shards of metal embedded in the door and even in the brick of the alley.

"My God," Jack said.

"These guys really mean business," Betty said.

"They sure do," Sam agreed. "We're lucky they didn't bring a bigger bomb. Probably didn't want the fuzz coming too soon," he growled out, then took a gun out from his belt and headed outside.

"Don't worry," Leroy said, far too flippantly for when there was a gun involved. "He's going to fire some warning shots. Those deadbeats will be hanging around to watch the place burn. Sammy's letting them know the show's over before it started."

"That's...terrifying," Jack said bluntly.

Betty privately agreed. This world where bombs and fires and guns were commonplace was no place for a farm boy and farm girl from Wisconsin. Yet here they were. They'd fought off a fire. Jack had coldcocked a giant of a man. Together they'd saved the damn speakeasy they worked for. Betty was so proud of them she could burst. Not bad for two rubes straight off the wheat field. Maybe she was a bit of a bearcat after all.

They set to cleaning up as much as they could, scrubbing the soot from the walls and taking closer stock of the damage that'd been caused. Thankfully, it remained surface level, with only one wall now sporting a hole where the fire must have burned too hot.

It was like this that Charlie found them. "Jesus fucking shit," he cursed, taking in the blackened walls and soot-covered cloths in their hands. "What the hell happened here?"

They retreated to the bar to tell him, and Betty laughed that Sam's story had a few embellishments that made them all sound a little bit more heroic. She liked the way Sam told things.

"Jack here's our house peeper now," Sam said, smiling in a fond way that made Betty smirk. Sam was oblivious to how he looked at Jack, all soft in the eyes like a love-struck Dora. "He saw Matchstick heading over this way and tipped us off. Saved the bar, I'd say."

"Hey now, let's not forget me!" Betty chimed in. Eva grinned at her, wrapping their hands together in a gentle squeeze and Betty was struck by how similar the look on her face was to the look on Sam's. It warmed her inside, but also made her hands sweat a bit. She hoped Eva couldn't feel her palm becoming damp against her own.

"Of course. Bets was the one who did most of the peeping," Jack agreed.

"Thank you both," Charlie breathed, pulling first Jack and then Betty in for an embrace. "Jesus, I don't know what would have happened if you hadn't seen them."

"We'd have been in much worse shape," Leroy said. "I think we oughta have a drink to Betty and Jack. Might settle our nerves a bit too."

And when Charlie went to pour them drinks, Jack asked for a gin fizz, which according to Sammy was "a bit of a cop-out, but still impressive, Money!" Betty on the other hand got pure whiskey. She sat damn near on top of Eva as they drank, still shaken from the whole ordeal.

To think what might have happened if they hadn't been walking in the right place at the right time.

CHAPTER NINE

It was late afternoon when Jack found himself at the Trespass. With no piano lessons to teach today, he had still wanted to play piano at home, but Betty had been fast asleep and he didn't want to wake her.

He was just finishing up when a voice startled him. "Aww, is the show over? I wanted to hear a song."

Jack looked over to find Sam standing there. He looked tired, which made sense. In the world of speakeasies, the afternoon was early to rise.

"Too late," Jack told him, "I'm packing up for the day."

Sam laughed and shrugged. "All right. You at least want to have a drink with me?" Jack rolled his eyes, but did head over to the bar. "I need some water. Which is what *you* should be drinking at—" He checked his watch. "Two in the afternoon."

"Water doesn't have much of a kick," Sam said. "I need somethin' a li'l stronger."

Jack shook his head but didn't press it, even when Sam poured himself a whiskey. "You're going to dehydrate," Jack said as he sipped his glass of water.

"Haven't yet," Sam said, then grinned and clinked his glass against Jack's. "You had a drink the other day!"

"That was a special circumstance," Jack said, his cheeks heating. "It doesn't mean I'm going to start acting wild like you."

"Come on, Money. Admit it, you like the speakeasy life," Sam said.

Jack took a second to consider. It wasn't the worst life, he supposed. He sort of enjoyed the danger of it in some strange way. But dangerous it was, and he worried sometimes about himself and Betty.

"I don't know," he said. This clearly surprised Sam. "This is a dangerous business. Like what happened with Bianchi before, and now this fire."

"You dealt with both of those things though," Sam said. "You were amazing."

Jack blinked, surprised at the praise. From Sam of all people. He was certain that Sam only thought of him as stuffy old Jack, but maybe that wasn't true. "Thanks, Sam," he said.

"Sure, Money." Sam looked like he was thinking for a moment, then he grinned and said, "Let me teach you something about fighting. Just in case you ever gotta defend yourself."

"I can defend myself just fine," Jack said. He hadn't expected the offer, and he was certain that even practicing fighting with Sam would end up with him injured.

"Aww come on, Money. Let me teach you a couple of things. It'll be fun, I swear."

Jack looked him over. "I don't know. You aren't going to hit me, are you?"

Sammy laughed. "No, Money. I only wanna teach you how to grapple a bit. Show you how to get out of a hold if someone grabs you from the front. Things like that. I've already taught Betty some. I bet you'd be just as good a student."

Well, Jack had just been thinking about the dangers of this business. He might as well try to learn something new.

"All right," he said, taking a long pull of his water. "As long as you aren't pulling my leg or something."

"Cross my heart, Money," Sam said, hopping to his feet.

Jack stood more reluctantly, following Sam out onto the dance floor.

"First thing you gotta do is try to choke me," Sam said.

"What? I'm not going to choke you," Jack said, horrified.

"You won't hurt me," Sam rolled his eyes.

"You might hurt me," Jack retorted, still nervous. Sam was something of a friend to him now, but he was still a rough-and-tumble kind of guy. He could hurt Jack without even meaning to.

"Come on, Money," Sam said, gesturing him forward. "Grab me. I won't throw you off, I promise."

"How about instead I teach you to play piano?" Jack said.

Sam rolled his eyes. "Would you please just choke me already?" he said.

Jack laughed nervously. "The number of times I've wanted to do just that..." he trailed off and then took a tentative step forward. "Okay. I just put my arms around you...like this?"

He wrapped his arm loosely around Sam's neck.

"Sure, Money. More of a hug than a choke hold, but that's okay. We can work with this," he said. He grinned when Jack halfheartedly tightened his grip. "Better."

Then Sam set to teaching Jack how he could throw him off. He spent the next hour and a half showing Jack the ropes. Teaching him how to aim for the tender areas. How to use his opponent's weight against them. Jack was surprised to find he was having a good time, and while he didn't put much force behind any of the moves Sam taught him, he did at least get them down.

Jack felt a rush of pride every time he managed to pin Sam to the floor. It was intoxicating. Sam was a hard line of muscle beneath him, his body warm and his skin soft. This was Sam, who fought like he was out for blood, pinned down by nothing more than the force of Jack's body. It felt good. Maybe too good. He hoped that Sam hadn't done this kind of grappling with Betty. But no, she would have torn him to pieces if he'd tried.

"Sometimes you gotta bite a guy," Sam told him as they stood. "I would have bit you there to get out of that hold, but I'm a nice guy."

"I have a feeling biting isn't something professional fighters would teach," Jack said, grimacing at the feeling of his shirt sticking to his back from sweat.

Sam grinned widely at him.

"Nah, but I'm better than some boxer or something," Sam said, "I've got experience in *real* fights."

Jack looked at him sideways, then grinned and shook his head. "You're something else, Sam."

Sam squinted at him suspiciously. "Thanks?" he said as though he didn't quite believe that Jack was complimenting him. Then he clapped Jack on the back. "Come have a drink with me! Let's celebrate you learning to brawl."

Jack smiled at him. "I'll have some water."

"All right," Sam said and wandered over to the bar to pour himself a stronger drink.

Jack hesitated, enough that Sam looked like he was about to say something. "Thank you, Sam. That was a good lesson."

"Any time, Money," Sam said back with a loose salute.

"So," Jack said, once he'd poured himself some more water. "How'd you learn to fight anyways?"

Sam shrugged. "The mob," he said like he was talking about the weather. "I learned to fight from mobsters like Baby Grand Bianchi. Guys who saw my scrappy style and who figured I had potential enough as an enforcer to be worth their time."

Jack nodded, taking a sip of his drink. Before he could figure out what to say, Sam continued.

"Fighting wasn't the only thing I learned through the mob though. Certain mobsters took a liking to me, despite the fact that I was nothing but a shitty thirteen-year-old with attitude problems. Hell, some of them thought that was funny. They'd razz me about it, how I was nothing but an angry little street kid, a ragamuffin with no class. And I'd razz them back about how old and ugly they were."

"Sounds dangerous, to razz mobsters," Jack said, frowning. Would they have hurt a kid if he got too mouthy? Because that's what Sam had been, just a kid, when he was picked up by the mob.

"Nah. They took care of their own, you know? They taught me how to drink. How to belch louder than anyone else, and how to gamble, though I've never really been a big fan of the gambling. For a homeless kid like me it seemed nuts for men to willingly give up their money just for a bit of a thrill. For me, thrills came from fighting. From punching a guy three times bigger than you and watching him fall. So, Bianchi taught me to slam people into walls, and Wiley Wilson taught me to shoot whiskey. Joey Benelli taught me to shoot a gun, and they all taught me how to survive."

"What about Zanetti?" Jack asked, morbidly curious.

"Ah," Sam said, looking down at his drink. "Zanetti was the one who taught me how to crack a safe. I can still remember him smiling that shark's smile of his as he took me by the shoulder. 'Come on, Sammy,' he said. 'Let's make a yeggman outta you, huh?' He was a scary fella, Jack. Even when I was on his side. He had a temper that was only rivaled by the pleasure he took in causing pain. But he was good to me. Taught me how to use nitroglycerine to crack a safe in no time, and even let me keep part of whatever was in the safes we practiced on. He was a temperamental teacher, but he never hit me. He'd scream when I messed up, sure, but his praise made it feel like I was flying high above the ground whenever I managed to earn it."

Jack felt cold at that. It sounded like Zanetti had been a friend to Sam. How could he have decided to put a hit out on him like that?

"I still remember the time Zanetti bought me a drink after we busted up a particularly difficult safe. He was boasting to the other guys how he'd made me into the best safecracker in New York. He ruffled my hair, and I shook him off, but I was so full of pride and excitement that I was fit to burst."

Sam snorted, shaking his head.

"Sounds like you were good friends," Jack said.

"Zanetti and I were close for years. At least, as close as you can get to someone like him. Hell, I'm man enough to admit that I hero-worshiped the guy. Zanetti taught me so much. He protected me when I needed it and he won my loyalty for it. I'm pretty sure I'd have done anything for him. Hell, I *killed* for him." Sam laughed bitterly.

"And then…" Jack paused, his heart hurting. "And then he tried to kill you."

"Yeah," Sam sighed, deflating slightly. Jack sort of wished he'd kept his mouth shut. "I trusted them like uncles, you know?"

"Yeah," Jack said. "I'm sorry, Sam."

"Nah, it's all in the past now. Nothing I can do but go on. And I found the Trespass! The people here are my real family."

Jack's breath caught in his throat. Did that include him? He couldn't be sure, but strangely, it was a nice thought.

"Well, I'm glad you're here," Jack said. "I should get going," he added and placed his water down. "Betty'll be expecting me."

"All right, Money. Thanks for the talk," Sam said as he poured himself another whiskey. "Come back and grapple with me anytime, okay?"

Jack shook his head, but he was smiling as he turned and headed toward the door.

❖

Being a singer meant Betty was asked to sing quite often. By friends, family, and even strangers. It was always the same. "Oh, you sing? Well, sing us a song then!"

She'd arbitrarily chosen "Baby Won't You Please Come Home" by Bessie Smith to sing whenever she got a request like that. Though she had been tempted to choose something silly like "Yes! We Have No Bananas" at first. Only, Bessie Smith was Jack's favorite, and she preferred a slower, sadder song anyway. The sad ones always felt best to sing.

But with Eva, she wanted only sweet songs. She'd find herself humming "Ain't We Got Fun" to herself while she did the dishes, thinking of Eva's smile and the way she danced. Or maybe it'd be "Let Me Call You Sweetheart," as she and Jack walked to work together, while she thought of Eva's eyes and the way she carried herself.

But she stopped herself whenever she caught herself at it. It was a bad idea to reinforce the feelings that were bubbling up inside. A bad idea to let herself feel anything other than lust for Eva.

"I love listening to you sing," Eva told her one night. They were lying wrapped in Eva's sheets, their bare legs intertwined as they looked at each other.

"Thank you," Betty said. "What about you? Can you sing?"

"Absolutely not." Eva laughed. "Couldn't even if you paid me."

"Oh come on," Betty replied. "You can't be that bad. Here. Repeat after me."

She thought of and discarded a dozen songs before settling on "Brown Bird Singing."

All through the night-time my lonely heart is singing
Sweeter songs of love than the brown bird ever knew
Sweeter songs of love than the brown bird ever knew
Would that the song of my heart could go a-winging
Could go a-winging to you, to you.

"Oh, Nightingale," Eva said, soft as the petals on a flower. "That was beautiful."

"You're beautiful," Betty shot back, cradling Eva's face with her hand. "Now you try."

And try Eva did, though it wasn't pretty. Still, Betty loved every ear-hurting moment of it, because it was Eva doing the singing.

"I told you," Eva said, cringing at the sound of her own voice.

"I liked it." Betty laughed. Then, at Eva's incredulous look she said, "It wasn't good. But it was a good start. And it was you. Sometimes, I wish I was a painter instead of a singer, just so I could paint you."

Eva laughed, that full perfect laugh of hers. "Thank you, Songbird. You flatter me."

Betty headed back down to the Trespass with her heart still singing. The smell of smoke and alcohol was almost like a hug now. It smelled of home.

Unfortunately, she wasn't paying attention to where she was walking. Betty's chunky heel caught on one of the shimmering black beads of a flapper's shawl, sending her tumbling to her knees.

"Bets! Are you all right?" Billy's voice called out. Betty looked up, a bit dazed, to see him standing above her. At his feet sat the charm bag Eva had made for her. It must have fallen out of her dress. She reached out and tucked it back into her cleavage before accepting Billy's hand up. He was grinning at her. "What was that?"

"Oh, just a little perfume bag," Betty laughed, feeling the bag nestled up against her chest. "I'm all right! Just bruised my knee up a little, that's all."

Billy grinned at her. "Be careful, doll," he told her. "Don't want you getting hurt."

Something about that rubbed Betty the wrong way. "I'll be absolutely fine, don't you worry about little ol' me," she said sweet as pie, biting back the sarcastic edge she wanted to use.

Billy nodded, seemingly none the wiser. "You looking for Jack? He's over by the stage."

Betty blinked, her annoyance dissipating to be replaced by intrigue. He and Jack sure had been spending a lot of time together. Betty wondered if Jack was catching feelings for him. "Thank you! I'll go get him. Good night, Billy."

"Night, Bets."

She collected Jack and walked home, feeling like she was flying from her visit with Eva. When she got home, she undressed and found her charm bag. The little stone in it was cracked. Betty frowned. Had Billy stepped on it? Or had it broken when she'd fallen?

"Well, darn," she said to herself. She'd have to ask Eva if she could fix it.

CHAPTER TEN

The speakeasy down the street was out of booze.

This much would have been clear just from the sheer number of bodies rushing into the Trespass Inn, mingling with the regulars. But it was especially obvious by the grumbling of these new visitors.

"They had a bottle of whiskey," one man said, his voice full of disdain. "One bottle for all of us. How in the world did they think that'd do?"

Jack watched with trepidation as more and more people filed in off the streets.

"Zanetti's crew intercepted their supply," Sam said. He shook his head as he watched with Jack. "Heard it from another runner. He said they're practically dry now over at Last Call. It's a cryin' shame."

"Shouldn't you be happy?" Jack asked. He was genuinely curious. "We're getting more business because of it."

Sam shrugged. "Maybe. But we were doing just fine before. If they don't get back up and running, how long do you think we can keep up the supply for all these folks?"

Jack looked around the crowded room. It seemed impossible to keep all of them happy, even after Sam had brought back a good haul of booze just the other night. "Right," he said. "I suppose that makes sense. What are we going to do about it?"

Sam looked at him and grinned. "Maybe I'll help 'em out. See if we can't get them back in business with a few reinforcements. But for now, I'm going to find me a pretty little doll to dance with. Shouldn't be too hard, with all the extra bodies around here tonight."

Jack rolled his eyes. Of course, Sam would see this as an opportunity to find a girl. He was just so typical.

"Make sure to play some slow songs, Money," Sam said with a wink. "I wanna be able to get in real close, if you know what I mean."

"Every day you horrify me," Jack told him as he took his leave. "Every single day."

"You're welcome, Money, old boy," Sam said gleefully, then tottered away to go be vile somewhere else. With a put-upon sigh, Jack made his way over to his piano. Sam was growing on him like mold on a damp surface, but he was still a pain in the butt. They had a big crowd to try to please tonight. Though if he had anything to say about it, he'd be playing nothing but fast songs this evening.

"Things are busy," Billy noted, moving to grab his trumpet from the case beside the piano. "Did something happen?"

Jack nodded. "Zanetti basically shut down Last Call," he said. "Seems like we'll be lucky if these folks don't drink us dry as well."

"Huh," Billy said, looking out at the crowd. "Well, I guess for now all we can do is show these folks a good time, right?"

Jack grinned, the telltale buzz of excitement that came from performing starting up inside him. "Let's do it," he said, running his fingers along the keys as Charlie shut off the gramophone.

They played like men on fire, and Betty sang her heart out. The place was packed, but despite the crush of bodies filling every corner of the speakeasy, it seemed everyone was in the mood to dance. Even the seating area was swarmed with moving bodies, and whoops and hollers accompanied every song they played.

By the time they'd finished their fourth encore, Jack was about ready to pass out right there on the keys. He made his way over to Billy, barely able to keep his eyes open.

"Whew, I'm exhausted," Billy said. "That was quite a night, but I think I'll head on home if that's all right with you, old boy."

"I think Betty and I will probably head out early too," Jack agreed with a nod. "That sure was something. Great playing, Bill."

"Thank you. Get home safe, all right? Good night, Jack." Billy beamed at him, his hand brushing against Jack's right before he moved away. Everything in Jack heated and swooped at the feeling, and for one wild moment he considered asking Billy to take him home with him. "Good night, Billy," he said instead, unsure where that wild thought had come from. "Take care."

Billy gave him a jaunty wave, and Jack waved weakly back. Lord, he really needed to get himself in order. The problem was that Billy was just so...so *Billy*. So pleasant and dashing. So attentive, at least when it came to Jack, that it was hard not to fall for him.

Jack was trying very hard not to fall for him.

He'd noticed that he was only interested in men when he was young enough that he barely knew what liking a person in that way meant. But after James...well, he didn't like to think about it much anymore. He didn't want to fall for anyone, no matter how kind and handsome they were.

"Sweetie," Betty sang out, in that way that meant Jack was about to lose an argument. "How would you feel about staying around just a tad longer."

Jack sighed.

"I'm guessing not so that you and I can sit around and chat," Jack said, knowing full well where Betty would be headed. He was surprised Eva was still awake at this hour.

"I won't be long, I promise," she said sweetly.

Jack laughed. "I've heard that one before," he said, thinking of that night when Sam had forced him to dance with that girl.

But in the end, he never could deny Betty anything she wanted. "All right. Go on up, tell Eva I say hello."

"You're my hero," she said, kissing his cheek before she rushed off toward the door.

Jack was too much of a gentleman to ever make Betty walk home alone, and if he was being honest, she made him feel safer when she was by his side. Like together they could take on whatever the night, or the world, had to throw at them. So, he waited, trying to avoid getting his toes stepped on by drunken dancers. Trying to find somewhere safe where he wouldn't be bothered.

On a night so busy, that was nearly impossible.

Every corner was filled with laughing girls or loud drunken men trying to show off or pick fights. He couldn't find a single seat, and even the tables were being perched on by flappers with tired feet or who'd had one too many drinks. Worse was that Charlie and Leroy were far too busy doling out drinks to talk to him. Hell, he couldn't even find Sam in the crowd, though he was sure that Sam wouldn't have time for him, if he was trying to seduce some girl.

Resignedly, Jack made his way back up onto the tiny platform they called a stage, turned off the gramophone, and sat down at his piano. He figured he might as well play, if there was no one around to talk to.

Halfway through a song, he finally located Sam, at precisely the moment he ended up getting punched in the gut by some little wannabe thug. But Jack only stuttered in his playing for a second, before jumping back on it. And if he played a little more frantically, it wasn't because he was worried about Sam. Sam could take care of himself. Jack was just…adding to the violent ambiance. That was the power of the piano. It could turn even a fight into a dance.

The dance floor cleared around the fight pretty darn quickly. It would almost be funny, except for the fact that Sammy split the guy's lip. The violence wasn't something Jack liked to see, and unfortunately it seemed to be getting worse. Everyone was on high alert lately with the mob violence increasing. It was like living in a powder keg and dancing with a candle. Things always felt one tiny misstep away from exploding.

It made him glad Sam had taught him to grapple. It'd even been fun, holding Sam down, learning to work with his body as they moved together. Intoxicating in some strange way.

Not that Jack could do much against someone in a fight. Not like Sam could.

Sammy won, of course. It seemed like Sammy couldn't lose a fight most days. The only time Jack had seen him come close was that night with Bianchi when he'd nearly been shot. But this time there was no gun, and the guy was given the bum's rush quick enough.

It seemed like a century later before he caught sight of Betty making her way over to him. By then, the crowd had thinned quite a bit, with only the most dedicated partiers left milling about. And even *they* had all stopped dancing, either too drunk or too tired to continue.

"Ready to go home, sweetie?" Betty asked, coming up behind him as he played the last notes of his song.

Jack sighed, feeling suddenly tired down to the bone. "Yeah, Bets," he said, gathering up his sheet music. "Can you grab the tips?"

They packed up together in amiable silence, though Jack felt it unfair that Betty kept smiling to herself while all he felt was tired and a little bit lonely. With a wave to the exhausted looking Charlie and Leroy, they headed out.

It wasn't until they'd reached the outer door and Jack felt the chill of the evening air, that he realized he'd forgotten his jacket in the back room.

"I'll wait here," Betty said, still humming to herself. It made Jack happy to see her so happy, of course. But deep down there was an ache of loneliness so vast that he felt liable to drown in it. And it seemed like her happiness only served to shine a brighter light on that low feeling.

"Sure," he said tiredly. "I'll be right back." He had maybe, just maybe, pushed himself a little too hard tonight. But with Billy playing horn for them they felt more like a band than they ever had, and it had inspired Jack to bring his best playing to the table every night since he'd started working with them. He smiled at that. It felt good to be a band. And ever since Betty had taken up with Eva, he'd been feeling that gnawing emptiness creep up on him. It was nice to have someone to talk to who wasn't a gangster.

He paused outside of the door to the back room when he heard a sound. Someone was in there.

They were making a lot of noise too, and though many people called Jack naive he wasn't under any illusions as to what whoever was in there was up to. He'd spent enough time in barns with James to know exactly what was happening in there. He dithered for a moment, unsure what to do. He'd seen more than his fair share of flappers and their fellas getting frisky since he started working here, but he didn't exactly relish the experience.

Still, it was far too cold to walk home without his coat. And besides, the Trespass was closing up now. They could take their rendezvous elsewhere. With that thought, Jack pushed the door open.

He'd expected to see a couple in some manner of undress, and he wasn't incorrect about that. What he *hadn't* expected was for one of them to be *Sam*.

Jack froze, staring transfixed at the scene before him.

There was a woman sitting on one of the chairs in the room with one breast out and her skirt hiked up round her waist. And there on the floor in front of her knelt Sam with his face nestled between her legs.

Something cold and horrible slithered in Jack's stomach. A feeling like being punched. Like being screamed at on a street corner when he'd been minding his own business. The worst part was that Sam didn't notice him come in. He just kept right on at it, until the woman stiffened up as she spotted Jack.

"Oh," she said in mortification, as Sam looked up at her in question. "Oh, sorry. We're nearly finished in here."

Jack blushed a deep red, from the roots of his hair all the way down to his chest. Sam turned then, and caught sight of him, grinning that stupidly crooked grin of his right at him. "Right. Well, we're closing so…" he said, then grabbed his coat and fled before Sam could say whatever horrible thing had clearly been on the tip of his tongue.

"Hey, Jacky boy," Betty started, before she caught sight of the look on his face. "What's going on?"

"Nothing," he said, too quickly. "Nothing. Let's just go home."

He grabbed her by the arm and hurried away from the bar as though Sam was about to emerge instead of sticking around in the back room and finishing what he'd started.

God.

"Jack Norval, you better tell me why we're running away like the fuzz are chasing us," Betty demanded, thankfully still moving at the pace he'd set. "What happened?"

"Nothing," he repeated, feeling more and more foolish as time went on. "It was nothing Betty. Really."

"Bushwa," she snapped, finally pulling him to a stop. "Jack, what's going on?" she said, softer now.

Strangely, Jack felt like he might cry. "Nothing, Bets, I swear. I just walked in on something I shouldn't have." He wasn't even sure why it'd upset him so much. He knew that Sam took ladies back there. He should have guessed that it'd been Sam in the first place. It wasn't like they let just anyone go back there.

But he'd forgotten. Or maybe he simply hadn't wanted to know.

Either way, the image of Sam on his knees, with that smile of his, was burned into Jack's brain. And for some reason, it made that yawning chasm of loneliness within him ache all the more.

Betty searched his face, and whatever she saw there she seemed to accept. "Okay," she said softly. "Let's go home and make something good for dinner-breakfast, yeah? Or maybe we can go out!"

Jack laughed weakly. "Sure, Bets. Let's go out. Why not, right?"

Betty gave him a bone-crushing hug and giggled. "Why, Jack, I think working at a juice joint might be good for you. Look at you out here, living your life to the fullest."

"Might as well," he said. "We've got some money now. And it's early enough for breakfast."

Betty pulled him along, chatting about which restaurant they should go to, while Jack stayed silent beside her. He wasn't sure why his mind kept replaying what he'd seen, but he was sure that he wanted it to stop. He didn't need to keep seeing Sam on his knees, that grin of his. The way he'd been flushed, his breathing heavy.

The ding of a bell brought him back to his senses. "Sorry, Betty," he said sheepishly. "I don't know what's wrong with me today. I must be tired."

Betty nodded, letting him use the excuse. "Of course, Jack. You played hard tonight. Come on now, let's get a good meal in us and then go home to bed."

Bed. Sure.

His bed where he'd sleep alone tonight. He wondered absently if Sam had gone to bed alone this evening. He wondered if Billy had.

He was quiet throughout breakfast, despite Betty's best efforts. Quiet on the walk home, and quiet as he fell into his lonely bed. And when he fell asleep, he dreamt of two very different smiles. One straight and gleaming, and the other lopsided but brighter than a summer's day.

❖

Betty needed a break from the nightlife. Things were getting far too wild for her liking, and all of the fighting was starting to get to her. Which meant that when Eva invited her out to help her browse a market, during the day no less, well, Betty couldn't possibly refuse.

They held hands as they went, and Betty secretly thrilled at how different the meaning of their linked hands was from that of most of the other ladies walking around with their friends. Though, she supposed that there might be some good friends who were no such thing, just like her and Eva. She wondered if she could spot them as they walked.

"What are you thinking about?" Eva asked her. They were starting to reach the better side of town, which meant they should probably let each other's hands go. After all, a white woman and a Black woman walking together was already bound to draw some attention, without the added physical contact. But Betty didn't want to let go. She wanted to hold on forever, no matter where they went.

"Wondering how many women are like us," she said, kissing Eva's hand before she let it go.

Eva laughed, eyeing her up with appreciation. "More than you would think, my Nightingale. I'm sure of it."

"So how about them?" she asked, giggling as she nodded to two women who were leaned in close to talk about something.

"It's possible," Eva replied, then, getting into the game, she nodded to a group of three women walking down the opposite sidewalk. "Which of them, do you think?"

"Oh, the blond one for certain." Betty giggled, then made a show of thinking about it. "And maybe the one in the blue plaid dress."

Eva looked them over critically. "Or all three?" she said, making Betty gasp in surprised delight.

"Eva! You're posi-lutely right! How could I have missed it." She laughed, wanting more than anything to lean against her. To kiss her cheek, or her lips, and not have anyone stare. But that wasn't something she could do, so she resigned herself to a day of not touching Eva, but at least making her laugh as much as she could as consolation.

The outdoor market that Eva led her to was beyond splendid. There were lines of vendors selling their wares, and each one adorned their booths with shimmering scarves and curtains of beads. The wares varied from booth to booth, with long rolls of beautiful fabrics, and glittering jewelry, and strange but beautiful carvings littering every visible surface. Everywhere the eye roamed was something delightful and dazzling and wonderful in every way, and Betty was struck through by the sight of it.

"Oh, Eva," Betty breathed. "It's beautiful here."

Eva smiled at her like she was the world. "Not as beautiful as you."

"Sappy," Betty said, wanting more than anything to reach out and grab her by the hand.

Eva giggled, but looked at her knowingly. "And yet you're blushing." Betty didn't have any comebacks for that one. She simply walked closer to Eva as they entered the little market, ostensibly due to the little crowd of women and men bustling along looking at the booths.

There were normal booths with fruits and vegetables and food of various varieties, but Eva led her straight to the tables with stones and runes and strange little figures on them. There was one that sold candles of all different colors, that smelled of jasmine and frankincense, and other earthy scents. Eva bought three yellow ones that Betty loved the smell of, and three jet-black ones for her work. Eva seemed delighted to pick out the things that Betty exclaimed over, like the long silver shawl that looked so beautiful against Eva's dark skin, or the large pink crystal that one man was selling for a price that Betty was quite frankly offended over. But Eva didn't seem bothered by the prices of anything. She just bought whatever tickled her fancy, smiling and humming happily whenever Betty found a new delight to fawn over.

Betty bought them both some little strawberry tarts from a booth, and they ate them as they walked. The sweetness on her tongue paired with the sweetness of the day was nearly too much for her to bear, but even here hidden among the flowing fabrics, she dared not hold Eva's hand. It wouldn't do to let her guard down now and have some passerby try to ruin their perfect day by objecting. But she wouldn't let that slight hint of bitterness ruin things for her.

While Eva bartered with a man over a long diamond-shaped pendant on a single chain, Betty wandered over to another booth, staring in awe at all the different decks of tarot cards laid out on it. There were cards covered in Egyptian drawings, ones that looked like Eva's decks, but with wildly different colors on the backs of them, and even some cards with wholly different designs to what she'd seen Eva use. But Betty felt herself most drawn to a deck with beautiful blue and gold geometric designs on the backs of them. They were the kind of cards that Eva already had, but Betty still found herself asking for the price.

They reminded her so much of Eva. The calming blue, and the regal gold. They were stunning, just like her.

"I might have bought you a present," Betty said sheepishly, returning to Eva's side with the cards in hand. Eva threw back her head and laughed in that full bodied way she did, and Betty's heart soared.

"I did the same for you, Songbird," she told her, making Betty laugh too. They were quite the pair.

"You open yours first," Eva said, handing her a small box, the kind that one would keep jewelry in. Betty opened it to find a necklace with a little bird pendant. The bird's body had a tiny blue stone set into it. Betty gasped softly, running the tip of her finger along the delicate wing of the bird. "Oh, Eva. It's beautiful."

"It made me think of you," she said. "A beautiful bird singing her tune to the world."

Betty blushed, her heart fluttering in her chest. "I love it. I feel silly now, I bought you these, even though you already have tarot cards at home. I should have gotten you something else." But Eva took the cards from her with a look of awed adoration on her face.

"Oh, darling," she whispered, barely audible above the bustle of the market. "They're wonderful."

Betty smiled, but that little bit of worry still tugged at her chest. "Are you sure you don't want something else? I could get you something you don't already have."

Eva brought the cards up to her chest, holding them close to her heart. It was almost comically adorable, like she was a small child afraid of her toy being taken away. Betty wanted to kiss her hands and promise her the world if she wanted it.

"No, no," Eva said quickly. "Tarot card decks each have their own voice. Every deck has its own personality, so one can never have too many decks. Each one will tell you the same story, just in a different way."

That sounded odd to Betty, but Eva was the expert. "So can you tell what this one is like yet?" she asked, genuinely curious. She hoped she'd picked a set with a good personality, and not one that would prove rude or belligerent or something of that nature. But then again, they were only cards, so perhaps that was a silly thing to worry about. Who had ever heard of cards being belligerent?

Eva laughed. "Not yet. I'll have to use them first. But I have a feeling that they'll be wonderful for love readings."

Betty's face heated. Maybe she was in love. Maybe she wasn't. But this wasn't the time or place to decide that. At least, that's what she told herself. Instead, she just leaned herself up against Eva and whispered, "Oh. How lovely."

They spent the rest of the day in much the same way, wandering amongst the booths as though they were in their own magical little world. Betty didn't buy anything else, but she delighted in helping Eva pick out many new little trinkets to brighten up her workspace in her apartment, cooing over how mystical they looked and making Eva smile.

"We should go for lunch," Betty said a while later, her arms laden with bags from the market. "I'll buy!"

Eva looked at her for a moment, then shook her head. "Sweet girl, where would we go?"

Betty bit back on her suggestion, suddenly remembering the problem. There were no restaurants where they could go together. No place that would allow them to sit with each other unmolested. Hell, most of the restaurants Betty frequented would turn Eva away before she even walked in the door. "Oh," Betty said softly. "I'm sorry. God, I didn't even think."

Eva cut her off with a quick press of her lips to Betty's, startling her silent. "It's all right, Nightingale. I have to believe it won't be this way forever. Maybe not in our lifetime, but you're worth the risk. And it is a risk, sweetheart. For me more than for you."

But despite the thrilling public kiss, it wasn't all right. It was a stark reminder of the reality they lived in. Betty knew she tended to live in her own little fantasy world, but the problem with living that way was that she would often forget the real world's injustices. And the reminder of them always brought her back down to earth *hard*. And Eva was right. The risk was far greater for Eva. It made Betty feel like fleeing. Sparing Eva would be the right thing to do, wouldn't it? But then again, that felt a lot like making a decision *for* Eva. It felt more like cowardice than bravery.

She had a funny feeling that she couldn't leave anyway. She was in too deep.

"We'll go back to my apartment," Eva said, looking worried. "We will always have the apartment and the Trespass as our safe places. I have some good food we can make there together."

"Of course," Betty said, though her heart wasn't in it. "That sounds like fun." She knew in her heart that she would forego dining out for the rest of her life if it meant that Eva could have a meal anywhere she wanted. But life didn't work like that. She couldn't bargain away the world's injustices.

"Maybe I could make you a surprise dessert," Betty suggested, trying to shake herself out of it. If anyone had the right to be upset, it was Eva and not her. And she didn't want Eva thinking the wrong thing, as though Betty was disappointed at not being able to go out, rather than disappointed at the entire world for being the way it was. The world was often a disappointment. Worse even than a disappointment.

"Dessert sounds lovely," Eva said with a small smile, although her eyes remained troubled.

They headed back to Eva's apartment with their arms pressed together, though the whole time Betty wished she could hold her hand.

Chapter Eleven

Jack loved Bessie Smith's voice. Not as much as Betty's voice, of course, but she was a very close second. "Down Hearted Blues" was one of his favorite songs in the world. He loved the feeling of it. The sad, down and out, but not ready to give up sound of it always brought him close to tears, even when he was playing.

He loved the lyrics of it too.

I ain't never loved but three men in my life
My father, my brother, and the man who wrecked my life

Jack shook his head as he played, feeling the lyrics in his heart. Wasn't that just the truth. Betty's voice was clear as a bell, sad as the voice of a woman whose heart was broken to bits. Which was funny, since Jack was pretty sure he'd never seen her happier than she was with Eva.

I got the world in a jug, the stopper's in my hands
I'm gonna hold it until you meet some of my demands

They didn't need Billy's horn for this song, so he sat out in the crowd at a table and watched them perform with a smile on his face and a look in his eyes like the fire of a candle, something flickering in the depths of them as he listened. When they were finished and had the gramophone set back up, Jack made a beeline toward Billy.

"Amazing as always, Jack," Billy told him sincerely. "Betty really sold that song too. You'd almost think a man had gone and broken her heart."

"Sure. Except that she's happy as a clam when she's not singing it." Jack laughed. Betty really did deserve to be happy, and it seemed like Eva was keeping her that way. Jack kind of wished he had someone to love him as much as Betty clearly loved Eva. Not that Betty seemed ready to admit that just yet.

Billy nodded. "It's good she's happy. What about you?"

Jack frowned. "What's there to be unhappy about?" he asked.

Just then, two men came up close to their table and paused there to chat. "You hear about that gangster who turned up dead?" one said. The other man nodded and took a long swig of his drink. "Someone slit his throat from side to side. Looked like he'd been beaten too, the poor son of a bitch."

Jack shuddered. What a gruesome conversation. Though he supposed that sort of thing was getting to be a common occurrence. It seemed like for all that the politicians and religious groups had promised that Prohibition would cut down on crime, all it had really done was increase it. And it was becoming even more violent than usual.

Billy frowned, clearly just as disturbed by the casual talk of violence as Jack was. Too many people stood around at the juice joint jawing about horrible things like murders and mysteries. Jack figured they loved the drama of being somewhere illegal talking about such dark topics. He doubted they'd be so calm if faced with the actual violence and horror of the seedy underbelly of New York crime.

"What do you say we go on out there, hmm?" Billy said. Jack had to replay his words in his mind, and *still* they made no sense. Was Billy…asking him on a date? Asking him to leave the speakeasy? He couldn't make heads or tails of it.

"Pardon?" he said, not sure if it was nerves or excitement swooping low in his stomach.

"Come on, Jack. Let's dance," Billy said with a laugh. That was not at all what Jack had expected.

"Pardon?" Jack spluttered again, certain that he'd heard it wrong. There was no way Billy wanted to dance with *him.*

"I said, let's dance!" Billy grinned, teeth white and eyes sparkling. And before Jack could say another word, Billy was pulling him out onto the dance floor.

Jack stood there like an extremely awkward woodland animal caught in the lights of an automobile, watching horrified as Billy started to dance with a wild sort of grace that he could never hope to copy.

"Come on, Jack," Billy prompted him, yelling over the croon of the gramophone.

Jack was frozen for a moment, but with jazz playing and people moving their feet all around him, there was no choice but to move along with them. So that's what Jack did, albeit stiffly. He'd never been one to dance, and he had no idea what he was doing, beyond desperately attempting to copy Billy's movements.

"Hey," Billy said, moving in close to speak to him. "You're so tense. Just relax. Here." He took Jack's hands and placed them on his shoulders. "Move with me."

So Jack did, breathless and thrilled, he let Billy press their bodies together. Let Billy's hands settle on his hips. Because why shouldn't he have fun? Everyone else always did. *Sam* sure did, with any lady who gave him the time of day. Why shouldn't Jack let this happen, just one time? So, he moved to the music, jostling against Billy as they moved deeper into the dance floor.

It wasn't that difficult to dance, now that he was getting the hang of things. With Billy leading, and the thrum and sway of the bodies around them, it was almost hypnotic. He just had to feel the music, like he did when he was playing. Let the rhythm translate through his whole body and let go.

"Hah!" he said into Billy's ear. "I'm dancing!"

"You sure are." Billy laughed. Pressed so close together his laughter rumbled through Jack like it was his own. He had such a low voice. Such a beautiful laugh. It felt so good, better than even the music to listen to. He wanted to hear it every day. Feel it as though it were his own like this again and again as they moved together. Then, as soon as it had all begun, Billy was moving back, his grin more subdued. "Sorry," he leaned in to say. "Got carried away. Let's go get some water."

Jack nodded, not sure how he felt. The shift in mood seemingly came from nowhere and had left him not so much reeling as feeling numb. "Is everything okay?" Jack asked when they reached the bar. There was a woman there, slumped on the floor, with her back against the wooden paneling, groaning. Completely sloshed. Billy looked at her with an expression Jack couldn't place. Somewhere between pity and revulsion maybe?

But then he was looking at Jack, that soft look back in his eyes. "Yeah, sorry. It was just a little much in there, with all those people."

Jack nodded, ordering some water from Charlie. "Yeah," he said as Charlie fetched them. "It sure is crowded tonight." Charlie slid them three glasses of water, and Jack bent down, offering one of them to the woman on the floor. She took it gratefully, with a weak smile.

"You're really something, you know that, Jack?" Billy said when Jack stood back up. He looked sincere and open.

"Hmm? Why?" he asked, his brow furrowed. From what he could tell he was about as regular Joe as a man could be, if not something of a stuffy type. He didn't know or understand what Billy saw in him to make him think that.

"You just are. I like you," Billy confessed. "You're a good man."

Jack felt his face warm and had to look away for a moment. "Thank you, Billy," he said, then gathered the courage to look back at him. "You're a good man too."

Billy smiled and tilted his glass of water to Jack but said nothing else.

❖

Betty adored Jack's smile.

He looked like a prince when he grinned, all charming and handsome and a little bit shy. She loved that about him.

And apparently so did Billy.

She could see that Jack was over the moon for the guy, certainly. And watching them tonight while they leaned against the far wall chatting, Betty was starting to suspect Billy felt the same way. It made her heart sing. Jack deserved good things, and the way Billy seemed to melt when Jack smiled was a good thing indeed.

She stood from her table, tossing back the last of her cocktail with a small secretive smile. Jack wasn't the only one who deserved good things.

The night was only starting, but they didn't have to play for another hour or so. So with music singing through her veins, Betty made her way across the dance floor. A man offered to dance with her, and she allowed herself to twirl into and then out of his arms with a laugh. The next time he spun her out, she kept right on spinning, away through the bodies on the dance floor.

She moved past couples and a group of women dancing wildly together who drew her willingly in for another precious second. Betty wasn't in a rush. She knew that Eva would only just be closing up shop. She'd be seeing her last guest out, if she had one, and blowing out her candles. Moving in that beautiful solidly graceful way she did through her space as she sought out each and every last flame. She'd be humming to herself, maybe, hearing the same music Betty was, though far more muffled up in her apartment. She'd be tidying her cards and placing the beautifully decorated black cloth with gold designs on it over her crystal ball. Betty liked to think of it as her putting it to sleep for the night. Tucking it in to bed.

Then she'd be retiring to her private space. Moving through her tiny little living area, past the kitchen and bathroom to her bedroom. And she'd be taking off her shawl…

Betty laughingly freed herself from the dancing group and finally made it to the edge of the dance floor. But she didn't stop dancing. Not when she was out the door, or even on her way up the stairs. She didn't stop even when Eva opened the door for her, just swept Eva laughingly up into her dance.

Betty had been slightly wrong.

Eva had still been wearing her shawl when she opened the door. But that was no big deal. Betty could help her take it off. And she did, almost the moment the door closed behind her, her lips pressed against Eva's as they swayed. God, she was so warm. So beautiful and perfect.

Betty had never carried a torch for anyone else like this.

They fell into bed together, all warmth and skin and stolen breath. Betty kissed her like she was starving for her. Like she was desperate for the taste of her lips, the light brush of her tongue. It took longer with a woman, to get her to that peak, but God was it ever worth it when Eva shuddered apart around her fingers, her cries muffled against Betty's lips. And it took less time than it ever had with men for Eva to get her there, using her mouth to work her over until she was practically sobbing, with the bedsheets tangled in her grasping hands.

Afterward they lay together, a tangle of limbs and happiness, soaking up each other's presence.

"Let me read your palm?" Eva asked when they'd both caught their breath, kissing the back of her hand first, then the palm.

"Let me pay you then," Betty countered, though she was flattered. Eva would never let her pay for any service. She'd read her cards, cast runes, and read her tea leaves all for free. And now it seemed she wanted to read her palm in quite the same way. But Betty wouldn't have it. This was Eva's living, and she didn't want to take money away from her.

"You allow me to practice," Eva protested, her smile soft. "And it makes me happy to do this for you, Nightingale."

Betty sighed, shifting in bed so that Eva could get a better angle, and gave in. "Okay, sweetheart. I suppose one palm reading won't kill me. By the time you're done with me I'm gonna be the most in-the-know lady alive." Eva just smiled at that and flipped her hand back over to look at her palm.

"This one here is your wisdom line," she said, tracing a line across her palm. "And here is your fate line." She moved her finger along a vertical line in her palm, her lips twitching upward. "I'll explain to you what they mean as we go."

Betty let her take her on a journey, following the roadways of the lines of her hands to destinations unknown, made clearer by Eva's low and soothing voice. "You have a strong love line," Eva said, and this time the shiver that ran through Betty wasn't only from the gentle drag of her finger.

"Oh," she said, her neck heating. She wondered how that could be possible when she'd given up on love a long time ago. She watched, fascinated as Eva moved on to another line. She couldn't bear to be rejected, or worse, betrayed by Eva. She wondered if there was a line that represented cowardice. She was sure that one would be strong. Then Eva frowned, worrying at another line with her fingertip. "There is betrayal in your future," she said. "Soon to come it seems. Be careful, my little songbird."

Betty shuddered. "Oh, that's very dramatic," she said, peering at her own hand like it could somehow translate its lines into images of the future Eva saw for her. "That gave me goose bumps. Look." She showed Eva her arm and was delighted when Eva pressed kisses up the length of it, as though chasing the tiny bumps away with her lips.

"I don't mean to scare you," she said, her lips soft against the inside of her elbow. "My fortunes are never meant to scare. They are meant to prepare you for what is to come." Betty shivered again, this time from the sucking kiss Eva pressed to her forearm. She didn't ask if Eva was telling the truth, or if this was simply a practice in cold-reading as Leroy had called it once. It didn't matter.

The only thing that mattered were the soft kisses Eva was pressing against her skin and the warmth of her body as Betty rolled to hover over her with a wide smile.

❖

"Hey there, Billy!" Betty called out, but Billy didn't turn. "Billy?" she said again, reaching out this time to tap him on the shoulder. He jolted, then looked at her, shaking his head ruefully.

"Sorry about that, Bets," he said, though he looked annoyed. "I was lost in thought."

"Penny for your thoughts?" Betty asked.

"Nothing worth a penny really. Just thinking about playing our next song," Billy replied, smiling at her now, all traces of annoyance gone. His eyes weren't on her though.

That was obviously bull, but Betty didn't push it. "I'm sure it'll be great," she said.

Billy still wasn't looking at her. But when Betty turned to see who he was staring at she was surprised to see Sammy instead of Jack.

"Sure will. Excuse me," Billy said, sounding distracted. "I'm going to go find Jack."

"All right," Betty said, shaking her head as he left. He sure was acting odd.

Sammy came over to join her the moment Billy walked away.

"Heya, Bets," he said, "How you doing?"

"I'm all right. What's going on, Sammy?"

"I don't like that fella," Sammy said. Betty followed his nod to see Billy across the room chatting with Jack. "I don't care if he came on the rum run with us, there's something wrong about him."

"He seems fine to me," Betty said. "Jack seems to like him."

"Jack's an easy mark. Grifters like Billy always go for an easy mark."

Betty shook her head. "Or are you jealous?"

Across the room Jack and Billy started to walk in their direction.

Sam glared at her. "Nothing to be jealous about," he said. "I'm just looking out for everyone."

Betty pressed her finger against her lip as Billy and Jack approached.

"Billy, you sure can blow that horn," Jack said, sounding starstruck as all get-out.

"Says the best piano player this side of Tin Pan Alley. You ought to be playing there, Jack. Not in this place," Billy said.

"You're working in this place," Sam pointed out.

"Of course. There isn't anything wrong with working here," Billy said amicably. "I just think Jack could take it professional, is all."

"Thank you," Jack said, all soft and pleased.

"Course he could," Sam said angrily. "But he'd have boring crowds if he went pro. At least here we keep things interesting."

Jack seemed touched for a moment, before laughing. "Maybe a little too interesting. Bunch of little gangsters running around here causing trouble. At least for a high-hat crowd I'd be away from all this madness."

Billy perked up at that, like a dog on point. "What kind of madness?" he asked.

"Nothing," Sam said forcefully. "Jack's just not used to living around people who know how to have fun."

"Excuse me?" Betty said, raising an eyebrow at Sammy.

"Sorry, Bets," he said. He looked at her contritely, and she waved her hand in forgiveness. She couldn't stay mad at Sammy. The poor bunny was obviously struggling with his feelings.

"Well, I'm going to go be boring over at the piano," Jack said. "Billy, you coming?"

"Just a minute," Billy said.

Jack looked between him and Sammy like he wasn't sure what was going to happen. "Okay, Betty?"

"Be right there, sweetie," she said. Whatever Billy had to say to Sammy, she wasn't about to miss it. Jack nodded, looking like a lost puppy as he wandered away.

"Betty, this conversation is for the men," Billy said.

Sammy scoffed before she could defend herself. "Whatever you have to say to me, you can say in front of her."

"That's right," Betty said.

"Fine," Billy said, a muscle in his jaw jumping. "What's your problem with me?"

"It's like I said. I don't trust you. I think you ought to consider working somewhere else."

Betty was shocked at the straightforward demand. Sammy really did hate Billy.

Billy sized him up, then laughed. "All right, sure. Where should I go work, huh?"

Sammy grunted. "I'm not joking. I want you out of here."

"And what about everyone else, hmm?" Billy asked, still smiling that carefree smile.

"Betty?" Sam said, clearly hoping for backup.

"I'm staying outta this, Sammy," she said.

Billy finally turned his attention to her. "Smart girl," he said.

Well. That was annoying. Why was she only a smart girl when she was siding with him, when before he hadn't even wanted her there as part of the conversation?

"Don't matter what anyone thinks," Sam growled, "They don't know from nothing. I've met people like you before. Charming pretty boys who lock on to the easiest target around and bleed 'em dry."

That finally made Billy frown. "You think Jack's an easy target, huh? Then why don't we call him over here and you can tell him that to his face?"

Sam narrowed his eyes. "You think you're clever," he said, to which Billy shrugged and nodded "Well, you aren't. I know you're up to something, and I'm watching you. You slip up, just once, and I'll beat the snot out of you. With pleasure."

"What a tough guy," Billy said flippantly. "I don't know what to tell you, Sam. I'm here to play and that's it. I can't be held responsible for your overactive imagination."

Sammy made a rude gesture and turned to walk away. Betty noticed that his other hand was clenched into a fist. "Stay away from Jack," he called back as he headed toward the bar.

"Excuse me," Betty said to Billy. He was grinning like he'd won a battle, and Betty felt a little bit uneasy with how nasty that grin had gone. "I'll go after him."

She followed in Sammy's wake and poured him a drink when Charlie proved to be busy with some customers. "Do you feel any better now?" Betty asked.

Sam shook his head. "No. That bastard's up to something. You gotta believe me, Bets."

"I will say that he doesn't seem to like you just as much as you dislike him," Betty agreed. "But I think he's good for Jack. He makes him smile."

"Anyone can make Jack smile. I can make Jack smile," Sam grumbled.

"Maybe you should work more on making him smile than you do trying to cause trouble with Billy," Betty suggested.

"Maybe. I don't know," Sam shook his head. "There's just something I don't like about Billy."

❖

There was something that Jack really liked about Billy. A certain charm to him that had won him over almost immediately. And he was fun. He made Jack laugh. Made him feel good. And when Billy laughed and smiled, he always looked at Jack like he was something special.

"Come on," Billy said, near the end of the night, after they were done playing for the evening. "We're going to dance again."

Jack breathed out heavily. "You've already seen how badly I dance," he said. "Are you sure you want that?"

"I'm going to teach you," he said as though it were simple as that. "Come with me." And Jack, God help him, followed him out onto the dance floor.

"Hold onto my shoulders," he directed. Jack complied and tried to breathe as Billy placed his hands on his waist. "Now just relax and move with the music."

"Easy for you to say," Jack said, "You actually know how to dance."

Billy shook his head, but he was still smiling at least. "You'll do fine. Just sway with me."

Jack tried. He tried to forget the crowd around him and focus on Billy. On the way he moved to the music. For someone so good at playing music, Jack was terrible at moving to it. He felt too aware of his movements, but not aware enough to match them to the beat. When he was playing he could fade away into the moment. When he was dancing he was *too* present, unable to relax.

But here he was, on the dance floor yet again, this time with Billy to copy. To lose himself in. And Billy knew what he was doing.

He moved with a grace that Jack could never hope to achieve, his body swaying and moving to the music like it was his natural state. Like he was meant to dance. Polished, unlike Betty's flowing motions. Precise in a way that Sam could never hope to be with his wild flailing and reckless abandon.

Billy leaned in, and Jack moved with him. Moved toward him. He was amazing, in a way that was stealing away Jack's ability to think.

And then, there in the crush of bodies, Billy kept right on leaning in until their lips were pressed together. The kiss lasted only a moment, but to Jack it felt like forever, frozen there, pressed together in an instant that he never wanted to end.

Then Billy was pulling away, his cheeks red. "Sorry," he said over the music. "Got carried away again." Jack stood there, still now in the middle of the dancing bodies, trying to process what had just happened. His heart beat heavily, and his hands were trembling. He hadn't been kissed in a long, long time. It was nice. Nicer even, than he remembered it being. And despite himself, Jack felt joy bubble up in his chest. He couldn't help but smile, his hands moving up to his lips.

"Let's go get some water," Billy said, leaning in close again, but just enough so Jack could hear him. Not close enough to kiss him again. Not close enough to feel the wild beating of Jack's heart.

They moved as if in a dream, heading to the bar. In silence, they grabbed their waters together, sipping them side by side. Jack tried to get his heartbeat under control. Tried to breathe. Tried to think of something, anything, to say.

"Sorry about that," Billy said, staring into his water glass.

He didn't provide anything else, so Jack took a deep breath and said, "That's all right. It was...nice."

Billy didn't meet his eyes for a moment. But when he finally looked back at him there was no sign of regret. Just a look like he was trying to figure out what made Jack tick. "I should head home," he said, patting Jack on the shoulder. His hand lingered there for a moment, warm and sweet, just like the kiss had been. "Good night, Jack."

"Good night, Billy," he said, and watched him walk to the door with his heart in his throat and his head in the clouds.

Chapter Twelve

What should we do tonight?" Eva asked Betty. They were sitting in her living room, still in their nightgowns, and they had at least a couple of hours before Betty had to be at the Trespass. They'd passed the day slowly, chatting and reading from Eva's selection of books in her parlor, sharing the occasional kiss as the sun made its way across the sky.

"Oh, I know!" Betty said. She grinned mischievously and sat up from the chaise where she had been semi reclined, shaking her dark hair from her eyes. "Let's nip down to the bar before it opens and liberate ourselves a bottle of the Trespass's best."

Eva grinned back. "I'm sure Leroy and Charlie won't mind too much," she said as she stood to offer Betty a hand up.

Giggling like schoolgirls, they left the apartment and snuck down the stairs. There wasn't likely to be anyone in yet, but the back door was usually left unlocked. The whole errand had a deliciously secret energy—even if the risk of being caught was miniscule. And even if getting caught would get them nothing more than an amused glance and maybe a teasing talking to. They went around the back, with only a little embarrassment at being out in their nightgowns, only to find the door ajar. That silenced their giggling.

Betty had the sinking feeling that something bad was going on just inside.

"Would Leroy or Charlie leave the door open?" Betty whispered.

Eva shook her head. "Not since I've lived here."

The sound of smashing glass made them both jump.

Someone was in there.

Someone none too friendly if the sound of another bottle smashing was any indication.

"We should go find someone," Eva whispered, as another crash came from the bar.

Betty shook her head. It'd be too late by then. It sounded like someone was destroying the place. They didn't have time to fetch one of the men. "Wait here," Betty said. She grabbed the broken slat of a crate and wrenched it the rest of the way off, arming herself with a plank of wood.

"No. If you're going in, so am I," Eva said as she searched the ground for a weapon. She found only a broken bottle, which she picked up by the neck gingerly. "I wish I'd brought my heater, but this'll do. Let's go."

Betty blinked. Eva had a gun? Well, that was interesting. Not that now was the time to discuss it. She nodded, then before she left the alley, she grabbed the metal lid of a garbage can. That should be good enough as a shield.

They crept through the door, Betty going first, to find a man with his back to them. He was smashing bottles of booze and muttering to himself, his white shirt baggy and torn.

"Damn stupid waste," he said. "But when Zanetti says destroy the liquor you destroy the liquor." He was taking his time, taking a swig from each bottle before he smashed it. What a fool. He could have just swept his arm across the bar and have been done with it. Betty thanked the Lord that mobsters didn't seem to be too bright.

Even with him muttering to himself, to cross the room would make too much noise. But maybe if they scared him enough while they had the element of surprise...Betty took a deep breath, and then slammed the wood against the garbage lid.

The loud bang made the mobster jump like a frightened cat, and he nearly overbalanced as he spun around to face them.

"Hey, asshole!" Betty shouted. "You have to pay for those drinks!"

"Who the hell are you?" he slurred. He was swaying on his feet, clearly drunk as a skunk. Still, he was much bigger than either Eva or Betty. This was going to be difficult.

"Who the hell are you?" Eva shot back as she brandished her bottle threateningly.

The man laughed, stepping out from behind the bar. "Just a buncha birds, huh? Why don't you ladies mind your own business and get outta here."

Betty huffed. Just a bunch of birds? She'd show him.

With a shout, she charged forward, pleased to see the gleam of fear in his eye right before she swung her piece of wood at his face. He blocked the attack, but the wood connected with a hard *thunk* against his forearm.

"Jesus!" he cried out. Then he doubled over as Betty used the trashcan lid to hit him in the gut. "Christ! What's wrong with you?"

Betty yelped as he straightened up and grabbed her wrist, hard. He backed her up against the bar and grabbed the trash lid. He wrested it from her fingers, throwing it off to the side with a loud clatter. She couldn't move, trapped between his body and the bar with his hands on both her wrists.

"You little bit—" He stopped suddenly, and everything went quiet as Eva pressed the sharp edge of the bottle she'd found against his pulse point.

"You're going to let her go," Eva said, quiet and serious as the grave. "Or I'll bleed you out and send your head back to Zanetti myself."

Betty watched, wide-eyed, as Eva pressed the bottle a little harder against his neck. Hard enough to draw blood.

"Okay," he said, taking a step back along with Eva. "Okay, she's free."

Betty grinned, and took the opportunity to smash him in the face with the plank of wood. It connected with a sickening crack and bright red blood gushed from his nose, dripping down his chin and onto the floor. He hunched down for a moment to gather his balance, and Eva kicked him in the rear. He stumbled forward and ran full-tilt toward the door.

"And stay out!" Betty called after him.

He didn't stop, just ran out the door like the devil was after him.

Betty collapsed against the bar, her hand trembling where she still held the piece of wood.

Eva flopped down beside her, breathing heavily. And then, she started to laugh.

"We just chased that big time mobster away! Us!" she said, making Betty laugh along with her.

"We did," Betty said, opening one of the bottles of gin and taking a drink.

There was blood, glass, and booze all over the floor. They'd have to tell Leroy and Charlie what happened. At least the missing gin bottle she was drinking would be chalked up to being one of the smashed bottles on the ground.

"Did you see that?" Eva cackled. "You got him right in the beezer!"

"I know," Betty said, "I broke it!"

"You sure did," Eva said.

The smell of alcohol was strong, but when Betty leaned in for a kiss all she could smell was Eva's jasmine perfume.

"Betty May Dewitt, you're the bee's knees, did you know that?" Eva said after the kiss.

Betty took a swig of gin, winced at the taste, then bit her lip. "Felton," she offered. "My real last name's Felton."

Eva's expression softened, and she ran her hand along Betty's cheek. "Betty May Felton, you're the bee's knees."

Betty leaned in and kissed her again, soft and sweet. "And so are you, Eva."

"Eva Waters," Eva provided. "I don't think I've told anyone what my last name is since I was a child."

"Thank you for sharing it with me," Betty said.

The air felt almost electric as they looked into each other's eyes. They'd just saved the bar together. And now, with everything quiet in the aftermath, the moment felt so intimate that Betty almost wanted to cry.

"I love you," Eva said.

Betty's heart leapt into her throat.

"Oh—" she said, unable to find the words to say. Love. Eva loved her. It should be the easiest thing in the world to say back, and yet...

"It's all right, Nightingale. You don't have to say anything." Her voice was kind, but her expression held a sadness that Betty wished she could kiss away. "I just wanted you to know."

"I...have a lovely time with you, Eva," she managed to say. "Thank you for telling me. I'm just not ready..."

"Of course. I understand," Eva said, smiling normally now. "Come on. I'd like to show you a new magazine I bought the other day. Let's go back upstairs. We'll catch Leroy and Charlie when they come in."

"Sure," Betty said, feeling strange. "Let's just grab another bottle."

Eva laughed, shaking her head. "I don't know. Don't you think they lost enough?"

Betty shrugged. "We saved the bar, didn't we? We deserve a treat."

When Betty eventually had to go back downstairs to work, Eva came with her. They found Charlie standing at the bar looking confused. "What in the hell happened here?" he said.

"Some fella from the mob tried to smash up all your liquor," Eva told him.

"Don't worry, we chased him off," Betty added.

Charlie looked at them, astounded.

"You two...chased off a mobster?"

"Sure did. Hope you can clean that up before opening," Betty singsonged. "I have to go warm up my voice."

But before she could get very far, Eva's hand was on her shoulder.

"You all right, Nightingale?" Eva asked her quietly. The whisper in her ear gave Betty a pleasant shiver down her spine.

"Of course," Betty replied. But she wasn't sure she was. Because as she walked over to the stage, smelling strongly of spirits, she couldn't help but think of the sweet smell of Eva's perfume. And the thought dawned on her, with a shiver of something she didn't want to name slipping down her spine. *Oh no. I think I'm falling in love.*

Chapter Thirteen

B illy kept teaching Jack how to dance. It became one of Jack's favorite parts of the evenings at the Trespass, when Billy would take him by the hand and bring him onto the dance floor after they'd finished playing for the night.

Billy was a good teacher, and strict. He'd correct Jack's missteps and ensure that he wasn't missing any beats. He'd cringe when Jack stepped on his toes and berate him in a way that made Jack laugh, but also try harder to get it right. He was better than any music teacher Jack had ever had in that respect.

"You're doing well," Billy told him one evening, a few dance lessons in, as they swayed together on the floor. "Maybe someday soon I can teach you how to do a real dance." He hadn't kissed him again after that first time, but Jack was tentatively hopeful he might. He just had to be patient. After all, this was the best he'd felt since back when James had first kissed him that day by the river.

God, just thinking about that now hurt like nothing else. James had been Jack's everything. Back then they'd met up in empty barns and corn fields. By the river, and in Jack's favorite apple tree. They were always so careful not to leave marks on each other's skin in any place that was visible above clothing. They were less careful with places that would be covered.

Jack had learned to touch and was touched in ways he'd never known before. They were both in their late teens and full of life and hormones. It was joyful, and hot, and the final nail in the coffin for Jack, who knew now that he'd never feel for a woman what he felt for James. But more than that, it was love. James had been Jack's very first love. Betty had been overjoyed when he told her.

"Jack Norval, you dog!" she'd said, hugging him in delight. "James? As in James Parsons? The handsomest boy in school? I'd be jealous if I wasn't so happy for you."

Jack had grinned nervously, and hushed her, even though they were in the safety of his own house. "Yeah, thanks, Bets. Just, please don't breathe a word of this to anyone. James wasn't even sure if I should tell you."

"Humph," she'd said, glaring a little bit. "Well, you did the right thing telling me. I'd have been madder than that old tomcat in the barn if you'd kept something this big from your best friend!"

Jack had laughed and shook his head. "I would never."

"Imagine us! Best friends going out with two best friends! It's like it was meant to be!"

Betty had kept the secret for him, and for a while, Jack had thought that James might be his future. And then—

Jack shook his head, not wanting to think about that right now.

"Has this not been real dancing?" Jack asked Billy incredulously. He was pretty certain that moving your body to music at all was dancing. As far as he knew.

"No," Billy laughed. "This has been the very basics. But you're a quick learner. I think we can get you there in no time." Jack grinned, letting Billy pull him around the floor faster, as the song picked up. He only stepped on his toes a few times in the process.

Laughing breathlessly, they moved to their table, flopping down beside each other as close as could be. "You're a sweet guy," Billy told him, their hands brushing on the table and setting Jack's whole world on fire. "How'd such a sweet guy get to working at a place like this?"

"I could ask you the same question," Jack said, thrilling at how Billy left his warm hand against his own.

"Like I said before, you could get a job in Tin Pan Alley, no problem," he told Jack. "I know you could."

Jack smiled, feeling suddenly shy. "Thanks, Billy. That's the dream. Someday maybe. But for now, I need the money I get working here. Besides, it's not such a bad place once you get used to it.

"No really, Jack, you gotta get out of this place," Billy pressed, leaning in close. "You're too good for this life."

"I kind of like it here," Jack said, inching his pinkie finger up on top of Billy's. He didn't move his hand away, and Jack's whole body sang with it.

"I'm serious," he said, this time urgently enough that Jack sat up and took notice. "You need to leave as soon as you can. Things are heating up, and I don't want to see you caught up in it." Jack felt cold all of a sudden, like someone had opened a door to a street covered in bitter snow.

"Billy, what are you talking about?"

"Look." Billy leaned in even further, but he moved his hand away from Jack's. "I like you, Jack. Otherwise, I wouldn't have said anything. But the Cherry has the police in their pockets, you understand? They're fixing to raid this place within the next few weeks."

"How in the world would you know that?" Jack asked, voice shaking. Things were going south far too quickly for him to follow. Or maybe he didn't *want* to understand what Billy was telling him.

"Damn it, Jack." Billy slammed his fist on the table between them, making Jack flinch. He flashed for a moment in his mind to another man's fist smashing into his nose. The feeling of that moment was sickeningly close to the one he was currently living.

"Shit. I'm not going to hit you or anything," Billy said, clearly reading something in Jack's body language. "Sorry. I'm just trying to help you. My bosses are getting impatient."

"Bosses," he said numbly. "So…so you've been working for the Cherry? For Zanetti?" he asked, horror clear in his voice.

"In a sense. I'm the police, Jack. The Cherry is paying me off. They're calling the shots as far as speakeasies go, and I've been getting the police to crack down hard on places that the mob doesn't like lately."

"Stop talking," Jack demanded, moving away as Billy reached out to touch his shoulder. "Get out."

"Jack, I'm serious."

"So am I. You need to leave."

"So do you," Billy insisted, purposefully ignoring Jack's demand in order to warn him again.

"Or you could stop giving the police your reports," Jack said. "You could stop working for the Cherry. *Please*, Billy. You've met everyone here. You know we're good people."

Billy stared at him like he was seeing him for the first time, and he didn't like what he saw. "You really don't know me, do you?"

Jack leaned forward, desperate now. "I do, Billy. You're a good man—"

"Mack," Billy interrupted him. "My name's Mack." Jack felt for a moment like he might cry. There was rage and betrayal, sure. But deeper than that was a sadness he thought might swallow him whole.

"Fine. Mack. Please. Don't do this."

"I do my job," he said. "I do what pays, Jack. It doesn't matter how naive you are, or how kind you think these gangsters are. They're gangsters, and they aren't paying me like Zanetti does."

"Money can't be the only thing you care about," Jack pleaded. "Please, you have to know that the Cherry sells *poison*, Mack. Sam told me—"

Mack laughed harshly. "Oh, *Sam* told you, did he?" he snarled. "Because Sam is so good and trustworthy. I've seen his criminal record and his file, Jack. And I wouldn't be surprised if there are things we don't know about." Jack felt cold. Sick. So the police likely knew that Sam had needed to kill before. "Putting him behind bars won't just win me favor with my bosses *and* the mob, it'll mean getting a criminal off the streets. It's a good career move, Jack. I'm not throwing that away just because you think he's *nice.*"

Something in Jack snapped. "Then get out. Now." How dare this asshole, who was in the pocket of the *mob*, decide that what they were doing was so wrong. That just because the Trespass sold illegal alcohol, they deserved jail. That because Sam had killed on the orders of the people who were *paying Mack off*, he deserved less respect.

"You can't be serious," Mack said in disbelief. But Jack was tired. He was so tired of being walked all over. He was tired of people thinking he was soft, that they could use him for their own means and then throw him away like yesterday's paper.

"If you don't leave right now, I'll be going over to the bar and telling Leroy what you just told me. He won't be *asking* you to leave like I am." The words were hard and cold as they left his mouth. "Leave. Now, while you can still walk out of here."

"I thought you were better than this," Mack said. He grabbed his coat as he stood. "I really did. Just consider what I told you. You ever want to change your mind, you can find me at the police station."

"I won't," Jack said firmly, standing as well. "Get out of my bar."

He walked Mack to the door silently, opening it for him and watching him ascend the stairs before he slammed it shut. Billy…*Mack* hadn't even looked back once.

"Jack? You okay?" Leroy asked when he stalked over.

"No. I'm not," he said through clenched teeth. "I need a drink. And to tell you something."

❖

"Jack, honey," Betty said, tentative and soft. She leaned in his doorway, taking in the sight of him sitting hunched over on the edge of his bed with his head in his hands.

"It's okay, Bets," he said, his voice rough. "I'll be fine. I just need some time on my own." That was all well and good, but Betty knew a little something about sadness, and facing it all on your own never helped. She couldn't let him face this alone.

"Don't be dumb. I'm here for you," she said, marching into the room and climbing up beside him. "Now come here. It might not actually solve any problems, but I think a good cuddle can go a long way toward making them feel a little less big."

Jack laughed wetly, a disbelieving sound, but he did sit up straighter and let her tuck herself under his arm. They didn't need to talk, but if Jack wanted to, she'd be sure to listen. She could only imagine how hard this was hitting him. Not that Billy and he had been together, but she'd watched them flirt enough to know it'd been heading that way. At least this had all come out before it had happened. She wasn't sure he could stand another betrayal by someone he was seeing. Especially not since the first one had ended with him in the hospital.

"I really believed him," Jack managed to say, pressing his wet cheek against her hair. "I thought for sure—" He cut himself off, pressing his nose into her hair. "Doesn't matter. At least he didn't pull a James and beat the snot outta me." He laughed humorlessly. "Small mercies."

"Oh, Jack," she said, carding her fingers through his hair. "I'm so sorry." And she was, but she was more angry. At Billy… *Mack*, whatever his name was. And at herself. She should have seen it. She should have noticed them getting closer and should have seen the inconsistencies in how Billy acted. But she'd been fooled. Caught up in her own whirlwind romance and the excitement of their new life in the glamorous world of working at a speakeasy. Maybe if she'd been paying attention, she would have noticed he was scum. Eva was too distracting by half.

"If he was still around, I swear—" she said. She gritted her teeth. But what would she do, really? Bump off a cop? Sock him in his ugly mug and get thrown in jail? It just wasn't fair.

"Thank you, Bets," Jack said. He sounded absolutely exhausted. "I know you would."

They just existed there together for a while, holding tight and crying out their pain and frustration and anger. Eventually, Betty wiped her hand across her face, trying to clear her tears. "Let me make you some dinner, sweetie," she said. She pressed a kiss against his hair.

"You're too good to me, Bets," Jack said. He had stopped crying for a moment.

Betty squeezed his shoulder but kept quiet. She wasn't too good to him. She could have done more. Should have done more. But she swore if there was any way that she could keep Jack safe, she would do it. After all, it was her fault he'd gotten caught up in this whole wild life in the first place.

She'd wanted to be in New York so badly. Wanted it for what felt like her whole life. She knew in her heart that she and Jack were going to be famous performers together. It was a foregone conclusion in her mind. The sky was blue, the grass was green, and she and Jack were going to be famous.

Then James had come along, and for a while it'd seemed like Jack might stay in Wisconsin forever. He'd been so in love with him. Over the moon, he'd kept saying. James had become Jack's everything. Just like Richard had been her everything. And then...well, Betty's blood boiled just thinking about it. What James had done, because Richard had found them together. It was more than Betty could bear.

She'd grabbed Jack's hand one night after that, and she'd told him her plan. And poor sweet Jack, had looked at her for a while, with this sad, sad look in his eyes, and he'd said. "Sure, Bets. Anywhere would be better than here."

And now it seemed history was repeating itself. She'd brought Jack to New York and gotten him into danger. She'd let him fall again for someone who could never ever deserve him.

Betty wasn't sure she could ever forgive herself. And if it could happen to Jack, who was to say it couldn't happen to her?

❖

The crunch of bone as his nose broke. That was what Jack remembered most about the day James had beat him within an inch of his life. The crunch of bone and the taste of blood, and the thought of how goddamn breakable everything in the world was. If you could break something as tough as a bone with one little punch, how easy would it be to break a man.

He'd found out on that day. The day when the man he'd fallen in love with and his friends, including Betty's boyfriend, had kicked and punched and spat on him. They'd beaten him bloody and left him there broken, in more ways than one.

He could still remember the pleading look in James's eyes, right before he'd landed the first punch, the one that had broken his nose. Like he wanted Jack to forgive him. Like he was stuck.

But he hadn't been. He could have been brave. He could have told his friend the truth when they'd been found by Richard in the cornfield the day before. He could have come clean, and taken the beating with Jack, or maybe they could've escaped it somehow. James had had choices. Instead, he threw the first punch. Instead, he cracked Jack's bones. Screamed and hurled insults at Jack for being a faggot, as he and his friends kicked Jack while he was down with snot and blood and tears streaming down his face.

James was a journalist now, back in Wisconsin. Jack was starting to think anyone who seemed halfway upstanding wasn't worth knowing. They certainly weren't worth trusting, that was for sure.

But Betty had always been so kind. She'd kept him alive after that day, with her love and her sunny disposition, the one she held so close despite the current of sadness that ran through her. She'd taken care of him, even though her own heart was just as broken. She'd saved him with her plans of moving to New York. "We'll get out of here, Jacky," she'd said with determination. "You and me. We're going to live in the Big Apple and be real musicians. Just you wait and see." And now here they were, living something close to like what they'd dreamed. Only he was still so easy to break, or at least he felt that way.

Chapter Fourteen

Jack and Betty kept playing and singing, but Jack's heart wasn't really in it. Every song they played reminded him of Billy blowing his horn along with them. He told Betty this, about two days after the betrayal, while they were out for dinner at their favorite place, trying to cheer themselves up. Betty changed their songs. It helped a little bit, and Jack took solace in the fact that at least he hadn't given Billy his heart.

Everyone who worked at the Trespass was subdued. The betrayal had hit them all hard, and Mack's confession had uncovered something they'd all already felt. Something big was coming. The violence of the Barber's gang was increasing with each new week that went by, and it felt like any moment now someone or something was going to pop off and explode.

"We need to know when it's going to happen," Charlie said as they gathered around the bar after another evening spent on high alert. "We can do something if we know when they'll be here."

"Starting with making sure Leroy and Sammy aren't working," Betty said firmly. They'd had this argument already a few times over. Jack was on her side, but Leroy and Sammy were harder to convince.

"If they get Sammy, he'll be in jail whether they find booze or not," he said. "And they aren't going to go easy on any of us, and especially not Leroy."

Betty nodded. "It's not fair, but it's true," she said.

"We're the best brawlers this place has," Sam said. A little frown appeared on his face. Like the thought of not being able to fight pained him.

"If we come up with a good enough plan we won't *need* to fight," Jack said. "Besides, I think you're not giving George enough credit as a brawler," he added. It was the first time he'd really joked since Mack had left, and it felt good. George lifted his glass to him at that.

"And how, exactly, are we going to make sure we don't have any liquor here on the right day?" Charlie asked. "If you think I'm serving water for a few weeks in a row until the coppers decide to show up…"

Even Betty was stumped by that one. But surprisingly, Jack wasn't. He knew what he had to do. It didn't matter that every instinct he had was screaming at him that it was a terrible idea. He had to help them out of this mess.

"I'll find out for us," he said. He felt reluctant but determined. "I can go to the police station and scope out who works there."

"Yeah? You're just gonna stroll into the police station?" Leroy said. "How's that gonna work?"

"Billy," Betty said grimly. She'd taken to saying his name like it caused a terrible taste in her mouth. Jack could relate.

Jack nodded in agreement, resolved now to what he had to do. "He told me to come see him at the station if I ever changed my mind about working here."

Sam nodded. "This could work," he said. "If Jack goes down there pretending he's finished with us, he can look around, see if he can find anything out. Play that sucker like he tried to play us. And I say tried because I *knew* he was a creep."

"That's enough, Sammy," Betty snapped. She shut him up right quick. Sam had been damn near insufferably smug about being right ever since he'd found out. It grated on everyone's nerves, not just Jack's.

"Jack, that sounds dangerous," she said. Jack shrugged helplessly at her. What could he do? This was their only choice.

Charlie looked to Leroy. "At the very least he can take a look at the faces he sees there. He can help us keep an eye out for any dry agents in the bar. Remember what we used to do?" Charlie asked.

"Right," Leroy answered. "Back in the days when we had a band, before the two of you, we used to have a song that they'd play if they noticed anything suspicious. The Prisoner's Song." The moment we'd hear it everyone would scram before the cops could grab us. They'd take the booze, sure, but at least none of us got busted."

"I know that one," Betty said, nodding. "We can do that. As long as we know who to look for." But she didn't look too happy about it.

"Money really *can* be our house peeper," Sam said, elbowing Jack in the side. "Who'd have thought we'd have our own private dick, huh?"

"Sure. I can give you all descriptions of the coppers I see there." Jack nodded. He could feel himself smiling now, which should probably worry him. Back in the day he would have been horrified at the very thought of spying on the police, and now here he was smiling about it. "We can all keep an eye open."

"Right. Then we can keep our losses to a minimum," Charlie said.

"Jack," Betty said. "Are you sure? You don't have to do this. We can find another way." She looked for all the world like she was going to cry.

Jack shook his head. "I can't think of any other way this could work, Bets. We won't be able to find out when they're coming unless we have a man on the inside."

"I could go," she said.

He shook his head again. "Bets, you know it makes more sense for it to be me. He offered me an invitation."

Betty nodded, but she didn't look pleased. "I just don't want you getting hurt."

Jack smiled. She was truly the best person he knew, always looking out for him. "No way around it. Least I can do is hurt him back, huh?"

She searched his face with her eyes, then slowly smiled. "Well, in that case," she said. "Let's get planning."

❖

Betty sometimes liked to go to the Trespass to think. She'd plunk herself down on the edge of the stage and just let the sounds of whoever else happened to be there wash over her while her mind wandered. Jack always worried when she got quiet like this, which was why she hated trying to think at home. It was hard be sad when Jack's concern was louder than the boisterous laughter of the boys at the Trespass. And bless them, the boys were always sweet enough to leave her alone when she got like this.

Right now she was thinking about Billy. Or Mack. Whatever his damn name was. The asshole who broke Jack's heart. She wondered if he even realized how badly he'd hurt Jack. Probably not. How could he have possibly known the way that Jack got quiet after James attacked him. How he'd barely spoken for weeks afterward, and how he'd lost that carefree attitude he'd had up until then. How anxious he still got when he saw someone in a crowd who looked even remotely like one of the boys who'd beat him. How he'd flinched when Betty told him she'd called things off with Richard. As though she'd have stayed with someone who beat her best friend to a pulp.

There was no way Mack could know how deeply Jack loved, and how terrified he was to open himself up again. How his stay in the hospital had made him seem so small and frail, and left him with wounds that ran much deeper than skin and bone. He couldn't have known what his betrayal would do to Jack. But she bet her ass he would have done it anyway, even if he *had* known.

"Miss Betty?" A voice just behind her startled her out of her grim reverie.

"Oh! George, hello," she said. George wasn't exactly the type to seek out conversation, and it was odd that he'd chosen this moment to come for a chat. If that was what he'd come over for. "What can I do ya for?"

He sat down beside her, surprisingly graceful for a man of his bulk. "Saw you looking sad," he said with a shrug. "Thought you could use some company." Well, Betty supposed, if she wanted any company right now it *would* be from someone as quiet as George. So why not?

"Why, thank you," she said. "I think I could."

He sat there beside her, silent and solid and unobtrusive. It was nice. It was exactly what she needed. Just someone to *be* there with her so that she didn't start bawling right there on stage at the Trespass.

"You know it's not your fault," George said after about half an hour of amicable silence.

Oh.

She had been hoping that she seemed aloof and dramatic, like she was thinking about all the ills of the world and having a moment to suffer the weight of them. But maybe she was a little more transparent than she'd thought she was. "You think so?" she asked, finding it easier to admit what she felt with him for some reason. Like she was talking to a vault of silence but could still let her emotions out into the world instead of letting them boil up in her chest. "I should have noticed."

"Not your job to notice," George told her, like it was a fact. He was so still the whole time, but now he shifted, turning to look at her. "If anything, it was mine," he added with a low self-deprecating chuckle.

She blinked. She hadn't even considered that he might be beating himself up over letting a copper into their midst.

"But you couldn't have known," Betty protested, placing her hand on his arm. "He was too good of an actor."

George nodded. "Neither could you," he pointed out. Hah. The clever jerk.

"I suppose you're right," she admitted. "Can't help feeling like I should have though."

He nodded silently, looking out toward the bar. Betty sighed and looked down at her hands. "George, do you ever just feel blue?"

He huffed a laugh. "All the time, Miss Betty," he said. "Just like you."

Unsolicited, tears rose to her eyes. "Well then, I guess us blue folks had better stick together, huh?" she said, wiping the back of her hand across her eyes. With a sigh, she leaned against him in an almost hug. He nodded, and put his arm around her, and they sat there together in silence until they both felt ready to get up.

"Thank you, Georgie," she said as he helped her to her feet. "For sitting with me."

"Anytime you need," he said. "Think about what I said." He paused, smiling at her. "Try blaming him instead, yeah?" It was the most words she had ever heard George speak before. She appreciated that he'd said them for her sake.

"Yeah," she replied. "Yeah, I think I will."

CHAPTER FIFTEEN

Jack took a deep, steadying breath as he adjusted his shirtsleeves. He'd worn one of his good suits and a nice dress shirt, but he was starting to regret it from how much he was sweating. He hadn't even arrived at the station yet. No, he'd chosen a little side street to duck down in order to have his silent little panic. He fixed his derby hat for the fifteenth time, knowing full well that he was stalling. He needed to just get this over with, but God was he terrified.

Seeing Billy, no, seeing *Mack* again was going to be hard enough. It was going to damn near break his heart all over again. But worse was the idea that every copper in the place was going to somehow know exactly why he was there. That they'd figure him out the moment he walked in the door and arrest him right there on the spot. God, he was not at all cut out for gumshoeing.

A final deep breath, and Jack turned down the right street, sighting the police station as he walked. There was no turning back now. He had to do this. So, he walked right on up the steps and entered the building, while his guts rearranged themselves the whole while.

"Hello," he greeted the receptionist. "I'd like to speak to Officer Mack, if he's here."

"Of course, sir, please take a seat."

He sat, trying to keep his leg from bouncing. He figured police officers were trained to notice if you were nervous. The waiting area was much the same as any doctor's office, with only a few old newspapers on the table to distract him. One of them boasted a new actress performing at a nearby theater. He picked it up, figuring he'd read for a while, only to be faced with a larger-than-life picture of Dimitri Zanetti in the paper underneath it. His heart jumped into his throat, and silently he put the newspaper back down.

Jack instead turned his attention to the few men he could see beyond the front desk. A man with blond hair and a distinctive mole on his cheek. A ginger man who was balding.

"Sir," a voice made him nearly jump out of his skin. It was the receptionist, looking at him like she wasn't sure if he was well. "Sorry to startle you. Officer Lindh will see you now."

Jack had tried to prepare for seeing him again, but nothing could have prepared him for the feeling he got as Mack walked out to get him. It was like a punch in the gut. The way he smiled, the way he moved. The way he'd taken Jack's heart, only to stomp on it with his betrayal.

"Jack!" he said, holding his hand out to shake. This time, when he lingered a second or two too long, Jack felt nothing but the sweat of his palm and the urge to snatch his own hand back. "I'm so glad to see you here. Come on in, there's an office where we can talk."

Mack led him back behind the desk, into the police station proper. It was a typical looking office, with men in suits sitting at desks and walking around like they were in a rush, and filing cabinets lining every wall. It was almost a letdown. Like the office his brother Edwin worked in and had given him a tour of once. There weren't criminals being detained, or men with their nightsticks out screaming for men to *freeze*. Mostly there was just paperwork on every surface.

Mack walked Jack toward a hallway lined with closed doors, but before they could get far, a loud voice stopped them in their tracks. "Mack! Where's my report on that speakeasy nonsense."

Jack stiffened, turning with Mack to look at the imposing-looking man who had hollered. Just the mention of a speakeasy had him sweating even harder in his already damp suit, and he was more than a little reluctant to look the man in the face. But luckily, the man acted as though Jack wasn't even there, glaring daggers at Mack instead. His face was red as could be, all the way up his bald forehead.

"On the way, Captain," Mack said, but his normal pleasant smile had an edge to it now that Jack had never seen before. "Just finishing up."

"Well, hurry it up. You've wasted enough time as it is with these investigations," he said disdainfully. There was clearly no love lost between these two. Even Mack, who was a great actor, clearly wasn't a fan of his captain. A muscle in his jaw worked, but otherwise there was no outward indication that Mack was upset about being berated. But Jack could tell.

"Yes, sir, but the chief—"

"I don't care about the goddamned chief," the man bellowed, spittle flying from his mouth. "We're wasting our resources on these juice joints. We aren't getting any closer to Zanetti. Just catching low-life thugs who don't mean nothing."

God. They were after the very man who was paying Mack to direct the police's attention elsewhere. Of course, they were, he was the biggest threat to peace in New York right now. But it was strange to hear it from Mack's superior, knowing what Jack knew.

"I know, sir," Mack said, which surprised Jack. He'd expected an impassioned speech about how it was necessary. How his job was important and more than necessary. Hell, he expected him to stand up for himself even a little. But Mack wasn't even man enough to stand his ground on the importance of the missions that gave him the *chance* to work for the mob in the first place.

How had Jack ever thought that this man had any moral standing? He was worse than the gangsters he was trying to catch. At least the gangsters were honest about what they did. "But I'm certain I'm onto something here. There's a gangster working at this joint who has connections to Zanetti. I think we can get him, and he might be the one who leads us right to him." Jack felt sick. He had a nasty suspicion that Mack was talking about Sam.

"Right. I'll believe that when I see it. Just hurry up with the report," the captain said disdainfully.

"Yes, sir," Mack said to the back of his head, rolling his eyes at Jack as though they were partners in crime. "Come on in with me, Mr...." Mack trailed off, and with a start, Jack realized that he didn't even know his last name. Well, there was no way he was telling him the real one now. "Brant," he volunteered the first name he could think of. Miss Brant had been his sixth-grade music teacher. She'd had a snaggletooth and a bad temper and a hand that was quick to rap on knuckles when it wasn't entirely necessary.

"Mr. Brant," Mack said, smiling around the word. Jack thought that it was only fair. One fake name deserved another, after all.

The room was sparsely furnished, with a long table, a few simple and uncomfortable looking chairs, and a wilting plant in the corner whose leaves were covered in a thick layer of dust. Jack sat, staring at a ring left behind from someone's coffee on the light wooden surface of the table. He wondered who had last been in this room. He wondered if they'd been there to see Mack.

"It's good to see you, Jack," he said, sitting across from him. Jack forced himself to look up, to look into his eyes. Sam had told him that people trusted you more when you did that. And after what he'd been saying about Mack the whole time he was there, Jack was inclined to trust him. Sam might have been insufferable ever since he was proven right, but he *had* been right.

"Good to see you too," he said, not certain which name he should address the other man by. He figured he should probably call him Mack, but when he looked at him, he only saw Billy. "I, um, I hope it's okay that I came over here. I didn't know where else to turn."

"What's going on?" Mack asked, aloof in that charming sort of way he'd always had. Like he could use his kindness and his dashing smile to keep you at least an arm's length away, while making you feel like he was pulling you in close.

"I talked to Sam," he said, closing his eyes like the words pained him. "About his criminal record. After what you said, I just...I had to know." When he opened his eyes, Mack was nodding like he understood completely.

"Let me guess," he said, or perhaps snarled was the better word for it. "He lied to your face." Like you did, Jack wanted to say. But he just shook his head.

"No, it was worse. He told me everything. About the people he killed. The things he's done." Jack took a deep breath. "He said it all like it was *nothing*. Like he was talking about the weather. He *laughed* at one point. I...I can't go back there. Not after that."

"I'm sorry, Jack," Mack said. He sounded anything but. "I tried to warn you about him."

A wave of rage rolled through him, but he played it off, not even flinching. "I know. I should have trusted you," he said. "I just didn't know that a man could get so low. I...I need your help."

Mack nodded, looking smug as the cat that got the cream. "Of course, Jack. What do you need?"

Jack sighed. "Time? To get Betty out of that place. She's still fooled by Sammy's act. I can't bear to tell her what he's done."

"You have to, Jack," Mack said. "It's the only way. She needs to know who she's working for, and right quick."

"Look, Mack," he said, his heart hammering in his chest. "I haven't even told Betty that I'm here. She's still all caught up in the life in a way I've never been. But I need *time* to get her out of there."

"Then you'd better get to it," he said, without sympathy. "We're planning on raiding the place Saturday, next week." Jack didn't bother trying to hide his shock. Christ, that was too soon. Did they have enough time to take care of everything before then?

"Next week? I have to get her out of there before then?" It suddenly hit him, how real this all was. He was there, in the police station, spying for a speakeasy. The police were going to *raid* that speakeasy. He could go to *jail*.

For a brief, shameful, moment he considered telling Mack everything. About the spying, and the plans they were making. About how much he missed him, and how he was still sometimes terrified of this life he'd found himself in. But he kept his mouth closed, letting his knowledge of Betty's loyalty to him wash over him. He knew, deep down, that he'd never betray his friends like that. He couldn't.

He'd never be able to live with himself.

"I'll do my best," he told Mack. He let out a shuddering breath.

Mack smiled at him, that smile that used to melt Jack's insides like butter. Now it felt like a knife to the gut. "I'm glad you came here, Jack."

"Me too," he agreed. Though for wildly different reasons.

"You can come call on me anytime." He sounded so sincere. So much like the Billy that Jack had thought he'd known, back before he'd heard him talk about working for the worst gangster he knew of like it was nothing. Before he'd snarled threats about Jack's friends, who were also gangsters, sure, but the best gangsters he'd ever had the pleasure to meet.

"Thanks, Mack. I will," he said, knowing that it was never going to happen. With any luck, he'd never see Mack again in his life. Because if he ever did see him again, he had no illusions as to how hard Mack would punch his face for this betrayal.

Jack gathered his jacket and hat, chatting aimlessly with Mack as his thoughts floated somewhere far, far away. And still, he kept his eyes on the men in the room, committing them to memory. The man with the mole, the ginger haired man, a man with graying hair and dark eyes. He needed to remember as many faces as he could.

He nearly vomited when he finally got a block away from the station, leaning over and trying not to dry heave. God, he was entirely nerves. Nothing he had ever done in his life had ever been so dangerously thrilling. He wasn't sure if he loved the feeling or hated it. Maybe a bit of both.

He wanted to run straight to the Trespass, to tell them everything he'd seen and heard. To tell them what Mack had told him. But he couldn't do that. Leroy and Charlie had been firm about him going home first, just in case Mack sent someone to tail him. So Jack set off toward his apartment, his heart beating hard in his chest.

He hadn't expected in a million years to get the actual date of the raid. He'd been banking on getting a rough estimate, but this was better than anything he could have hoped for. And he'd taken stock of the faces of the men he'd seen there. Kept tabs on who he'd seen coming and going. The man with blond hair and the mole, the man with the large belly and a balding head of sparse red hair. The man with salt-and-pepper hair with dark hooded eyes. He ran through them in his head over and over as he walked.

Tomorrow he'd break the news to Charlie and Leroy. He'd spread the word to everyone, give them word of who to look for. But tonight he had a feeling he'd be sleepless. Maybe he'd play piano, soft enough that it wouldn't bother any of their neighbors or Betty.

Tomorrow they'd start their planning.

Chapter Sixteen

The Trespass Inn was just as bustling as any other Saturday night on the day that the raid was to take place. Betty felt positively nauseous with each face who came into the bar, certain that any one of them was going to be a copper, there to shut the place down.

She sent a little smile George's way, and he gave her a friendly wave back. He really was a sweetheart. She just hoped he'd be safe during whatever was about to happen. He was scanning every face, telling anyone who quite obviously didn't match a description of any of the coppers which song to look out for. Betty had even caught him singing a few bars to those who didn't know it, his voice low and melodic and not half bad.

Her hands were shaking as she climbed up onto the stage. It was more than stage fright this evening, that was for damn sure. There were so many things that could go wrong.

What if the tiny stairwell was overwhelmed by people fleeing in a panic? Sure, the plan was for everyone who worked there to head out the back door, but Betty knew that a frantic crowd was unpredictable and often violent. What if the dry agents were disguised? How would they know to play the song if they couldn't recognize anyone suspicious in the crowd?

And almost worse was the worry that Mack had been lying. That maybe the raid *wasn't* happening tonight. That they'd have done all this preparation for nothing, only to live in fear for who knew how many more weeks, knowing what was coming.

Betty hated uncertainty. She'd had enough of it for a lifetime at this point. The uncertainty of whether or not she'd make it. The strange, lingering sadness that made her feel as though she might never be happy again. The fear for herself, for Jack, for Eva. For the whole damn world, it felt like. She hated it all. She hated not knowing what would happen.

But that's why she sang.

Whether she was up on a stage or sitting by herself in her room, song was always a certainty for her. She knew the lyrics she had to sing, the notes she needed to follow. The melody could carry her places she wasn't expecting, certainly, but she was always in control. She made the decision to linger over this note, to breathe that one out for effect. Song was her domain, and she never felt lost there.

She tugged at her overly modest dress self-consciously. This wasn't what a gal at a flapper club should be wearing, but it would make their escape ten times easier if they got caught on the street. There was no way she could explain away a sexy little beaded dress if a copper questioned her.

Over by the doorway Betty startled as Eva entered and began whispering to George. She looked calm enough, but something like a premonition of dread swept through Betty, and she knew with a sudden certainty that Mack hadn't lied. It was happening tonight. Eva waved to her, nodding her head twice very deliberately. A shiver of fear made its way through Betty. They were here. They hadn't entered the building yet, but Eva had obviously seen them on the street.

Betty took a steadying breath and moved to whisper to Jack. "They're here. George is going to let them in, so play a short one," she muttered. Jack paled, but his nod was firm and unwavering. God, Betty loved him. He was so brave, though she was sure he'd never believe it if she told him.

Jack played an instrumental as Betty made a show of grabbing her water from the side of the stage. She tried to act natural, but she couldn't stop herself from scanning the crowd for any sign of danger. She looked to George then, trying to steady herself. He was such a solid presence, and she was certain that the moment the dry agents entered he would be looking to her to let her know. Eva had wandered casually over to the bar and was leaning in to whisper to Charlie. To any casual observer it would look like she was flirting with him, especially when he smiled and laughed, but Betty was certain she'd just let him know that she'd seen them outside.

Her eyes flicked back to George, widening slightly as three men who perfectly matched Jack's description sauntered through the door. On any other night she wouldn't have given them a second glance. A blond man, a man with thinning red hair, and a man with black and gray hair. They were dressed in the same kind of finery as all of the other fellas here, the only difference being that they weren't as wobbly in their steps as most. George nodded to her, and she gently touched Jack's shoulder.

Over at the bar, Charlie was making an excuse, and there he went, heading toward the back door to the alley.

So, Betty took a deep breath, and she sang.

Oh, I wish I had someone to love me
Someone to call me their own
Oh, I wish I had someone to live with
'Cause I'm tired of livin' alone

A few of the smarter patrons took notice, and Betty watched them try to casually head toward the entrance. Good. Maybe there would be less of a rush if some of the crowd had thinned.

Oh, please meet me tonight in the moonlight
Please meet me tonight all alone
For I have a sad story to tell you
It's a story that's never been told

More and more people began to head to the doors, the rush becoming more obvious now.

I'll be carried to the new jail tomorrow
Leaving my poor darling all alone

Then, like a dam breaking, everyone began to run. Everyone including her and Jack. She grabbed her hat off the stool and fled to the back door as the police began to scream at patrons to stop. That they were under arrest.

But when she turned back, one of the officers had his hand around Eva's arm.

"Go, Jacky," she yelled over the sound of the crowd, pushing him toward the back door. "Just go!"

Jack said something in response, but it was drowned out by the crowd and the beating of her heart in her ears. The man was manhandling Eva toward the door, shouting at her. Betty's blood nearly boiled in her veins. How *dare* he touch her.

Betty could barely run fast enough. "Eva!"

She was close enough now to hear Eva shouting, "Get your hands off of me!" She swore when he only tugged at her harder, nearly tripping her.

Eva drew her fist back, and Betty took the opportunity to jump onto the policeman's back, grabbing his free arm and leaving him open to the punch. He staggered backward, hand freeing Eva to cradle his own cheek.

"Run!" Betty shouted, as she fell to the sticky floor, having finally been thrown off. She hit the ground with a thud that knocked the wind out of her. She lay there for a moment, certain that she'd be arrested as soon as the officer got his wits about him. Then there was a hand in her own, and Eva was tugging her to her feet.

"I told you to run," Betty said as they wove their way through the crowd, running for the back door where there were fewer policemen congregated.

"I am," Eva said. She grinned, not at all sorry.

Hand in hand, they ran as the police whistles started up and the shouts of the crowd grew louder. She set her sights on the door and didn't look back. Even once they were in the alley, she kept her eyes straight ahead, for fear that she'd look behind them and see Mack or one of the other dry agents giving chase. Not that Mack had even come, the coward.

Lord, she just hoped that everyone else had escaped unscathed.

They slowed to a walk once they were a few streets away, holding each other's trembling hands. "Go, sweetheart," Eva told her. She squeezed Betty's hand, then let go. Betty grabbed her hand back.

"I'm not leaving you," Betty said.

"We draw too much attention together. Go, darling. I'll be safe, I promise," she said, though Betty knew she had no way of knowing that for sure.

"Okay," she said. Her heart ached almost worse than her back did from the fall. What would happen to Eva if she got caught? With her heart in her throat, she left Eva and headed back to the street she and Jack had meant to take together.

Betty found Jack a block away, dithering. Waiting for her.

"Oh, Jack," she said. She walked as fast as she could without running and fell into his arms.

"Eva. Is she—"

"She's all right. She said we should go separately to the safehouse," Betty told him. She felt tears gathering in her eyes.

"She'll be okay, Bets. She's hard-boiled, just like me, huh?" Jack said.

"God, Jack," Betty whispered. "It really happened."

"I know," he said, squeezing her hand. "Do you think everyone got out?"

Jack let out a breath, his whole body taut as a bowstring beside her. He seemed filled with just as much adrenaline as she was.

"I sure hope so."

They took a meandering path through the streets, the only thing hinting that they weren't two lovebirds was their terrified silence. Betty wished they could just make a beeline to Leroy's, but this was safer. They couldn't be followed. Betty took a few deep breaths, willing herself to relax. It was working too, right up until a whistle echoed through the night. Betty had to squeeze Jack's hand hard to keep herself from running wildly in the opposite direction of the sound. Instead, she froze, holding tight to Jack as a police officer approached them.

"Can I help you, Officer?" Jack asked, looking the picture of confused and concerned. Betty had never really considered what a good actor he was before. But this was amazing to behold. No wonder he'd had such luck at the police station.

"You folks better get yourselves home," the blond man said. The mole on his face was just like Jack had described it. Betty felt a chill run through her that had nothing to do with the night air.

"I was about to take her home," Jack said, cool as a cucumber. How could he be so calm when Betty was trembling? "Is everything all right?" The man looked them over but didn't seem to be concerned.

"We just busted up a juice joint," he said. Then added, "You weren't there, were you?"

"Of course not!" Jack protested, with just enough annoyance in his voice that it read as sincere, but not overblown. "I would never go to a place like that, let alone bring a lady there!"

"Good for you, son," he said, nodding sternly. Then he turned to look at Betty. "Hmm, have I seen you somewhere before?"

Betty blinked, fear coiling like a snake in her stomach. Was she imagining the dark spot on his cheek or was this the officer they'd defended themselves from? "I shouldn't think so, sir," she said as calmly as she could. Still, her voice had the slightest tremble to it, and for one tense moment, Betty was sure that they'd been caught.

But then the police officer laughed. "I know! You remind me of my wife when she was younger," he said, "She was quite the looker then too, you know." He winked at her merrily.

"I'm sure she still is," Jack said with an amicable smile. "Well, I really should be getting her home now. Hope that you catch those miscreant drunkards."

"Thanks, son. Good night, folks," the officer said, and let them walk away. Somehow, impossibly, Jack kept them walking at a sedate pace, when all Betty wanted to do was run as fast as she could away from there.

"Quickly, let's get to Leroy's," Jack said. "It seems like they haven't had much luck." He paused, giving Betty's hand a squeeze. "I think we just might have gotten out of this one, Bets."

Betty certainly hoped so.

❖

The plan had been to gather at Leroy's apartment after the raid. Betty had never been there, but they knew the address, and even though it was on a side of town they never went to, it was easy enough to find.

Leroy's apartment wasn't what she was expecting. She'd come to associate everyone who worked at the Trespass with the speakeasy so much that it was hard to think of them existing anywhere else in the regular world. But Leroy's apartment was about as plain as they came, and his wife, Mary, was just about the sweetest lady Betty had ever met. She was beautiful, with a kind face and tired eyes. She greeted them with the most hospitality Betty had experienced since visiting Jack's grandmother back in Wisconsin, taking their coats and fussing over them like a mother hen. She led them into the hallway and down to the living room where she got them all fed and watered as they gathered to talk.

Betty looked around the room. Eva was missing. She felt like she could scream. "Has anyone seen Eva?" she asked instead.

"Not yet," Leroy said.

She scanned the worried faces of everyone in the room, but it seemed no one had seen her.

Just then there was a knock at the door. Forgetting all semblance of manners, Betty rushed past Mary to open it. She nearly collapsed in relief at the sight of Eva's face.

"Eva," she breathed, collapsing into her arms. "Oh, I was so worried."

"I told you I'd be all right, didn't I?" Eva said against Betty's hair.

"Please come in," Mary said, the smile on her face betraying that she wasn't at all put out about Betty pushing past her.

"Sorry, Mary," Betty said, contrite.

Mary waved away the apology and led them back to the living room.

"Whoo boy, Mack is going to be *furious*!" Sam cackled and threw himself down on the sofa with the familiarity of someone who spent a lot of time there. "We sure pulled one over on him."

"What if they start coming down harder on us now?" Betty asked. She wasn't letting go of Eva's hand for a second, but Eva didn't seem to mind.

"I don't think they will," Jack said, "The captain there seemed pretty irritated that they were wasting time trying to shut us down in the first place. I don't think he'll take it well, finding all that water when he's expecting liquor." Because while they'd lost a few bottles, sure, the rest of the gleaming bottles of liquor were filled to the brim with normal drinking water. They'd spent the day before hauling the real booze over to Charlie's place and replacing the bottles with empties filled with water. They'd only kept enough actual alcohol to keep the guests nice and drunk for an hour or so, which had cut their losses considerably.

"Damn good job you did, Money!" Sam laughed and gestured at him to sit beside him. "Can you imagine the look on his stupid face when he realizes?"

"Yeah," Jack said. "Yeah, I really can."

Betty kissed Eva's cheek, also silently pleased at the thought of Billy getting what was coming to him.

They spent the rest of their working hours at Leroy's, talking about the raid and enjoying some delicious food. And, of course, there was some alcohol that Charlie had picked out specifically for the occasion. Betty, Eva, and Mary migrated to the kitchen after a while, to escape the drunken antics of the men.

"I stopped drinking even before I got pregnant," Mary said as she handed Betty a tumbler of whiskey. "I had a friend who went for a night of drinking and never made it back home."

"No," Betty said, horrified. "Oh, Mary, I'm so sorry."

Mary smiled sadly, leaning into the hand Betty placed on her shoulder. "She was a good woman. But they use poison in so many speakeasies that it's a gamble with your life just to go out for a night of fun. Leroy has told me some real horror stories."

"God. Why is it so dangerous?" Eva asked.

Betty wanted to know too. She had seen people at the Trespass so blackout blotto that she'd been afraid for them, but the way everyone talked around poisoned alcohol made her wonder.

"It's industrial alcohol," Mary explained. "Ever since prohibition there's been such a demand for booze that people will distill damn near anything that they can turn into alcohol. Even if it ain't meant for humans to eat. It's labeled as poison when it's sold, but there's ways to make it into booze."

"Sam mentioned something about people going blind once," Jack said from the doorway. Betty wondered how long he'd been listening. "I had always thought that was just a myth." Betty put her arm around Eva's waist. Her other hand was still holding her untouched drink.

"It's true," Mary said. "Wood alcohol. That one's a sneaky one too. You'll be feelin' all right the next day, and then all of a sudden, you're losing your mind, going blind. From what I hear it's killed a lot of good folks."

"Does Leroy know how you feel about alcohol?" Betty asked.

She chuckled in a long-suffering way that spoke to many conversations between the two of them in the past. "He knows. He tries his best to make safe drinks, but I still worry."

"But it's a living," Betty put in. "It's a tough spot to be in, for sure." From the other room there was the sound of loud laughter, so at odds with the somber conversation they were having that it felt almost surreal. But Betty supposed it was fitting, in some way. Merriment and happiness marred by something so grim. She wondered if that was how those who'd been poisoned felt, the surrealness of a night of fun turned deadly. Laughter and gaiety turning somber by morning. She figured that was the way of life at a speakeasy. Maybe that was even the draw for some people, that danger. Dancing merrily on the edge of a sharpened knife. Betty understood that. The call of it was almost as intoxicating as the illegal liquor itself was. It was a little bit like how she felt about Eva. Falling for her when she shouldn't but unwilling to let her go. She held Eva tighter thinking about it. Someday soon she'd have to figure out what to do about the feelings rushing through her.

Someday, but not today.

CHAPTER SEVENTEEN

The next night everyone was tense, but nothing exciting happened. Jack kept scanning the crowds for weeks afterward, and he could see that all the others were doing the same, but no other police officers showed up. Not even Mack.

He couldn't even be bothered to confront Jack for the betrayal. For once in his life, Jack felt like the braver man.

Eventually, they all stopped worrying about it as much. After all, they had other things to worry about. The Cherry didn't seem to be taking the failure of the raid very well, if the frequency of attacks against the Trespass was anything to go by. Sam was arriving at the bar more and more bloodied every time he went out to bring in a shipment. Jack was concerned, and even more concerning were the attacks on the bar itself.

The Cherry sending goons to cause trouble became a weekly occurrence. So far, Jack and Betty had stayed safe, but in Jack's opinion it was only a matter of time before they got in the way of some big lug with more muscle than brains.

One interesting thing that the frequent attacks *did* give him was an opportunity to see the different ways that everyone who worked at the Trespass fought. There was Charlie, who used cunning more than brawn, taking men twice his size down with sleight of hand and trickery.

Leroy fought like a bear, pure rage making it easy for him to throw his body weight around and slam even the biggest opponent to the floor.

George approached every scuffle with a silent, single-minded focus that was efficient and uncomplicated. He saw someone, he punched them. It was as simple as that.

And Sam. Well, Sam fought like a scrappy little dog, all fists and teeth and fury. He was the one who drew the most blood too, with his wild punches and dirty tactics. Jack had watched him damn near bite the finger off one guy, who had decided to cut his losses fast and had run out of there with blood pooling between his hands.

Speaking of Sam, he was headed over toward him, swaying slightly as he went.

"Heya, Money," he slurred, nearly tripping over his own legs as he approached the table Jack was sitting at. "How's yer night?"

"It's fine. Looks like you've been having some fun," he said. He wasn't a huge fan of how much Sam drank. It seemed to be getting worse lately, and Jack would be lying if he said he wasn't worried. "Maybe you should drink some water, Sam."

"You're such a milquetoast," Sam said even as he climbed like a deranged squirrel right up onto Jack's lap. Jack's entire world froze, narrowing down to Sam. Sam in his lap. What in the world?

He wasn't sure what to do. He wasn't sure what was happening or where to put his hands. He wasn't sure of much of anything, other than the fact that Sam was now *in his lap* out of nowhere.

As a man faced with the dual indignity of having a little snit of a gangster both intrude on his personal space *and* insult him, Jack did the obvious thing and addressed the most pressing matter first. "I'm not a milquetoast, I just have more than a pinch of dignity in my body, unlike *you,*" he said. "And what are you doing? Get off me!"

Sam cackled, making a show of pretending to think about it. "Hmmm. No can do, buddy. You might be a scrawny little thing, but somehow you still make a half decent pillow."

If Jack had possessed even the slightest bit of presence of mind, he would have shoved Sam to the floor. But he was far too consumed by...well, a lot of things. Frustration at having this little ragamuffin curled up in his space like he somehow had a right to be there. As though he could just come into his life and make himself comfortable wherever he pleased, with no thought of how it would affect anyone but himself. And something else, that made his blood run hot. Something he'd been trying to deny he felt for a long time now.

Said ragamuffin then went a step further in whatever godless game he was playing and laid his head right on Jack's *chest*. Jack looked around frantically, in a panic, but no one cast them a second glance, too busy dancing and drinking and carrying on. The gramophone crooned a steady stream of horns and piano, but for the life of him Jack couldn't say what song was playing, too focused on what the heck he was meant to do with his sweating hands as Sam made a sap out of him.

"Hah. Your heart's beating out a ragtime tune," Sam said, his words slurred. His gremlin claws scrabbled at Jack's shirt, and for one crazy moment Jack was almost sure he was trying to divest him of it. But thankfully he settled, still gripping the fabric.

"Jesus, you're zozzled aren't you?" Jack shook his head, trying to calm himself. He was being ridiculous. This was just Sam trying to get a rise outta him, and he refused to give him the satisfaction.

"...always zozzled..." Sam cackled, his breath hot through Jack's thin shirt. "We're in a juice joint. It's what's supposed to happen. Lighten up. Have some fun for once."

"I have fun! I just don't need to get blackout drunk to do it," Jack protested primly, still doing absolutely nothing to divest his lap of the rum-soaked gangster. Sam giggled against him again, shifting to find a more comfortable position. Everything in Jack went cold, then hot all in a rush. If someone saw something like this—

Jack shoved helplessly at him, not hard enough to move him, but enough that he'd get the picture and hopefully climb down. "Sam. Sammy, get the hell off! You're fried."

"Mm-hmm," Sam murmured, almost sounding irritated now. "So's your old man." Then he added injury to insult by brushing the tip of his nose against Jack's neck.

God.

Did Sam even know what he was doing to him?

In his panic he didn't notice when Sam began to still, half slumped on Jack's left arm. It wasn't until Sam started snoring that he clued into it. "Oh God," he muttered, trying to shake him awake without fully dislodging him from his lap. The last thing he needed was a hothead like Sam waking up on the floor and deciding to beat him to a pulp for the trouble. "Wake up. Get off me you little—"

"Having fun, Jack?" Betty's voice nearly sent him jolting out of his seat, his annoyingly drunk blanket be damned.

"No!" he said, eyes wide with panic. "Could you get him offa me? Please, before anyone sees."

Betty snorted. "Don't be stupid. No one here cares where Sammy sleeps. Nor, baby, who sleeps with you," she said, expression knowing.

"He's not sleeping *with* me!" Jack yelped, "He's sleeping *on* me! There's a big difference."

"Oh, you poor little bunny," she cooed as she petted his head. "Just try to have some fun, okay? I'll get you 'round three and we'll head home."

"Betty May! Betty May Felton, don't you dare leave me here," he said. "Don't you walk away you...you..." he trailed off as Sam grumbled out a displeased noise and nuzzled into his chest. "Christ."

Jack wanted to die. He wanted to burst into flames and burn up Sam, himself, and the whole damn speakeasy. He wanted anything but to feel like he was melting through the chair. Anything but this big warm feeling swelling in his chest, all over this man who by rights he should hate. After all, he'd witnessed him doing horrendous things, and heard about worse. He should want to run as far away from the sin of this whole place, and all the violence and everything that went with it.

Instead, he wanted to stay forever, frozen in the moment like a statue with Sam sleeping peacefully in his lap, in an illegal speakeasy that felt more like home than his own apartment.

He couldn't even check his watch to see what time it was, or risk disturbing Sam. Which...now that he thought about it, wasn't a terrible idea. If the unholy terror could torture him, the least Jack could do was torture him back.

"Hey," he half-whispered, gingerly poking Sam in the back with his free hand. "Hey, wake up." Nothing. Nada. The drunk asshole just remained passed out on his lap, snoring loudly. Somehow, even when asleep, he managed to be just as infuriating as he was when he was awake. Jack poked him again, harder. Then again.

Sam grumbled, squirming impossibly closer to the warmth of his body in his sleep. Jack's face blazed, every muscle tensed like the skin of a drum. "Oh my God. This is it. I'm done for. I'm going to die here in this speakeasy, with no good standing left to my name."

"You 'n' me both," a rather ruffled woman slurred at him and giggled as her friend pulled her along toward the dance floor.

Chapter Eighteen

"Zanetti's attacks are getting worse," Charlie said. He sounded tired. God, Jack was tired too. There was only so much excitement one could take before it started to take its toll.

Sammy grunted in agreement. "Excuse the swearing for the delicate ears here, but fuck that guy."

Betty grimaced at him. "I'm certain you weren't calling *my* ears delicate, now, were you?"

Sometimes Jack thought Betty might be the only person in the world who could put the fear of God into Sam. "Sorry, Bets," Sam said sheepishly. "I didn't mean you. I was talking about Jack."

Jack spluttered. "You little—my ears are *not* delicate. Not after working here with you, you foul-mouthed little goblin," he huffed. He was certain that his face was turning rosy. At times like this he envied Sam for his darker complexion. He'd never seen *him* blush, though perhaps that came down more to a lack of grace and good sense than his skin color.

"Hah," Sam said, looking delighted. "Ain't that just a compliment. Thanks, Money. You don't know the half of how dirty this mouth can get."

"Sammy!" Betty laughed, which saved Jack from dying a fiery death right on the spot. She swatted his arm and slapped a hand over his mouth, hard enough that Sam gave a muffled *ow* against her skin. "Remember, there's delicate ears here. How about some manners." Sam said something, and Jack was fiercely grateful that it was muffled by Betty's hand. Whatever it was, it hadn't sounded very nice.

"As much as I hate to agree with Sam, he's right," Leroy said, ignoring the indignant sound Sam made from behind Betty's hand. "About the attacks, not his big mouth. We can't let these no-good louses keep disrupting our business like this." Right. These constant attacks were losing business for the Trespass. And they all relied on that business. Leroy even had a baby on the way. How was he going to feed his family if they ended up having to close up shop?

How would most of them feed themselves, really. He and Betty would be fine, eventually. And Charlie too probably. Some of the other bartenders that came and went might be all right, but the guys like Leroy, Sammy, and George had criminal records. If they lost the bar, they'd have few other choices. He suddenly fiercely wanted to protect them from that. Leroy with his wife and kid on the way, and George with his kind and almost sweet attitude that he kept hidden behind his bulk. Sam, who never wanted to be back on the streets cracking safes and murdering for money. Sam, who looked at him like he was someone worthy of respect, someone whose opinion mattered, even if he razzed him something awful.

"'Specially when it gets in the way of me bringing home the ladies," said the newly released Sam, which promptly extinguished Jack's momentary good regard for him. It also earned him a warning hand from Betty. He shut his mouth and shuffled away from her.

"We could talk to the guys at the Queen's," Charlie suggested. "You've seen the security they've got there. And they're only up and running some nights."

Leroy looked thoughtful at that. "Right. They're trustworthy too. Accepting of all types."

"Pfft, yeah. I'll say." Sam laughed, but Jack didn't quite get the joke.

"We couldn't go," Charlie continued, as though Sam hadn't spoken. "They know we own the Trespass. They'd block us at the door just in case we were there to cause trouble."

"We could always wait outside. Let them know we need to talk to Julian," Leroy said. "He's the owner of the Queen's. He'll be the one who makes the call. If he can spare some men we would have a lot better chance against Zanetti and his men."

"I can go," Sam said, grinning ear to ear. "I love that place. Could even bring Betty," he added, grinning at her. "Show you a good time."

"Oh, dry up, Sammy," Betty said. Finally, Sam was getting under someone else's skin as much as he got under Jack's. "Besides," she added slyly after a moment. "Wouldn't you rather take Jack?"

"All right," Jack said, that excited buzz of adrenaline already picking up under his skin. "I think we make a good team."

"Yeah. That's a good idea actually," Sam said after a moment, his face lighting up with a smile. "I can show you what a good time it is! How's about it, Money? Wanna have a fun night at the Queen's Legs with me?"

"Of course," he said even though he was certain that Sam's idea of a good time didn't quite align with his. "I'll come along. Long as Leroy and Charlie arm me with a full gin bottle, I'm sure I can hold my own."

They all laughed at that, Sam's laughter louder and brighter than anyone's, and Jack was struck once more with how much these people made him feel like he *belonged*. For someone like him, that meant the world.

"All right. The two of you can go there next time they have a ball on. I think it should be next week sometime," Leroy said. He patted Jack on the back. "Thanks for going with him. Hopefully you'll be able to keep him outta trouble."

"Can anyone?" Betty scoffed.

Sam grinned crookedly. "Nah. But it's fun to watch them try."

"Are you sure you don't want to come along?" Jack asked Betty. He was nervous now, thinking on it. Just him and Sam, alone at what he guessed was another speakeasy? It felt too intimate somehow. "Might look less odd if we have a doll along, after all."

For some reason that made Sam laugh, but he didn't explain himself. Just winked and said, "Sure. Bring Eva along too. She loves it there."

Betty looked displeased for a moment, looking at Jack like he ought to have picked up some sort of hint. "Well, all right. I won't pass up a night out," she said, shaking her head at Jack.

Jack felt a little silly about asking Betty along. It wasn't like he'd never been alone with Sam before. But for some reason it felt safer to have her and Eva there. Like maybe they'd make Sam behave.

Jack doubted it, but at least he could hope.

❖

The night of their mission to go to the Queen's Legs found Jack fidgety with nerves. He had no idea what to expect, and he was starting to think that Sam might have chosen the wrong guy to go with him. Hell, he was glad Betty and Eva were coming along. Even they could probably do a better job in a fight than he could. And if the security here was anything like the others had said, well, Jack hoped they didn't get into any kind of trouble. With Sam along, that hope seemed far-fetched at best.

The night was cold enough that Jack could see his breath misting up like the smoke from a cigarette. It swirled and danced, and he found that if he focused on it, it helped a little with his nerves. And he wasn't only nervous about going to the Queen's Legs. Sam was walking close to him. Close enough that their arms brushed with every step. Sam walked fast. That was another thing he was learning. Eva and Betty didn't bother keeping up, giggling together behind them and holding hands under the cover of night. It made him feel like it was just him and Sam.

Sometimes Jack felt like Sam was only really supposed to exist within the dark wooden walls of the Trespass, where music and liquor and smoke were all poured out with equal zeal. It was strangely intimate to be out with him, heading somewhere new.

Sam had greeted him with a "Well, don't you look spiffy!" and a slap on the shoulder when he'd arrived at the Trespass to meet them. Jack had dressed in a good starched white shirt, with suspenders and a reasonably nice jacket. Nothing more or less fancy than he normally wore, but perhaps it was the novelty of seeing each other on the street.

Sam seemed smaller somehow when they were outside. His personality was so big that he always seemed to fill the whole space with it. But as they walked along out here on the cold New York streets, they were just four random people, passing by in the night. None of the people passing them had ever seen Sam punch a man in the face, or smash someone's head against the ground. They'd never seen him with the muzzle of a gun against his head. It was an odd thought. It was also a little bit thrilling. Jack felt like he was in on a secret that only the two of them knew.

Leroy had told him the Queen's Legs was about twenty or so minutes away from the Trespass, but with the way Sam was practically sprinting in excitement, Jack assumed it might be more like fifteen. They moved through the frosty streets at a brisk pace, passing a surprising number of people still out at this time of night, dressed to the nines under their warm winter jackets.

"You sure are eager," Jack said, not sure if the feeling in his chest was excitement, anxiety, or both.

"'Course I am, Money!" Sam laughed, spinning around to face him without faltering his pace. And just like that, the people coming the opposite way down the street moved out of his way as he walked backward down the sidewalk.

Jack had a feeling if he tried that same move, he'd be trampled to death by some overly zealous pedestrian.

"We're gonna have a great time," Sam continued with a wide and genuinely happy grin on his face. "Just you wait and see."

"So, this is another speakeasy?" Jack asked, rushing to keep up with Sam as he spun around to face forward again and practically skipped down the street.

"Something like that," Sam said. His tone was full of mischief. "Come on. We're almost there.

❖

"So where are we going? Sammy's been so tight-lipped," Betty said. The night was cold and Betty was thankful that she'd worn a pink cape coat that was trimmed with fur. Eva was a vision in a patterned, shin-length coat with a matching hat and a fur muff that she held in one hand in order to hold Betty's hand with the other. Eva's hand was warm and Betty's heart felt light as a feather as they walked together.

"You sure you don't want it to be a surprise?" Eva said.

"Jack can be surprised. I want to know," she replied primly. Eva laughed, her beautiful full-bodied laugh, and relented.

"It's a drag ball, darling. The Queen's holds just about the best drag ball in the whole city. It's a pansy club."

"Drag ball?" Betty asked.

"Yes. Where men dress up as women and entertain. It's a place for people like us," Eva explained.

Oh.

She'd had no idea such a place existed, which meant Jack wouldn't either. He was either going to be thrilled or horrified. But Betty was guessing he'd land more on the side of thrilled.

"Does Sammy know?"

"Of course," Eva said. "He visits the Queen's almost as often as I do."

How interesting. Betty smirked, certain that her plan to get Sammy and Jack together tonight was going to work.

It wasn't much farther before they arrived. The outside of the Queen's was about as nondescript as it got, which was to be expected really. Betty figured they sold illegal alcohol just like the rest of them. They couldn't go making it all glitzy and attracting police attention. But they did have a pair of women's tights hanging from the light mounted above their door. A sign for those looking for the ball that they'd found the right place.

A bouncer opened the door for them, and Sammy thanked him with a nod and a grin. He'd already been drinking before they left the Trespass, as had Betty and Eva. It made them sway together and giggle louder than they ought to, but that was okay. It was to be expected really, on a night out like this. Jack was the only one sober, but the bouncer either didn't notice or didn't care.

After the bouncer, they faced a few big men, who patted Sammy and Jack down in search of any weapons. Betty was of the opinion that she and Eva could have had weapons too, but she supposed she ought to be grateful she didn't need to be patted down and that they only took their coats. The guards looked like they could rip someone's head off with their bare hands. Betty grinned at the thought. This was why they were here, to get guys like this for the Trespass.

After the pat down they were free to go into the next room, which was where the magic really happened. Sam grabbed Jack's arm and practically dragged him along with him in his excitement. Eva and Betty followed behind them and Betty gasped as they entered the room.

It was hard to pick out something to look at first, but the grand chandelier hanging above the otherwise simple bar was a strong contender. It hung high above the revelers and cast rainbow flecks down upon their heads. It was closer to Betty and Eva up where they'd entered, and as they stood at the top of the stairs that led down into the bar, Betty almost felt like she could reach out and touch one of the crystal drops hanging from it.

The chandelier wasn't the only thing covered in jewels. Ladies and men alike were dressed to the nines, with feathers and pearls and beads everywhere the eye could see. But the grand dresses of the assorted attendees were outshone by a mile by the gorgeous dresses of the twenty or so drag queens wandering amongst them, flirting and cajoling and showing off for adoring eyes. Wigs and perfume and dangling earrings created a miasma of color and scent and experience that had more people than only Betty gasping as they entered.

"Pretty neat, right, Jack?" Sammy elbowed Jack in the side. Betty tore her eyes away from the spectacle to see Jack's expression. He was standing still as a statue, eyes wide with wonder. Betty wasn't all that religious, but the look on Jack's face was what she figured an epiphany looked like. He was practically glowing, his expression raw and amazed and tender. Like he couldn't believe his own damn eyes but couldn't argue against the proof in front of him.

And standing next to him, Sammy stared at Jack like he was seeing him for the first time.

Betty grinned and elbowed Eva, only to turn and find her with much the same look on her face as she stared at Betty.

"Oh," Betty breathed, as a shiver worked its way down her spine. "Oh, Eva."

"C'mon, Money. Let's go have a good time." Sammy laughed loudly, snapping Betty out of it. He grabbed Jack's hand and tugged him forward down the stairs. "Let's lead the ladies downstairs."

"Shall we?" Eva asked Betty, holding out her arm. Betty took it, feeling like a princess as they descended the steps after Sammy and Jack.

"Right," she heard Jack saying, his expression going from awed wonder to pure disbelieving joy. "Right, just…what is this?" he asked, voice soft and stunned.

"It's a drag ball, Money. They do them every few Saturdays here at the Queen's. It's what this place is all about." Sammy laughed, tugging Jack along behind him. "This is a pansy club. I think you can figure out what that means, yeah?"

"Yeah," Jack breathed. "I didn't know there were clubs like this."

"Me neither," Betty said, looking around with wonder at all of the women dancing with women and men dancing with men, too close and too sultry to be just friends having a good time.

"Really?" Sam asked. "Your loss. This is my second favorite place. Second only to the Trespass of course," he said proudly.

"I'm...is everyone here..." Jack trailed off, clearly unsure as to how to finish his sentence.

"Queer?" Sam finished for him. "Dunno. Most are I'm guessing. The drag queens definitely are, I'll tell you that much."

Jack breathed out shakily, then turned to Sam with a smile so big that Sammy looked like he might lose his breath under it. "Thank you for bringing me here," he said, so sincerely. So sweetly.

Betty tugged at Eva's arm, pulling her away from them. "Come on. Let's leave them to it," she said. "I think I ought to get us some drinks."

When she returned to Eva with two Bee's Knees cocktails, she found her in deep conversation with a woman who was dressed in a man's suit and top hat. She was quite attractive. The kind of girl that normally Betty would go wild for. But Betty frowned when the woman placed her hand over Eva's as they laughed together. Suddenly she didn't seem as alluring.

"Betty, this is Dolores. Dolores, Betty May. She's the singer over at the Trespass," Eva introduced them. Betty curtseyed, then snaked her arm around Eva's shoulders, leaning against her with her hip cocked. The singer at the Trespass? Was that all?

"Lovely to meet you," Dolores said. She was eyeing them up, and eventually smiled. "Well, Eva, it's been lovely to see you," she said, then kissed Eva's hand. Something hot and angry flashed through Betty at the casual show of intimacy. "Betty May, good to meet you."

Betty didn't offer her hand for a kiss. "You too, Dolores."

Eva was grinning as Dolores walked away, and Betty huffed.

"Someone's feeling possessive," Eva teased her, lacing her fingers with Betty's where they rested on Eva's shoulder.

"Maybe just a little," Betty admitted. She moved around to stand in front of Eva, tilted her chin up with her finger, and kissed the daylights out of her. Eva made a soft sound into the kiss, sexy and quiet and just for Betty. It was intoxicating. Betty wanted to make Eva make more sounds like that for her. But they were in public. With great effort, Betty pulled herself away from Eva's lips. They could neck later, when they didn't have an audience.

Perhaps a distraction was in order. Out of the corner of her eye, Betty spotted Jack and Sammy through the crowd. "Let's go spy on the boys, shall we?" she said. Eva looked at her with a dazed expression, then grinned wickedly and nodded.

"Lead the way, Nightingale."

Betty felt like laughing. Sam and Jack were face-to-face, speaking quietly to each other. Then Sam held out his hand, grinning that lopsided grin of his. It looked like they were just about to dance, when Jack went ahead and bumped into a queen in an evening gown.

"Oh! I'm so sorry," he said, then seemed to freeze as he took in the sight of her. Betty couldn't help but admire her as well. She was tall and built, but the dress she was wearing helped make her look smaller and more like a woman. It glittered in the light, pink and pretty and covered from top to bottom in sequins and hanging beads. Her hair was all done up in curls that were pinned up behind her head, and a beautiful white feathered hairband held the whole thing in place. Everything about her seemed to glow, and behind her cherry red lipstick she was smiling brightly at Jack.

"Well, aren't you polite. Don't you worry about it, honey. I get bumped around all the time."

Jack continued to stare, just a little bit too long. Betty moved in closer, ready to save him, when he finally spoke. "You're… you're a man, right? You look so much like a woman," he said. Sammy started laughing at that, and Betty couldn't help but join him, while Eva watched with a smirk on her face.

The queen he was talking to didn't seem to mind at all. In fact, she threw her head back and laughed right along with them.

"Oh, honey, you must be new here," she said, kind and indulgent. "I'm Miss Dolly. I'm the headliner here, sweetie. And aren't you just the cutest little thing."

"Oh," Jack said, his face red as an apple. "Thank you. You're...very beautiful."

Dolly placed her hand on her heart and batted her lashes at them dramatically. "Why, sir, aren't you the biggest charmer. What's your name, honey?"

"Jack Norval," Jack responded immediately. It was like he was hypnotized by Dolly's large green eyes.

"Betty May," Betty introduced herself with a little curtsey.

"My name's Eva."

"And I'm Sammy." Sammy laughed as he patted Jack on the back. "It's his first time here. Excuse him for being a little out of touch with how things work."

Dolly eyed Sam up critically, then smiled wide at him too. "My, my, two beautiful women *and* two handsome men? Three who know what they're doing and one inexperienced but eager? The heavens are shining down upon me today."

Betty cackled at the punched-out sound Jack made at that, and the spluttering way he tried to explain that he wasn't *inexperienced* so much as he just hadn't experienced this before.

"I understand completely, honey. Since tonight's your first time, why don't you come on up on stage with me," Dolly said, grinning widely. Jack looked to Sam for guidance on the matter and found him grinning just as wide.

"Go ahead, Money. Have a good time," he said as Jack turned beet red and sputtered.

"Yeah, have some fun, Jack," Betty agreed, patting his shoulder.

Jack looked between them, then back up at Dolly. "I—I mean, I don't...don't have to dance, do I?"

Dolly threw her head back and laughed again, carefree and robust. "Oh, sweetie, you're too cute for words!" she said. "No, honey, you can just sit there and I'll do all the dancing."

"Okay," Jack said, hesitating for a second before taking her hand and letting her lead him toward the stage.

Betty whooped joyfully, grabbing Eva's arm. "Look at him go!"

"Have a good time, Money!" Sam hollered after him, getting a helpless look in return. God that was adorable. Poor Jack was like a puppy set loose in a marketplace. All excitement and terror in equal measures.

"Come on, ladies," Sam said, working his way through the crowd. "We ought to watch this before we go looking for Julian. Business can wait."

"Poor sweet Jack," Eva said, her breath hot against Betty's ear. "He looked like he might burn up from embarrassment."

"He'll be all right," Betty said. "And maybe you and I can sneak away again and—"

"Ladies, gentlemen, and people of all ages," a drag queen's voice rang out over the crowd. "May I present to you our first act of the night, the always lovely Clairette!"

Betty pouted, but the crowd roared, alight with hoots and hollers as a drag queen took to the stage, already doing a little dance to a jaunty tune. As far as female impersonators went, she was so good that Betty wouldn't have known she was a man if she'd walked into her at the Trespass or on the streets. The crowd cheered and applauded her, with a few shouting out some truly saucy things that were enough to make a Betty blush. But Clairette took it in stride, and even flashed them some leg for their troubles. And she had some *nice* gams on her. Once she'd finished her dance, another two queens took to the stage, bantering about the housework they were doing and complaining about their husbands. Betty and Eva weren't the only people in the audience laughing up a storm by the time they were through.

"Sort of wish Jack was here watching this," Sam shouted through the din. "But I guess we'll see him soon enough."

And speaking of, the next act was the headliner Miss Dolly herself!

"Good evening, kittens," she purred, doing a little spin so that the beadwork of her dress fanned out and rattled. "I want to thank the lovely ladies who opened for me, first and foremost. Weren't they just the elephant's adenoids?"

"More like the elephant's trunk, honey," someone called from the audience, earning them a wave of laughter throughout the crowd.

"Now what in the world could that possibly mean," Dolly said, eyes gleaming mischievously. "Those must have been some small trunks, I could barely see them! A lot like my last boyfriend really." The crowd hollered at that, but Betty's eyes were scanning the stage. Where was Jack?

"Speaking of boyfriends, I just met the cutest little thing in the crowd tonight, and I simply *had* to have him! So, joining me on stage tonight, please welcome my new friend, Jack."

The crowd erupted into applause, but none louder than Betty's, Eva's, and Sammy's. Sammy even wolf-whistled as Jack came onto stage, red-faced but smiling from ear to ear.

Dolly led him up to the front with her, making a show of inspecting him to the crowd. "Doesn't he have a face you could die for?" she gushed, then gestured him toward the chair. Jack turned, and Dolly smacked his butt lightly. "And those *cheeks*," she added to raucous applause.

When Jack sat down he was smiling wide, despite his awkward posture. It was like he couldn't decide whether he was delighted or horrified to be up there on the stage.

"Now, darlings," Dolly went on as she walked in Jack's footsteps toward his chair, "does anyone here know why they call me Miss Dolly?"

The crowd had some suggestions, but it was hard to hear any one clearly over the clamor of voices calling out. Dolly raised her hand, waiting for silence. Or at least, as close to silence as she'd get in a packed room. "I have no idea what any of you just said, but I can tell you right now, you were all wrong," she said, her voice dipping low on the word "wrong." "Of course, it's because

I'm not only pretty, but also fun to play with!" She emphasized this by giving Jack's shoulders a squeeze, then running her hands sensually down to his chest.

Betty's eyes darted over to Sammy, who was frowning now. "She's laying it on a bit thick isn't she?" he said. Although Jack really didn't seem to mind, with his eyes all wide and his smile huge and bright on his lips.

Betty wanted to razz him for being jealous, but she took pity and stayed quiet. He really did look upset.

"I think I'd like to sing you a song, Button. What do you think?" Dolly asked Jack on stage. Standing behind his chair still, she bent low to sling her arms around his neck as she asked the question. Jack's mouth moved, but Betty couldn't quite hear him. But he was nodding, going along with it. Betty laughed at the look of mixed horror and excitement on his face.

This was going to be *good*.

Miss Dolly moved around him in a slow circle, crooning out a Josephine Baker song at him like she was trying to get him into bed.

"Show that boy a good time, mama!" someone in the crowd hollered. And Jack might be beet red, but he was smiling up a storm. Hell, it looked like Jack might even be happy to sleep with Dolly, if she asked him to.

Betty bit her lip, looking over to Sammy again. Sammy, who was leaning into her to whisper something.

"I didn't figure Jack was the type," he said, "But I guess it'd be good for him to get some action."

He didn't sound so sure. Betty wanted to smack him in the head, or maybe just shake him.

"Sammy—" she said, leaning in close so that he could hear her.

"He's never looked at no one at the Trespass like that," Sammy interrupted her. "Except that scumbag Mack."

Eva took notice now, leaning in to hear. Betty was momentarily distracted by the soft press of Eva's breasts against her arm.

"This guy could be working for Zanetti. He could be anyone."

"Sammy. I think you know that's not true," Betty said.

But Sammy shook her off, looking increasingly agitated. "I need some air," he snapped, and stormed out, disappearing into the crowd.

Betty shared a look with Eva and sighed. "You look after Jack, I'll go get Sammy," Betty said into Eva's ear. She pressed a quick kiss to her lips, then made her way across the room to the nearest door.

It took her a few moments to find him, but she eventually located him leaning against the brick wall in the alley. He was rubbing his palms against the rough brick, glaring at the wall across from him like it'd done him wrong.

"Sammy," Betty called out, startling him.

"Jeez, Bets," he said. "Don't sneak up on a guy like that."

"I was hardly sneaking," she replied. "Are you all right?"

"Sure. Why wouldn't I be?"

Betty frowned at him. Was he really as dumb as he pretended to be, or was it just an act? Because he had to know by now how he felt for Jack. Everyone else could see it, clear as day. Betty leaned against the wall next to him, just letting Sammy breathe for a few minutes.

"Look, Sammy. You don't have to pretend with me. I know how you feel about Jack," she finally gathered the courage to say, about fifteen minutes later.

Sam glared at her. "Yeah? And how's that?"

Before Betty could answer, Jack's voice startled them both.

"Sam?" he called out. "Jesus, Sam. Are you all right? Eva said you went tearing out of there like the hounds of hell were after you."

"I'm fine. Needed some air," Sammy said, looking embarrassed now. "Let's just go inside and find Julian." He still had his back to the wall, and Betty noticed that he was still scraping at the brick hard enough that his hands were likely to start bleeding soon.

"Sammy's right. Let's go back inside," Betty said. Something about the way Sammy was standing reminded her of a caged animal. Like he was one word away from snapping.

"Sam, are you sure you're all right?" Jack asked. Betty wanted to tug at her hair. Didn't Jack see that pushing him right now was a bad idea?

And sure enough, Sammy snapped. "I said I was fine, didn't I?" He shoved himself away from the wall and glared daggers at Jack.

Jack looked startled for a moment, before frowning. "All right. You don't have to get all worked up about it. I just wanted to make sure you weren't in trouble or anything."

Betty sighed. Now he'd gone and done it. Sam snorted a laugh. "And what would you do if I had been, huh? I don't see any bottles around here to smash someone's head with. I don't need you, Jack. I'm hard-boiled enough to take care of myself."

Jack took a step back, clearly confused by Sam's outburst. Confused and upset. "Jesus, Sammy. I never said you couldn't. But you're also hard-headed enough to get yourself killed."

"Boys, please," Betty said.

"Stay out of it, Betty May," Sammy said. It was the first time he'd ever spoken to her with any sort of anger in his voice. "I've survived this long without you, Jack," he spat, clearly itching for a fight. "I don't need you to be my mommy."

Jack flinched at that, then glared. Getting angry now too. "What's that supposed to mean?" he asked, his voice cold.

"Means what it sounds like. I don't need you to take care of me. So why don't you go back inside and have a dance or two with whatever his name is."

Betty watched as the color drained from Jack's face, and his expression went from horrified shock to cold and removed. "So that's your problem. You think that I...that I'm..."

"Jack. Sam," Betty tried, but Sam was fired up. He spoke over her, his voice a growl. "It's none of my business *what* you are," he said. "My business is to talk to Julian and save my goddamn speakeasy. That's it."

"That's bull," Jack said, taking a step forward now. "You know I care about the Trespass too. You're not the only person in the world who gives a damn."

Sam scoffed. "Sure. This coming from the guy who acted like he was gonna catch a disease just from looking at the place. None of us were fooled, Jack. We all saw the way you looked at us when you first got there," Sam said.

"I—I wasn't," Jack started, then paused. "That was then. It's my home now too."

"You don't have to pretend like you care, Jack," Sammy said. "You can go back in there and do whatever the hell you want. I'm going to find Julian and then get myself out of this damn place."

Jack was shaking now, likely from anger and not from the cold. "What are you implying?" His voice was ice cold and sounded almost dangerous. Betty had never heard him sound like that before.

"Look, no one cares if you're a pansy," Sam said flippantly. "But we do care about you walking around like you haven't had any nookie in your life and you're mad at anyone else who has."

Jack went from angry to looking like he'd been slapped across the face. His face was pale and his eyes wide, and Sam suddenly looked like he regretted everything he'd just said. But instead of shutting up like Betty was sure he should, he kept talking.

"It ain't that hard to just let loose every once in a while. I mean, you're always so uptight," he said, and just like that Jack was back to angry.

"Why the hell wouldn't I be, spending all my time with you lowlife goons and grifters, huh?" he snapped back, getting up in Sammy's face. "Don't pretend like you care about what I do in my spare time. You're just a no-good, selfish gangster who doesn't have a single care in the world for anyone but yourself."

Betty took a step back, not sure now if they were going to come to blows.

"That's how you see us, is it? Just a bunch of lowlifes? You're too good for us, with your fancy piano playing and your *I'm so sweet and innocent* rube schtick?"

"Maybe I am," Jack said, his teeth gritted and body tense as a bowstring. "I know I'm better than *you*, at least."

Betty gasped. Jack didn't mean that. But Sammy didn't know any better.

"Screw you," Sammy spat. "You were more than happy to slum it with us when that copper was around. If you weren't so uptight, I wouldn't have been surprised if the two of you were making the beast with two backs the whole time he was there."

Jack's expression cracked, just a bit. Just enough for Sam to get his fingers into that vulnerable spot and *pull*. "Or were you? Hauling ashes with him and leaking all our secrets to the cops. Christ. It's a wonder we didn't all end up in the can."

"Sam!" Betty snapped. "How dare you."

"You—" Jack bit back whatever he was about to say, a muscle working in his jaw. Betty noticed that his eyes were wet. "Never mind. You aren't worth the time."

And with that he spun and left. Sammy looked stunned.

"What's your problem?" he called after him, hands balling into fists. "Hey! Come back here! Jack, you goddamn piker! Get back here and face me like a man you—"

"Sammy! That's enough!" Betty snapped, satisfied when Sammy seemed to shrink in on himself and shut his mouth. "Stay here."

She ran after Jack, catching up with him as he exited to the street.

"Jack, honey!" She put her hand on Jack's shoulder, only to have him roughly shake her off.

"Don't touch me. Just leave it alone, Betty," he said. "Just leave me alone."

Betty stopped walking, watching as he stormed away. God. He was so stupid. He and Sam both.

She turned back, only to find Miss Dolly and Eva talking to Sammy in the alley. Betty wanted to fly into Eva's arms, but she held back, instead sidling up to her and pressing their arms together.

"Oh, honey, he's not coming back tonight," Miss Dolly drawled, placing her hand on Sam's shoulder. "You really balled that up, didn't you?"

"Says you!" Sammy said through a clenched jaw. "I didn't do anything, but he sure managed to make a sap outta me anyways."

Miss Dolly tsked. "They always do, baby. Any good man'll make you look like a fool. But don't you worry. He'll come back to you. I saw the way he looked at you. Y'all will be just fine."

"She's right, Sammy," Betty said. "But you really did make a mess of things."

"Like Jack was any better than me," he huffed. "God. This got all balled up fast."

He was right. They'd come here with a simple goal, and to have a little fun on the side, and now Jack was gone. And they hadn't found Julian either.

"Hey," Betty said, turning to Dolly. "You wouldn't happen to know where Julian is, would you?"

"Right. Guy who owns this place? I need to talk to him," Sammy added.

"Then talk away, sweetie." Dolly laughed. Then, in a lower voice he added, "Because you've found him."

Sam laughed humorlessly. "Of course. Damn it, of course you found us first. Shit."

"Why exactly were the four of you looking for little old me?" she asked, her voice stern enough that Betty had no illusions as to what would happen to them if she didn't like their answer, dress be damned.

"We're looking for some extra security down at the Trespass Inn," Eva told him. "We thought maybe you'd know some people since your drag ball security is so tight."

Julian surveyed them mistrustfully. "And why do y'all need extra security? Last I heard you did just fine for yourselves."

Betty bit her lip. She knew that telling Julian about Zanetti was a risk, but it was better than lying. Most people got nervous when the name Dimitri Zanetti came up. But they didn't have much of a choice. They needed help, and they didn't need to start it off on false pretenses.

"Zanetti's been throwing his full force at us," she said, watching Julian's face for any reaction. But he stayed stone cold beneath his makeup.

"That, uh, might be my fault, just a little. I used to work for him. He doesn't like the *used to* part," Sammy added bashfully.

Julian nodded, then finally, *finally* cracked a smile. "Oh, honey," he said kindly. "We hate that fucker here just as much as he seems to hate you. I'll ask some of the girls, but I'm positive they'd want to help just out of spite. Though you *will* still have to pay them."

"Thank you," Sam gushed, "We sure do appreciate it."

"Of course, peanut. I'll send someone to the Trespass tomorrow night to let you know how many want to help out. I wouldn't mind taking out some of my frustrations on some goons either," he said, gritting his teeth. Right. The Queen's Legs was a favorite for entertainment, but there were some, including Zanetti, who didn't so much like what went on there. It was no wonder so many of the people who frequented the place had learned to fight.

Betty wondered if Zanetti had tried to get the place shut down. Or maybe he'd never bothered. Probably because the police and the KKK already did that for him. Or maybe he wasn't threatened by them? Who knew? The man was a psychopath.

"We really do appreciate this," Betty told Julian.

"It's awfully kind of you," Eva agreed.

Julian laughed, his voice high and airy once again. "It's no problem really. You'd be surprised what a woman will do for two beautiful ladies and two handsome fellas if they ask politely."

Betty giggled, but stopped smiling quickly enough. Jack was probably walking back home on his own and liable to get mugged for his efforts.

"Damnit, Jack's alone," Sam said, echoing Betty's thoughts.

"Don't worry about him, honey," Julian said. "He's a good man, I can tell. He'll forgive you, and you'll forgive him, yeah?"

Sam sighed, slumping in exhaustion. "Yeah," he said. "I don't even know if he's got anything to apologize for, if I'm being honest."

"Well, he's gone for now," Julian said, patting him on the back.

Betty looked at Julian again. He was so damn *tall*. It was hard to tell when he was up on stage with other queens, but when Jack had been up there, he'd looked practically tiny in comparison. Julian was a big guy, despite trying to look like a small woman. And he seemed kind. Betty liked him already.

Julian gestured to the three of them. "You want to come back in? Drinks are on me, since you're so down and out right now, peanut."

Sammy smiled a sad smile, shaking his head. Betty was surprised. Sammy, turning down a drink? He really must be feeling bad.

"Nah, I'd better get the girls home," he said, clapping Julian's arm. "Thanks for the offer. We'll see you soon at the Trespass?"

"Sure thing, honey," Julian said before disappearing back into the fantasy land of glitter and glamour. Betty wished she could follow. She wished the night had ended better. But that was okay. She'd talk with Sammy about it later. Now it was time to head home.

❖

Betty cornered Sam the next day. She'd just finished singing and was still freshly smiling from her performance as she stomped over toward where he was lounging in a seat. But her smile was painted on, and she was on a goddamn mission. "Come with me," she snarled through her clenched teeth, gripping Sam's shirtsleeve and hauling him to his feet.

"Whoa, hey!" Sammy yelped, looking more frightened than he ever did when faced with a huge hulking boob with a gun. "Where's the fire?"

Betty made her way through the crowd with ease, her smile and the look in her eyes paired with her hauling Sammy Esposito behind her enough to make people step aside right quick as she passed.

"You're about to be on fire if you don't go apologize to Jack," she said, pushing him against the wall in the rum room behind the bar.

"I didn't do nothing!"

"I was there, Sammy! I know exactly what you did. Pipe down and listen to me," Betty said. "Jack has been through enough. He doesn't need to be in a fight with you right now. So, you're going to go tell him that you're sorry, and tell him that you didn't mean a word you said, got it?"

All the fight went out of Sam at that. "Fine. I'll do that." He sighed. "Punching people is so much easier than this."

❖

Jack sat on the piano bench, staring down at the keys of the baby grand as though they could solve all of his problems. He was exhausted from the night out and from the fight with Sam, and he wanted some peace for a little while.

So, of course, Sam came to find him.

"Hi, Money," he said, standing awkwardly off to one side of the bench. Jack grunted out what might charitably be considered a greeting but refused to look at him. He didn't want to see that anger there. The disdain of the other night.

"Can we talk?"

Jack finally looked up at that. "About what?" he asked.

"I just wanted to apologize," Sam started, shuffling his feet awkwardly. Jack noticed that he was playing with the hem of his shirt. "All that stuff I said at the Queen's, that was nasty of me."

Jack stared at him. That was not at all what he was expecting. Hell, he wasn't sure what he'd been expecting, but an apology from Sam wasn't it.

"I get real mad sometimes for no reason," Sam admitted. "But I shouldn't have taken it out on you. I ruined our night." His fingers twisted in his hem. He was going to ruin his shirt like that.

Jack took a deep breath, steadying himself. "I understand," he said. "I get that way sometimes too. And I got so caught up having fun that I forgot we were there for a reason. And then I up and left you all on your own…"

"No no, it's okay, really. I found Julian, so, it all worked out," Sam said. "You know, sort of. Except for the part with you and me."

Jack's heart lurched at that. The part with you and me. God.

"Right. Well, it's all right" Jack said, shrugging. "We're fine now."

"Sure," Sammy said, scuffing his shoe against the ground. "We're copacetic."

But it didn't *feel* copacetic to Jack. It felt like they'd had a conversation sideways. Like they'd been talking about two different things at the same time.

"Why don't we go grab a drink," Jack said. "Charlie'll be over the moon to know I'm drinking too."

"Sure thing, Money," Sam said. He sounded sad. Jack could relate. It felt like whatever they'd had before had been broken. "Let's go grab that drink."

CHAPTER NINETEEN

The drag queen security were all dressed as men when they came to visit the Trespass. Betty wasn't certain if all of them were drag queens or if some of them were just men who worked there.

Betty had to admit that as a man, Julian was rather handsome. He was also incredibly tall and built like a stallion. How he had managed to pull off a dress the night before was beyond her.

"Good to see you," he said, shaking Sam's hand. Then, he turned to Jack, beaming. "And you too, my sweet little thing." Jack, bless his soul, blushed to the roots of his hair.

"Hello, Miss Dolly," he said. Julian looked so delighted that Betty was almost scared he was going to try to kiss Jack right then and there in front of everyone.

When she looked over, Sammy was glaring daggers at him, but only until he noticed her looking. The moment he caught her eye he startled, then became intensely fascinated with his glass of whiskey. What a silly old fool he was, thinking that he was hiding his feelings for Jack from anyone except for Jack himself.

"This here is Leroy," Jack continued as Julian moved to shake his hand without hesitation.

"Good to meet you," Julian said, his smile friendly. "You're the owner of this fine establishment?

"Part owner," Leroy said, "Charlie will be in later this evening. It's good to meet you too."

Julian introduced the other men he'd brought along as Randy Jenkins, Francis Walters, and Happy. They were all three huge men, with muscles of a size Betty had never seen before. They made the table they were sitting at look comically tiny. It was truly a sight, and she suddenly understood why they'd turned to the security at the Queen's Legs.

Randy was a large Black man who had a scar across his left eyebrow but was no less handsome for it. Francis, another Black man, was unmarred, at least from what she could see. But Happy, the white man who hadn't smiled once since they'd arrived, was sporting a shiner that rivaled even the worst ones Sammy had gotten while she'd worked here.

"We'd be willing to pay you a fair wage to help us out with our mobster problem," Leroy said, sitting down with them at the table. Betty and Jack went to fetch everyone drinks, whispering to each other as they did.

"They're so big!" Betty said. She paid more attention to the men at the table than the drinks she was pouring. "Do you recognize anyone else who was dressed like a woman?"

Jack shook his head. "They look so *different* in drag, don't they, Bets? I swear if they weren't so enormous, you'd think you were talking to a lady."

Betty laughed and swatted his arm. "You don't think a lady can get muscle like that? I bet there's plenty of ladies out there with big strong arms." The thought was privately very appealing to Betty, but she didn't need to share that with Jack.

"Sure," he said easily. "But there's something about just *knowing* that she's a man under all that makeup…"

Betty giggled into her hand, looking at Jack knowingly as his cheeks heated. "Oh, sweetie," she said, making him turn even redder. "Come on, let's bring these over."

"I'm sure we can come to some kind of arrangement," Julian was saying as they approached. "After all, I don't think there's any love lost between any of us and Dimitri Zanetti."

Betty breathed a sigh of relief. God, she would feel so much better knowing that these huge gentlemen were in the crowd, keeping things safe.

"We really can't thank you enough," Leroy said, sounding just as relieved as Betty felt.

"As long as we're getting paid," Happy replied. He contorted his face into a grimace. Betty was starting to understand why they'd given him his name.

"Course you are," Sammy said belligerently. He was in some kind of foul mood, and for a second Betty thought he might start a fight, but he seemed to settle at the inquisitive look that both she and Jack shot him. "We're honest folks, unlike Zanetti."

"I'll drink to that," Randy said, raising his glass in a toast. "To fucking with Zanetti."

"To fucking with Zanetti!"

They all drank, even Jack.

❖

The Trespass Inn was quiet during the day. It was one of the things Jack loved the most about practicing there. The open space, usually so bustling and vibrant and loud, settled into a soft and companionable silence in the afternoon. No flappers dancing and giggling, or men throwing back drinks and clamoring for their attention. Just the occasional gentle creaking that came from old wood settling, and Jack's own footsteps as he walked across the dance floor to the stage.

It was, paradoxically, darker there during the day without the bar lights shining down, and Jack never bothered to turn anything but the stage lights on. He liked the isolation of it. The feeling of being in his own private world, alone and at peace, with no one's eyes on him and only himself to prove anything to.

He sat at the piano bench and ran his fingers across the wood above the keys reverently. "Just you an' me today, old girl," he said fondly. Pianos were simple. Jack trusted them. You could always count on a piano to make the right sound when you pressed the right key. And if it didn't, you only needed a tuner to fix her up again, right as rain. People were a lot more complicated. He never had gotten the knack of reading them or knowing what they'd do. And it took a lot more than tuning to fix things up when they broke.

He sighed, fingers hovering now, over the keys. Touching them just softly enough to avoid pressing them down. What to play.

There were pages and pages of sheet music available to him, but none of it felt right today. No, today was the type of day that Jack wanted to let his fingers fly over the keys and create something from nothing. He had some lyrics he'd been working over in his head for a day or so now, and he was itching to make them into something beautiful. To pour out his soul in song the way he could never quite manage with mere words.

So he sat, with all the hurt of the past few days welling up in his chest like flood water. And he sang.

You took my heart
Oh yes you took it
When I was looking away
And now's the part
Where I shoulda shook it
But I'm wanting you to stay

Oh and I'm lost
And I am lonely
And I thought I'd found me a home
But I'm still lost
And I'm still lonely
Because no matter where I may roam
I'm always thinking of you
Always thinking of you

He caressed each key with a lover's touch, letting his fingers bounce and trip and run over the ivory as he sang. He ran his hand down the keys, pouring himself into the glissando. Pouring everything he had into the music as he sang the last chorus. Jack finished playing, the last notes ringing out clear and true. God, he was crying. He felt so stupid. So ridiculous and weak and—

Loud clapping made him jump nearly clear off the piano bench. He'd been certain he was alone, but no. It seemed someone had snuck in to witness his stupid outburst. "Wow, Money," Sam said with a whistle. "That was somethin'."

Of course. Of course it had to be him. Why not? It made some twisted sort of sense really, since the whole damn thing was about him in the first place. Because Jack couldn't deny it any longer. He'd fallen for the damned gangster. Hard. It was impossible to deny after their conversation at the Queen's Legs had damn near torn his heart right out of his chest.

"I didn't know you could sing, old boy! You've got some pipes on you," he said. "You been having dame troubles?" Sam continued, ruining any possible chance that this interaction was going to go well.

For a moment, rage flared in Jack's chest like a fire. How dare Sam taunt him with this. It was like poking a fresh wound, and Jack had had enough. But then the fire banked, all at once, and all that was left was emptiness. Emptiness and *hurt* so deep he thought it might kill him.

"Stop," he managed to say, voice cracking around the word. "Just don't, Sam."

"Whoa, hey," Sam said, suddenly lurching from his seat. "Hey, what's wrong? It isn't actually a dame thing, is it?" Jack shook his head and sighed. So, he wasn't being malevolent. He was just being *stupid* and oblivious. That was somehow worse.

"Sammy, just leave well enough alone for once," Jack said, desperation coloring his tone. "Please. Just go away."

"Hey, look," Sam said, sounding irritated now. "I'm sorry I walked in on your practice. I wasn't trying to be a jerk. I just like hearin' you play." That twinged something within Jack. Sam liked to hear him play. Sam cared about his music, at least on some level. But he'd already proved that he wasn't exactly a fan of Jack himself.

"It's not too uptight for you?" Jack asked, hearing the bitterness in his voice but not caring. Why should he hide it? He was bitter and angry and hurt, and no matter what he'd said to Sam before, he hadn't forgotten anything. Not the way Sam had looked at him like he thought Jack was a goddamn joke. Or how simply and efficiently he'd made him feel small again, like he'd felt when he was young. Weird. Uptight. The strange, stuffy little kid who'd loved pianos more than playing with children his age, and whose lingering looks at the workers in the field spurred gossip and speculation. The boy who'd poured his heart out to someone only to have him beat the trust out of him after using him for some fun.

"I mean, your playing isn't," Sam said, then frowned. "But really. You're fantastic, Jack. You have to know that." Sam reached out, placing his hand on Jack's shoulder. Jack flinched, but all he did was hold him there, staring deep into his eyes.

Jack shivered as Sam's fingers moved in an attempt to massage away the stiffness of his shoulders. He hadn't even realized how stiff he was until Sam touched him. Jack's face heated, and kept heating the longer Sam looked at him. God, why couldn't he just be a bastard all of the time? Then maybe Jack wouldn't feel this way about the little snit.

But he wasn't always a jerk, so Jack did feel. He felt *so much*, and Sam kept breaking his heart every day without even knowing it. Now here he was, staring into his eyes like he could find the secret to life in them, and standing so close that it'd be easy as anything to press forward. To breathe his air, and lean in, and—

"And hey, if you're having problems with a doll, I'm here for you," Sam said, breaking the moment and leaving Jack feeling like he'd been splashed with a glass of cold water. "Or problems with a fella," he added with a wink, his hand moving from Jack's shoulder down to pat his behind. Sammy looked so good, so ruffled and handsome and perfect. And so goddamn amused.

Jack shoved him away.

"Get away from me," he said, so mad that he could barely stand the feeling. It was like everything in him wanted to explode but was trapped by his skin and bone. And he wanted to punch Sam. God, he wanted to punch Sam more than he'd ever wanted to punch anyone in his life.

"Just let me be, Sam. Please," he begged, on the verge of tears. "Just leave."

Sam stared at him, completely confused. Oblivious, as per usual. Then he nodded. "Okay, I'm going."

He turned, and Jack watched him walk across the room with wet eyes. Nothing but the sound of Sam's footsteps and his own ragged breathing to fill the empty space. But Sam paused when he reached the door and turned back to look at him. "I don't know what I did," he called out across the empty room, sounding just as heartbroken as Jack felt. "But I'm real sorry that I did it."

And with that, he walked out the door, and left Jack heartbroken and crying on the stage.

❖

Betty twirled around Eva's tiny apartment, dancing like a flapper to the music of Eva's gramophone.

"I love watching you move," Eva said. She was smiling with an expression that was almost too sweet and soft.

"It's too bad we never got to dance at the ball," Betty said. "That would have been the bee's knees."

"It would have," Eva agreed. "It's a fun place to be. I've gone dancing there a few times."

"With Dolores?" Betty found herself saying.

"Sometimes," Eva said. She looked concerned now. "Are you upset about that?"

"No, no! I was just thinking maybe I should have flirted with someone at the Queen's Legs too," Betty said. She meant it to be teasing, but it made Eva frown instead of smile.

"I wasn't flirting with her, Nightingale," Eva said.

"She was flirting with you," Betty replied, trying to sound casual.

"So you *are* upset about it," Eva said.

"No! Of course not," Betty replied flippantly. "You can flirt with whoever you want."

Eva's frown deepened. "That's not the point, Betty."

Now it was Betty's turn to frown. "What is the point then?" she asked, bristling.

"You know I don't want to flirt with anyone else," Eva said.

Betty felt her chest tighten, a shiver of dread working its way through her. Love. Eva had said she loved her. Betty couldn't handle hearing that again. She couldn't be in love. She'd sworn love wasn't for her after Richard. And maybe if she hadn't been playing at love with Eva she would have noticed Mack earlier. Maybe Eva was bad for her.

Or maybe Betty felt the same way. And maybe she was a coward.

"Look. I'm sorry I said anything," Betty said. "Should I go?"

Eva looked like she was considering it, but then she shook her head. "It's fine. Let's just make some dinner."

"All right," Betty said.

But the shadow didn't lift, and when she left the next morning, it felt like she couldn't paste her smile on correctly. She just wanted to get home without talking to anyone.

Unfortunately, she ran into Sammy on her way out.

"Hey, Bets! Can we talk?"

Betty sighed out her nose but slowed her walk so that Sam could catch up with her.

"Maybe, uh, not on the street?" he said, looking around like he thought there might be spies at the mouth of the alley.

"All right. In the Trespass then?" she asked. He nodded, and Betty followed him down the stairs. No one was around, it being past closing time by quite a bit. She wondered if Sam had been waiting for her. "What is it, Sammy?"

"Look, I'm bad at dealing with people," Sam said. "I'm better at beating them up than understanding them. I mean, it's probably because I joined the mob when I was thirteen, now that I think about it. But anyways. I think I messed up with Jack."

"Again?" Betty asked. Lord, he was exasperating.

"I'm not proud of it, okay?" Sam bristled. "It's not like I was *trying* to annoy him. It just sort of happened."

"Okay. What did you do?" Betty asked, taking a seat at the least sticky-looking table she could find. Sam sat down across from her and shrugged.

"That's the problem!" Sam said, scrubbing his hands down his face. "I don't know what I did. I know that it's my fault, I don't know what I did to set him off. Maybe it's because of the fight we just had? I don't know, Betty. That's why I need your help. Jack hates me."

"Jack doesn't have a hateful bone in his body," Betty told him. "Just tell me what happened, and I'll see if I can help you figure it out." On the tail end of a disagreement with Eva, she wasn't exactly feeling like acting like an agony aunt.

"Except for me," Sam insisted. "All I did was listen to him play and he...I don't know. Maybe I said the wrong thing."

"Likely," Betty agreed. But when Sam didn't laugh along she sobered a little. "Tell me exactly what happened. It seems like you're all torn up about it."

Sam nodded. "He was playing piano and it was real soulful, so I asked him if he was having doll troubles, and then I asked if it was trouble with a fella instead because at the Queen's he was dancing really close with Julian before we got into our fight and—"

"Oh, Sammy," Betty sighed. "I can already see why he was upset. Look, can you tell me why you got so angry at the Queen's Legs?"

Sam swallowed. "I don't know." He shrugged helplessly. "I guess I just didn't like the way Julian was roping Jack in. I've never seen him so happy, and it was sort of annoying, you know? Because the only other person he's acted like that around was Mack, and we all know how *that* went."

"Enough about Mack," Betty snapped. "This is about you and Jack. And what I'm *hearing* is that you were jealous."

"Of what?" Sam asked, nose crumpled up in confusion.

This was going nowhere. It was time to tell him. "You're stuck on him," Betty said.

Sam snorted a laugh. "Funny. You know I love dolls."

"And you love Jack."

Sam's brow furrowed. "I mean sure, I've been around with a few fellas, but it's not like that's the same as going around with a doll. You're not a pansy if you like to fool around with women."

Betty burst into laughter, hooting as she patted at Sammy's shoulder.

"What?"

"You can like to fool with both, Sammy," Betty said, voice still shaking with laughter as she wiped her eyes with the back of her arm.

"What d'ya mean?" Sammy asked. "Of course, you can fool around with both men and women, but that don't make you queer. Just means that necking is fun. But if you want women that means you'll date women."

"You can hold a candle for men and for women. If you like necking with men, you can be with them romantically too," Betty explained, still far too amused, but at least a little less hysterical now. "You don't only have to go around dating women. Think about it. How does Jack make you feel?"

Sam made a face. "Really? Do we have to talk about it?"

"If you want to figure out what to do, then yes," Betty said with a shrug. "So. How's he make you feel?"

"Angry. Annoyed. Like I wanna shake him," Sam listed, scuffing his foot against the floor. "Or...or hug him."

Betty nodded encouragingly. She had to let him get there himself, if it was at all possible.

Sam huffed, but he was still thinking about it. "I guess, I guess I feel happy when he's around," he admitted, voice softer. "And damn, can he play. I could listen to him all day long and never get tired of it. And he's fun to razz. Fun to talk to, too. When he's not being a stick in the mud." Sam paused, still trying to put his thoughts into words, and Betty waited patiently for him this time. "I like being close to him. He's infuriating and amazing all at once, you know? And he's handsome, sure. I wouldn't mind kissing him, or more really." He grinned, and Betty rolled her eyes at him.

"I want to make him happy," he said, like it was a revelation. "I guess…I guess I just want him to think about me as much as I think about him. He's ridiculous, but he's got an arm on him, and a mouth when he wants to. And I…damn it. Betty, I'm stuck on him."

"Of course you are," Betty said, shaking her head fondly. "Now what're you going to do about it?"

"Do about it?" Sammy squeaked. "What's there to do? He hates me! And even if he didn't, I don't know the first thing about wooing a man."

Betty grinned. "That's where I come in. You have to do something nice for him. Something romantic, so that he knows you're being more than friendly."

"Uh, take him to the pictures? Or…or get him some flowers?" Sammy asked.

"Flowers will do nicely," Betty said.

"Okay. Flowers," he said, "I can do flowers."

"Tomorrow," Betty declared. "I'll meet you here in the early afternoon and we'll go pick them out together."

"That's…very nice of you, Bets. But it's a bit soon, don't you think?" Sammy squeaked.

"Is it now?" she asked, her eyebrows raised. "And when exactly would be a good time to do it?"

"I was thinking maybe ten to twenty years from now. A good reasonable amount of time," he said.

Betty nodded sternly. "Right. We'll go tomorrow. Pick him out a nice bouquet. You won't be picking him flowers off the side of the road, not on my watch," she said, pointing at him accusingly.

"I...okay," Sam said. He stood, grabbing his hat. "Tomorrow."

Betty smiled tiredly as she watched him leave. At least it seemed Jack would be getting his happy ending.

CHAPTER TWENTY

The queens from the Queen's Legs were fond of their booze, and their smokes. They were loud and wild, and they all loved to dance whenever they weren't beating in heads. Well, all of them except for Happy, who seemed to enjoy sitting and looking moody more than anything else. But Happy's surliness aside, the new security's presence brought a new level of gaiety to the Trespass Inn.

"Being a fairy isn't all glumness and blues," Julian told them while they all sat around what had become the queens' regular table. "A lot of folks expect it to be, since we can't go around telling just anyone."

Betty nodded. She felt like that with Eva sometimes. That feeling of sadness that she couldn't quite define. The one she felt when she walked in public with Eva and had to stay far enough apart to look respectable.

"Is it rough?" Jack asked, sounding almost shy. "Being with men, I mean. When people don't think it's all right?"

"Oh it's not that bad." Julian shrugged, giving him a little pat on the shoulder. "Most of the neighbors just call me a strange bachelor or say I'm *temperamental* and let it go. Doesn't matter to them that I bring home men, beyond the gossip," he said. "There're some folks who'll try to beat on you, sure, but they don't know who they're messing with when they go for me."

Betty couldn't imagine anyone being brave enough to try to bother Julian. His biceps were big enough that she imagined them as their very own warning signs. "Do not attempt to fight him or he will crush your head like an egg."

"I suppose that wouldn't work so well for guys like me, who aren't as hard," Jack said ruefully. But instead of agreeing, Julian looked him over thoughtfully.

"I don't know," he said after a moment. "Seems to me that you can hold your own. Sammy told me you once clocked a guy in the head so hard you knocked him clear out. That's not half bad."

Jack blushed, just a light dusting of pink, but Betty could tell. "He told you that?"

"Sure did," Julian said. "He talks about you a lot, you know."

Betty squinted at Julian. She'd thought that she was the only one who'd picked up how Jack felt about Sammy, but maybe she wasn't. With Sammy planning to bring him flowers in the afternoon, Betty felt that she ought to encourage Jack a little bit more. But before she could chip in, there was the sound of a scuffle at the door.

Happy was forcefully removing a real Bruno, but instead of acting at all concerned, Julian laughed happily. "Well, duty calls," he said, tossing back the rest of his drink like it was water. It wasn't. Betty was relatively certain it was straight whiskey.

"They sure don't mess around," Betty said, watching as both Julian and Sammy gravitated toward the fight like there was nowhere else they'd rather be. Fists slammed into flesh with solid thuds, and the sounds of men shouting filled the space, nearly as loud as the music. And still, the dancers kept dancing, with only those on the edge stopping to watch or shuffle away from the action in concern.

"They don't," Jack said, flinching as Sammy and Julian both landed a particularly hard punch each to the same guy's head. Julian was truly a force to be reckoned with, and with the help of Sam and Happy they easily incapacitated the mobsters who had dared try to get past George, without George even needing to lift a finger. He waved merrily to Betty, who waved back. She had the funny feeling that despite being good at it, George wasn't particularly stuck on fighting. Which meant their new arrangement suited him just fine.

"He sure is something," Randy said, coming up beside them and looking over at the door where the fight seemed to be wrapping up.

"Who, Julian?" Jack asked, sounding somewhat dreamy. Betty had to hide her laugh with a cough. Poor sweet Jack, he was smitten so easily.

Randy laughed. "Nah, I've seen Jules fight a thousand times. I mean that little guy. Sammy," he said, grinning. "You think he'd go for a fella?"

Jack remained suspiciously silent, staring too hard at the no longer interesting remnants of the fight.

"He might," Betty said amicably. Jack turned to stare at her, quick as a shot.

"Sam?!" he asked, "There's no way."

"Maybe I ought to ask," Randy said, his grin wicked as he headed toward the group of men by the door. "See you folks later."

Jack watched with wide eyes as Randy approached Sam, placing his large hand on his shoulder. "There's no way," he repeated, narrowing his eyes when Sam laughed at something Randy said. "Is there?"

"I don't know, sweetie," Betty said quietly. "Maybe *you* ought to try asking him."

Jack looked at her with wide, pleading eyes. "Betty," he said softly. "Please. Not right now."

She nodded. "Okay. Not right now." It didn't matter. She'd be helping Sammy get flowers today anyway.

After the party from the Queen's left, Betty made her excuses and headed up to Eva's apartment. She hoped that she would be free for a little while. Maybe if she didn't have any clients they could spend some time together.

But Eva didn't seem to want company.

"Another day, Nightingale," she said when Betty knocked, only to find that the door was locked. Eva never locked the door, not even once she was done seeing customers. Something wasn't right.

"Eva, sweetheart?" she said. "Is something wrong?"

Eva was silent for a moment, but then there was the sound of footsteps and the door unlocking. Betty frowned, her hand hesitating over the knob just like it had the first time she'd ascended these old stairs to meet the titular Madame La Utirips. "Okay, sweetheart," she said, closing her hand around it. "I'm coming in."

The apartment was dark, with only a few candles lit this evening. And at first, Betty could barely even see her. She was nothing but a dark shadow standing over by the entrance to her apartment.

Betty stood frozen, fear gnawing at her insides for some unknown reason. Maybe it was because Eva was acting strangely, or maybe it was intuition, but she knew somehow that something had happened.

"Come on in, Nightingale," Eva said when Betty didn't move from the front door. "It's okay. I just have a little injury. Nothing major."

If she'd felt frozen before, now she moved like a rushing river, surging forward to Eva and holding her tight. "Oh, sweetie, what happened?" she asked, when Eva hissed as she kissed her cheek. "Come into the light, darling."

Eva backed into the apartment, and Betty couldn't stop herself from gasping. Eva had a bruise on her wrist. A bruise like someone had grabbed her. And she had a black eye.

"Eva, honey!" Betty said, horrified. "What happened?!"

Eva frowned, her hand moving to hover over her eye. "It's nothing, Songbird. Just a disgruntled customer." Anger so fierce it felt like a roaring fire flared up in Betty's chest. How dare someone touch her beautiful Eva? How dare they *hurt* her like this.

"Disgruntled? Someone hit you! That's beyond disgruntled, Eva!"

"Things happen," Eva said, strangely calm for a woman with a black eye. "Not all of the people who come to see me are nice folks, and not all of them take kindly to hearing they won't end up with the girl they want. I think he was one of the boys from the Cherry too. Kept asking me questions about the 'joint I live above.' He wasn't happy about how tight-lipped I was."

"My God, Eva," Betty gasped, reaching out for her. For one blessed moment, Eva stepped into her arms, and despite everything, it felt like being home. Like Betty's arms would be enough to protect Eva from the world. Then Betty went ahead and opened her big mouth.

"You can't keep doing this work," she said, so mad she could barely see. "It's too dangerous."

Eva drew back, looking at her like she was seeing her for the first time. Like she'd been betrayed. "This is my job," she said, tone shaky but expression mad. "This is what I love to do. And I'm damn good at it."

"You're up here all alone all day and night," Betty protested, frowning. "Anything could happen! It's not safe!"

Eva glared at her. It was the first time Betty had seen the expression on her face. She was usually so happy, or at the very least peaceful and focused. She'd never seen her this mad before. "So, your work in an illegal speakeasy is safe, then?" she shot back. Betty noticed that her hands were shaking.

"Safer than this! No one has grabbed me," Betty protested, grabbing at her own wrists. She wanted to reach out to Eva, but she was scared. She couldn't be sure that Eva wouldn't smack her hands away right now. "And at least downstairs if they did I'd have a whole bar full of men coming to my rescue." Eva stared hard at her until Betty started to fidget under her gaze. "I'm just saying that I'm worried about you."

"That's what my gun is for. I chased him out of here before he could do any worse," Eva snapped.

"That's not good enough! What if he'd had a gun too? What if he'd hurt you before you'd grabbed yours?"

"Look. I know you love me, but you can't control what I do, Nightingale," Eva said, her expression fierce.

Betty came up short at that, like she'd been doused with cold water. Love. Again.

"I never said I loved you," she said before her mind could catch up with her mouth.

There was a beat of silence, during which Betty felt she could almost hear Eva's heart breaking. She could certainly see it on her face. Eva looked like she'd been slapped.

"Of course, my mistake," Eva said.

"Eva—" Betty started, but found she had nothing to say to make this better.

"I think you had better go," Eva said, her tone brooking no argument. She was crying, and Betty was too damned scared to reach out to her. "I want to be alone for a while."

"Eva, sweetheart…" she said, but Eva's expression was like a closed book that Betty dared not try to pry open. "I'm sorry. I'm so sorry. I'll go."

Betty left with a sinking feeling in her stomach, her head bowed. God, she'd really balled that up. She'd panicked at the word *love*. She'd panicked, and now she was paying for it.

God, she was such an idiot. She couldn't even comfort her lover with that one word when she needed it the most.

With tears in her eyes, Betty took herself home.

❖

Betty decided that just because her love life was in shambles, that didn't mean that Jack's and Sammy's had to be too. So, in the early afternoon before any of them had to work, she went and fetched Sam from the Trespass and took him to buy some flowers.

"You look different," Sammy said in greeting. Betty shrugged. Gone were the beaded dresses and feathered hair pieces that she normally wore, replaced by a blue cotton dress and her black stockings, with her makeup more subtle than he'd likely ever seen her wear it before.

"Come on, sweetie. Let's get you your man," she replied, grinning..

"You know," Sammy said, browsing the brightly colored blooms for sale at the flower shop. "Leaving the Family was really hard. I mean, sure, they betrayed me and tried to bump me off, but still. They were the only family I had, you know?"

Betty nodded, not sure where Sammy was going with this. But as long as he kept looking at flowers, she was happy enough to listen. It gave her a distraction from replaying what had happened with Eva over and over in her head.

"I learned to do a lot of hard things with the mob. Like cracking safes. Killing. Leaving them, knowing I was on their hitlist."

"Mm-hmm. What about these ones?" Betty asked, pointing to a cluster of chrysanthemums and sweet peas.

"Nah. Something blue. Like his eyes, you know?" Sammy said. Betty smiled to herself, turning away before Sammy could see it and get embarrassed.

"Well, there are no blue flowers here. What about these?" She held out a bouquet of aster. "Purple's close, right?"

"Yeah. Yeah, those'll do," Sammy said, nodding decisively. "Anyways. The mob. It was a rough place. And I'm just saying… this is harder than anything I ever had to do there."

Betty barked out a laugh. "Sammy, you killed people. Giving Jack some flowers is nothing."

"It's not nothing," he mumbled under his breath.

No. Betty supposed it wasn't nothing. Maybe…maybe she should pick up some flowers for Eva? Try to apologize?

"You're right. It's not nothing. But I just know Jack will love them," Betty said, bringing the flowers up to the front for Sammy to pay for them.

Sammy was nearly silent the whole walk to Betty and Jack's apartment. Betty took the flowers from him around the third time he tried to wipe his sweating palms on his slacks with them still in his hand. "They're going to lose all their petals if you keep on like that," she said, but she couldn't be too hard on him. The guy was clearly a wreck.

They arrived at the door, and Betty turned to beam at Sammy.

"Okay. Now all you have to do is knock."

Sammy nodded, raised his fist, then lowered it back down to his side.

"Sammy. You have to knock," Betty said, handing him the flowers. "He can't answer if you don't knock."

Sam took a deep, steadying breath and knocked on the door. "Just a second," Jack's voice called from the other side. Sammy looked like he might run, so Betty put a steadying hand on his arm, then stepped aside as the door swung open.

"Sammy?" Jack said.

"Hello, Jack," Sam said, hat in his hand held against his chest, flowers held out like an offering. "I'm, uh, I'm here to call on you?" he said, fidgeting with the flowers. A few of the purple petals fell to the ground.

Jack was still in his striped pajamas, looking sleep-rumpled and cute. Betty wished she has warned him to get dressed, but she figured Sammy must think he looked cute too, given the way he was staring at him awestruck. Jack blinked, like he couldn't quite believe what his eyes were showing him, and quickly moved to straighten out his shirt.

"Just got to fetch something from my room," Betty said in delight, scooching around Sammy and practically sprinting down the hallway to her bedroom. Once there, she peeked out from behind the door, watching Jack and Sam as they stood awkwardly across from each other.

Jack was fidgeting with his hands, like he didn't know what to do with them. "Uh, hello, Sam," he said, eyes trained on the bouquet in Sammy's hands.

"I brought you these," Sammy croaked out, handing the flowers to Jack without ceremony.

Betty wanted to slap her own forehead, but that would make too much sound. Lord, but Sammy was a fool.

"Oh," Jack replied, taking the flowers like he wasn't exactly sure what they were. "Thank you? They're very nice," he said cautiously. "Did you hit your head again?"

Sam frowned. "No!"

Jack was looking for all the world like he might cry, staring at the flowers like he could make them turn into something else through sheer force of will. Betty's heart ached at that look. He had been through so much.

"Then what's going on?" Jack asked helplessly. "Why would you bring me these? You aren't razzing me, are you?"

He looked so sweet and confused, and just the tiniest bit hopeful.

"I'm not razzing you," Sammy said, so softly that Betty could barely hear him.

Jack held the flowers nervously, still looking far too confused. "So, then you must have hit your head. Or these are for Betty. Maybe?"

"They're for you, Jack," Sam said firmly.

Jack took a deep shuddering breath. "Why?" he asked.

Sam rolled his eyes. "Why do you think, Money?"

"I don't know! You confuse the hell out of me, Sam!" he said, shaking the flowers at him. More purple petals rained down onto the floor, and Betty cringed. Those were expensive, and even if she hadn't paid for them, she still didn't want to see them ruined. "Is this...an apology? God, if it is you've missed the entire point—"

"Damn it, Jack," Sam snapped, "I'm trying to woo you!"

There was a beat of silence in which no one dared to even breathe, the tick of the clock on the wall loud in Betty's ears.

"You're what?" Jack laughed. "You...you hate me! You can't be wooing me."

"I never said I hated you," Sammy said, wrinkling his nose up. "I've never hated you. I thought you were an asshole for a bit, sure, but I never hated you."

Betty wanted to chip in so badly that she had to bite her lip to stop herself. Sammy could do this. He wasn't great at it, but he could do it.

"Could'a fooled me," Jack muttered, then looked down to the flowers in his hands. "You keep telling me how stuffy and uptight and boring I am. What's a guy supposed to think?" He paused, but before Sam could speak to defend himself, he continued. "You...you actually are trying to woo me, aren't you?" he said in disbelief. "You wouldn't have gotten me flowers if you were razzing me."

Sam grunted. "Of course I am. Are you going to make a sap out of me or what? Because I can go if you're not interested. I—"

Betty nearly cheered as Jack surged forward and pressed his lips against Sammy's. It was a quick kiss. Shy and awkward. But it was cute as all get-out.

"Whoa," Sammy said quietly.

"Yeah," Jack said. His cheeks were pink and his smile was big enough to be seen from Jersey.

Sam swallowed, and tried to catch his shallow breath. "So, uh. We should probably do that again. Maybe a few times."

Jack laughed brightly and reeled him in, kissing him more soundly this time, long and deep. Betty very nearly squealed for joy. Especially when Sammy said, "Holy crap, you're good at that."

"You're not so bad yourself," Jack replied

Sam took a step forward, trying to get in closer, and immediately stubbed his toe on a crack in the floorboards. "Jesus fucking shit!" he said as Jack flipped back and forth between apologizing for his floor's treachery and laughing at him.

Betty couldn't take it any longer, dashing out into the room to throw her arms around them both. "Finally," she breathed, squeezing them for all she was worth. "I thought you two boneheads would never get here."

"Let me just put these in a vase," Jack said, face red as he took the flowers over to their tiny kitchen.

"This is going to be good for you both," Betty said, nodding with determination.

"Yeah," Sam agreed, watching Jack watch him from across the room. "Yeah, I think it will be."

Betty smiled, but it felt hollow. This was how she and Eva should be. Why had she decided that it should be anything other than good between them? Eva wasn't Richard. Eva was her own person, a beautiful person. And Betty loved her. She could finally admit it fully and completely. Jack was brave enough to let someone in, even after what had happened with James. Why couldn't she be brave too? Why couldn't she take a risk like Sammy did, and tell Eva how she felt?

She loved Eva. She just hoped she wasn't too late to tell her so.

❖

Things between Jack and Sam remained the same, and yet they became completely different at the same time. Sam still drove Jack crazy, but now when he wanted him to shut up, he could press a kiss to his lips and ensure that Sam wouldn't talk for a good solid few minutes. Sam was still handsy as ever, but now it was something Jack craved, and he shook him off far less often.

He was also ready to get handsy in a new way. It sent excitement curling through him at the thought of it. They hadn't quite gotten there yet, but they were working toward it. Necking was fun, and hands had wandered south a few times. Jack had even managed to get Sam's pants undone once right before Betty had walked into the house and nearly laughed her head off at his flustered spluttering and bright red face.

So, Jack was a little bit worried about the way that things were progressing right in the middle of the Trespass Inn. They were sitting together on the piano bench during midday, closer than strictly necessary, and Sam kept on distracting Jack from practicing.

Sam kissed him, then kissed him again, slow and sweet. Making it hard for Jack to do much more than kiss him back as best he could. He left the keys ignored for the moment to focus, and soon enough they were necking like teenagers, all else forgotten. Then Sam reached for his belt, and Jack froze up.

It wasn't like he *didn't* want what Sam was offering. It was just that they were technically in public. Anyone could walk in on them right now, and if that happened, Jack would absolutely burn up into ashes from pure embarrassment.

Sam, to his credit, froze as well. "You okay? You want to stop?"

"Ah. See, I want to keep going, I, um…. it's just we're in public." Jack felt his face heat.

Sam looked around the empty bar, then looked around again for good measure. Then he laughed. "I oughta razz you something awful," he cackled. "We're inside. There isn't anyone else here, Money."

Jack huffed, but it was hard to muster any real annoyance when Sam's fingers were still resting at his belt loops. "Someone could walk in."

"Oh no," Sam said, leaning in to breathe the words against the shell of Jack's ear. "Whatever would we do?" Jack shivered, then shivered again as Sam moved to press biting little kisses to his neck, right below his ear. Jack held onto Sam's shoulders, his nails digging into his back as he teased, before he remembered himself.

"No. Nope, banks closed," Jack said, shaking his head and untangling himself so that he could stand up. Sam went sprawling overly dramatically across the bench, making sure that he landed at least partially on the keys with a cringeworthy clang. Jack flinched at the discordant sound, but didn't pause in backing toward the stage stairs. Hoping that Sam would follow. Unfortunately, he stayed put, grinning like he didn't believe Jack would actually walk out on him.

"Oh come on, Money, I'm calling bull," Sam said, confirming what Jack had thought.

Well, the joke was on him, because Jack could and would walk out, and nothing Sam could do would stop him. He'd reached the edge of the stage now and made to step down off it. "Sorry."

"Aww, no, come on," Sam said, "you're not actually going to leave me all high and dry now, are you?"

Jack grinned. He'd never known a bit of nookie could be so much *fun* before. "I just might," he replied, having made it down to the dance floor. "Unless of course you want to come back home with me."

"Come on, Money," Sam said. "Come join me."

Something about the way he said it gave Jack a premonition of doom. And a shiver of something else, lower.

Then Sam was undressing. First, his oversized sweater came off, then his pants, until he was left in only his white dress shirt, suspenders, underwear, and his hose.

Jack's mouth went dry as the desert. "Sam," he whisper-shouted, watching him unbutton his shirt. "What in the world are you doing?"

"What's it look like, Money?" Sam laughed, shucked off his underwear, and stole Jack's breath away. "I'm getting undressed. Last chance to join me."

"On the *piano?*" Jack said, not sure if he was deeply horrified or something else. Or maybe both. Yeah, both sounded right.

"Sure am," Sam practically sang, as he sat his bare ass down on the lid. "Too bad no one else is up here to help me out. Guess I'll have to take care of myself." And with that, Sam took it upon himself to put on a show. He was on a stage, after all.

Jack watched with rapt attention and a dry mouth as Sam shucked off his hose. His legs were so nice. So well-shaped and strong. Dark and lean, and longer than they seemed when he had pants on. God, he didn't have pants on. Sam licked his palm, and Jack followed his hand's descent with his eyes until he couldn't help but look at the one spot he'd been studiously avoiding. Sam was ridiculously attractive, and also getting to be ridiculously hard. It took Jack's breath away. And then Sam stroked himself with practiced ease, and Jack nearly choked on his own tongue.

No. This was absolutely too much.

Jack marched back up onto stage, determined to do something about this lewd display. What he did turned out to be grasping Sam by the lapels and pulling him in for a deep, desperate kiss.

"You're such a good little moll, ain'tcha?" Sam said between kisses, his hand still working between them. "You know just how to take care of me."

"Shut up," Jack whined. "Just, be quiet. This doesn't go any further unless you stop talking."

"Oh," came a voice from the door. "Sorry to interrupt!"

Jack whipped around to face the door, face burning when he saw Eva standing there. She looked like she was torn between laughing and fleeing.

"I had just wondered if Betty was…but I can see she's not," Eva continued. "My apologies." She looked more delighted to have caught them than embarrassed, but there was an edge of sadness to the way she said Betty's name. Jack's heart ached for them both. Betty had been saying Eva's name the same way lately. Then Eva turned and was gone, leaving Jack and Sam alone once more. "Sorry about that, Money," Sam said. He didn't sound that sorry at all. "Looks like you were right. We weren't alone after all."

Sam's hands moved toward his clothes, but Jack stopped him.

"Maybe you could take me into the back room," Jack said. He was feeling ridiculously shy considering what they'd just been doing. "You know, like one of your dates?"

Sam looked at him and smiled in a way Jack was still getting used to. "You're a lot more than just one of my dates, Jack."

But nonetheless, Sam held Jack's hand and led him to the back room, leaving his clothes strewn across the piano.

As soon as Sam was seated, Jack took him into his mouth.

"Jack," Sam groaned, in a way Jack had never heard him say his name before. A way he wanted to hear again and again, now that he'd been introduced to it. "Oh God, Jack." Jack shivered, gripping Sam's thighs tighter in what he hoped was an encouraging manner. As long as Sam kept saying his name like that, Jack would be happy to keep working him over the whole night through. And work him over he did, using his mouth in all of the ways he'd learned back when he was in high school when he and James had first learned each other's bodies. Only this was somehow a thousand times better, with Sam, a hardened gangster, turning to mush at Jack's ministrations. It was a heady rush, and one that Jack wouldn't have given up for anything.

He touched himself as he worked, shuddering as the pleasure he gave Sam translated itself into ragged moans and breathless gasps. Each one made him take Sam in deeper, made him pump his hand harder between his legs, until they were both falling apart.

Afterward, Jack shook his head. "I've lost all good standing I had with myself because of you. I hope you know that," he told Sam, still trembling slightly.

Sam practically giggled against Jack's neck.

"Good," he said. "You don't need it."

Chapter Twenty-one

Betty hummed a tune to herself as she headed toward the door to the Trespass Inn. The speakeasy was closed tonight, a rare occasion, but necessary. Their drag queen protection was indisposed this evening, as it was the night of their monthly ball. Betty would have loved to go back, but tonight she had other plans. The threat from Zanetti and the mob was too big for the Trespass to remain open without the extra security. But Betty wasn't headed to the bar. She wanted to go see Eva. She hadn't gone back since their fight the week before, and she needed to apologize. She'd spoken out of fear, and she'd hurt Eva. Her sweet Eva, who had already been physically hurt that day. Betty couldn't live with herself for doing that. It was time for her to confess her feelings and pray Eva would take her back.

She wondered if Eva would know she was coming, being a psychic and all. Her little joke made her smile to herself. She was so caught up in thought that she barely noticed the sound of footsteps falling in line with her.

"Hello, beautiful," a man said, coming up behind her, finally snapping her out of her reverie. She kept walking, going a little bit faster now. God, she hated men on the streets who thought their compliments were worth her time. She just wanted to go for a walk without having to fear a man twice her size trying to *be nice* by scaring the living daylights out of her.

She didn't answer him, just kept on walking a little quicker now, hoping he'd take the hint.

"Hey, don't ignore me," the man said, "I'm talking to you."

She was nearly at the Trespass, but to get in she'd need to go down an alley. There was no way she was doing that while being followed. She had to consider her options here. Maybe she could duck into a store and hope this creepy jerk wouldn't follow. Or she could wait there, where there were other people around.

"Hey, Songbird, I said I'm talking to you," the man said. Betty barely had time to jolt at the nickname before a huge hand was closing around her arm, and another was over her mouth. She tried to scream, but she couldn't. She tried to struggle, but he was too strong for her. She was helpless. And she *hated* it.

"There, now it seems like you're listening, doesn't it, beautiful?"

The voice didn't come from the man holding her. It came from beside him. She tried to turn her head, but the hand over her mouth kept her still. The knot of terror grew in her stomach as she realized there was less than no chance of escape. She was trapped. And two men against one of her was no fair fight. They maneuvered her into the alley, and the moment they got into the darkness was the moment she realized that no one had seen them grab her. No one was coming to help her.

"Now you're going to stay nice and quiet," the man said, still just out of her view. "And we're going to go see who's home right now. Let's hope for everyone's sake that it's that little shithead Sammy."

Oh God.

She knew now, exactly who this had to be. Or at least, who had to have sent them.

In the alley there were three men standing against the wall, but Betty's struggling was fruitless. The men behind her greeted them warmly. "Lucky, Wiley, Joey, good to see you. I hope you brought all of your tools," he said, stepping forward to give them each an embrace and a pat on the back.

When he turned around, Betty's heart sank. She'd seen this face before. Standing smiling, or sometimes frowning in the papers under headlines about murder and embezzlement and all manner of crime. Dimitri Zanetti. The Barber himself.

She prayed that everyone had come in today. That it would be six against five. Or that Leroy or George were there, at least. They were the two strongest. Then again, maybe it would be better if Sammy wasn't there. Maybe they'd let her go. She doubted it though.

At the very least she prayed that Jack wasn't there. God, what was Jack going to do if these men killed her. If they killed Sammy? And what would she do if they killed Jack but left her alive?

Worse, what if Eva was there? The thought sent a bolt of renewed fear through her. What if these men hurt her? No. No. She needed to think positively. She needed to keep her head cool, just like Sammy had taught her. He'd been telling her more and more about his adventures lately, giving her tips and tricks should she find herself in a rough situation. Those adventures had seemed so fantastical, but were suddenly sharp and real, rather than just stories Sammy told to brag. "The moment you panic is the moment you've lost," he'd said, his eyes dark and intense. "If you ever find yourself in a situation, that's the first thing to remember."

She needed to keep her head.

"Of course, boss," one of the men said, grinning at her in a way that made her skin crawl. She knew exactly what he was thinking, and she hated it. But she refused to look away, glaring at him so fiercely that his nasty little grin began to falter, and he looked away first.

"Then let's go in," Zanetti said. "Ladies first."

The large man holding her, who had to be Bianchi based on his sheer size, wrangled her inside, and Betty realized why. If anyone happened to be at the Trespass, they wouldn't open fire if she was there in front of everyone. God, she was a shield.

Bianchi tried the knob, and the door swung open with no resistance. In her near-hysterical state Betty thought that was rather rude of it, to not even resist. After all, these men were here to destroy the place and everyone who worked here. The least it could have done was stuck a little bit.

"Betty!" Jack called before he'd even turned around, but Sammy was quicker. He'd seen what was happening and had his gun leveled their way in an instant. Jack's face twisted in horror, and she tried with everything she had to shake her head. To do *something* to reassure him, to get that horrible expression of terror off his face. But she knew nothing would help. This was beyond fixing for any of them, except maybe Sam. But even for him, outnumbered this much and with her as a hostage, it didn't look good. She knew enough to know that.

She scanned the bar quickly, her heart sinking to find it empty besides the two of them. Without anyone else there, she doubted they had a chance. "Zanetti," Sammy spat out, the hate in his voice honestly jarring. She'd never heard him sound like this before. "Let her go. You don't have a problem with her, it's me you want."

"Sure is, Sammy," Zanetti said cheerfully. "But is that any way to greet your old family? I thought you cared about us, Sammy boy, yet here you are, still disrespecting me. After all I've done for you."

Sammy looked like he'd rather just shoot him in the head than answer, but Betty felt the cold muzzle of a gun pressed against her head instead. God, she was trying so hard not to cry. She couldn't give these monsters anything more than they already had. But the gun was so hard and solid, and it was against her temple. It was real.

She was going to die. They were all going to die.

"I'll go with you," Sammy said. "Willingly. Just let her go."

Jack took a step forward, grabbing Sammy's arm. He muttered something, too low for Betty to hear, and Zanetti clearly didn't like it. "I'd step back, if I were you," he said to Jack, his voice cold like steel. "Wiley, you go hold him. Lucky, you can have the distinguished pleasure of holding onto our lovely friend here while Bianchi has a little chat with our guest of honor."

Betty made sure to stomp *hard* on the new man's toes as Bianchi handed her over. She struggled, kicking out at her captor as she was passed over to him like she was nothing but a piece of meat.

"Feisty one you've got there, Sammy," Zanetti said calmly, with the air of a man who didn't doubt for a second that he had full control over the situation.

But Betty smiled at the angry hiss she got when she stomped on this new captor's toes again, just for good measure. He shook her, but he wasn't as strong as Bianchi. Still, she couldn't escape, and she distinctly remembered the way he'd looked at her outside. She didn't want to give him any excuse to hold her more tightly. Reluctantly, she stopped fighting.

"Take her over there," Zanetti ordered, nodding over to where Jack was being restrained by Wiley. He'd gone willingly, probably at the nod from Sammy. Sammy who looked more dangerous than she'd ever seen him. Like a caged tiger. All helpless aggression and simmering rage. The man named Joey stood off to the side, his hand on his gun and a nasty smile on his lips.

"Now," Zanetti said, once they were all in place where he wanted them, like pieces on a chess board. "Let's have a little talk, shall we?"

❖

Sammy slammed face first into the wall with a sickening thud. Betty wanted to cry. Instead, she shouted. "Stop!"

Bianchi slammed him against the wall again. "Shut the hell up, or I'll crack his damn skull open!"

That silenced her quick enough.

"Better," Bianchi said.

Zanetti chuckled, like this was the most amusing thing he'd witnessed all week. Like this was a show they were putting on just for him. "Now, the two of you are gonna be real quiet while I talk to our good friend Sammy here, and if you can do that then *maybe* you can walk after this is all over," Zanetti said to Betty and Jack. "The two of you, not this little snit." Bianchi ground Sammy's face into the brick to emphasize Zanetti's point, leaving more abrasions across his cheek.

Betty just prayed Eva didn't come downstairs. That she was safe until this was all over. She hoped Eva wouldn't be the one to find her body.

"Jesus, Baby Grand, my beautiful complexion! You're gonna lose me my modeling career," Sammy said through gritted teeth. God, his head must hurt. His face was bleeding, and he looked and sounded dazed. Betty was scared beyond anything she'd ever felt before. Could Sammy survive another blow to the head?

"Oh, Sammy," Zanetti laughed. "Always with a wisecrack. That's one of the things I like about you."

Betty winced as Sammy spat blood onto the floor. "Funny, I can't think of a single thing I like about you," he growled in response.

"That's not very nice of you," Wiley said from Jack's side. He was keeping him restrained, but not so much with strength. Betty could see the knife digging into Jack's back.

"No," Zanetti said thoughtfully. "Not very nice at all. Perhaps it's all this roughing him up we're doing. Maybe we ought to switch tactics." Dread shivered cold and vile through Betty. She wasn't sure what was about to happen, but she knew it'd be unpleasant at best.

Then her absolute worst fears were realized with the sound of footsteps, and Eva's voice.

"I thought I heard shout—" Eva froze in the doorway, a look of horror on her face as she walked in on the scene. She was wearing her nightgown and a robe, her hair wild and eyes wilder as she stared at Betty in Lucky's hold.

"Joey, looks like you've got a dance partner for the evening," Zanetti said. Joey already had his gun pointed toward Eva, and he crossed the room to grab her roughly and drag her inside.

"That's good. I was starting to feel left out," Joey said to his boss.

Eva gave Betty a desperate look across the dance floor. Out of all of them, she was the only one with a gun drawn on her. If anything happened to her...

"You don't have to do this," Sammy tried, but he sounded resigned. Betty was certain that Zanetti couldn't be reasoned with.

"I know," Zanetti said simply, "But I enjoy it. You remember that, don't you, Sammy? Or has it been too long since you *left* the Family."

"You tried to bump me off," Sammy protested.

Zanetti laughed. "I think you're misremembering. Too many knocks to the head. But that's all right. The past is the past, right? All we have is the now. And right now, I think we oughta see how Sammy reacts to us roughing up that doll over there." He nodded toward Betty, thank God, not Eva. But still, Betty's blood ran cold. What were they going to do to her?

Before anyone could say anything, Jack was breaking free of Wiley's hold, trying to get to her. "Don't you touch her," he yelled, and clocked Lucky right in the face. The thud of his fist was just audible over the yelling of Zanetti's cronies. Lucky cried out in pain, and Betty wriggled, trying her best to escape, but Wiley was too quick. He had Jack back at knifepoint before Jack could help her get out.

Betty watched Sammy struggle across the room, but Bianchi had him too tight. He'd doubled his efforts at keeping Sam still the moment Jack had broken free.

"Stay fucking still or I'll gut you," Wiley said, clearly digging the tip of the knife into Jack, just hard enough to hurt, but not hard enough to break the skin. Betty had never been prouder of Jack. He'd gotten in a good punch.

"Maybe we cut *him* up instead?" Lucky suggested gruffly, holding Betty with one hand, and his already swollen eye with the other. Even one-handed, he was too strong for her. She was helpless.

"Don't," Sammy said, then winced as though he hadn't meant to say it.

Zanetti looked between Sammy and Jack, a slow and nasty smile spreading on his face. "Huh. That's not a half bad idea. I think we'd all feel real bad treating a lady with such disrespect. But this fella here seems more than willing to take her place."

"Leave him alone," Eva demanded, but it was too late. Zanetti had found Sammy's weakness. And Zanetti seemed like the type who, once he found a sore spot, liked to poke it. Hard.

"Quiet, or you'll be next," Joey said, then put his hand over Eva's mouth for good measure. Lucky did the same to Betty, making sure she couldn't shout anything else and ruin the show. He was lucky that Betty didn't have a heater, or hell even a knife. She'd have had him and Joey dead on the floor if she did. If she survived this, she'd have to ask Sammy about getting a weapon for herself. She wished Eva had brought her gun with her.

"Wiley, why don't we let you play with your knife a little, hmm?" Zanetti said casually. Like he was discussing the weather.

Jack was pale when he chanced a glance in Sammy's direction, but had a look of such determination on his face that Betty's heart swelled with it. God, he was so brave. If only he'd managed to get Wiley's knife out of his hands before, when he'd broken free.

"Nothing would bring me more pleasure," Wiley said, grinning as he readjusted his hold, pressing the knife hard against Jack's forearm through his shirtsleeve as he waited for instructions. Zanetti nodded, and Wiley made the cut.

The knife sliced across Jack's skin, shredding the fabric of his shirt and staining it bright red. Jack hissed, but that was it. Silent as he could be, he'd barely even flinched. Betty watched a muscle in his jaw jump. He was gritting his teeth. She was gritting hers, too.

"Zanetti," Sammy said, before he could order another cut. "Dimitri. What if I wanted to come back?"

Zanetti laughed, like he'd never heard a better joke before in his life. "Oh, Sammy, you know it's too late for that. Now be quiet, I'm watching the show."

Zanetti nodded, and Wiley sliced Jack again, deeper this time. Jack's whole body twitched, but he stayed mostly quiet once again. Just a small grunt of pain, his eyes blazing as he stared Zanetti down. The mob boss watched him, looking at him like he was some interesting plaything. "This guy's real hard-boiled," he said, nodding to Wiley to cut him again. "He doesn't look it, does he."

Eva sucked air through her teeth. Betty tried to watch her instead of the butchering of her best friend, but it hurt just as much to see a man holding a gun to Eva's beautiful head as it did to watch Jack bleeding.

Zanetti moved toward Jack, and Sammy struggled to break free of Bianchi's grip. To lurch forward and get Zanetti on the ground. But Bianchi held him like steel chains. Betty knew it was hopeless. Zanetti ignored him, moving to stand in front of Jack. "It's too bad, you fell in with this bad company," he said, nodding at Sammy. "You could have had a real good career with us."

Jack, to his credit, didn't even look down. He stared Zanetti in the face, and quietly said, "No thank you."

Zanetti laughed and turned away, walking back to Sammy. "What an interesting man," he said. "No wonder Sammy took him as a crony. Cut him again, deeper."

Another hiss, and Jack's heavy breathing.

Zanetti came to a stop in front of Sammy. "That is what he is to you, right, Sammy? Or were you trying to make yourself a little family here?"

"Go fuck yourself," Sammy spat, looking pleased when flecks of blood sprayed onto Zanetti's face. Zanetti tilted his head, growling as he took a handkerchief out of his pocket. He didn't move back an inch.

"Cut him," he barked, and this time Jack cried out. Only a little *ah*, but it was enough to make Zanetti smile. Betty wanted to vomit. Behind Lucky's hand she tried to shout, but there was nothing that she could do. Nothing any of them could do.

"Dimitri," Sammy started, only to be cut off by a hand around his throat. Fingers squeezed down hard on his windpipe. He choked spluttering, his legs kicking helplessly.

"Yes, Sammy?" he said, almost sweetly. "What is it?"

Sammy continued to choke, as Jack screamed his name. Betty tried to bite the palm of the hand over her mouth, to no avail.

Then Zanetti loosened his grip. Sammy shuddered visibly, gasping for breath. Zanetti laughed. "Well? Spit it out."

"I can get this place shut down," Sammy rasped, struggling to breathe. "I'll shut it all down…"

"Oh, it'll shut down," Zanetti said, letting go of Sammy's neck. "They won't be able to keep up business with their best rumrunner dead and buried. Maybe we'll take out the band too, just for good measure."

Betty let herself cry then. It truly was hopeless. Sammy was looking over at Jack, whose sleeve was torn to shreds, deep cuts and shallow peppering all the way up his arm and his shoulder. Eva stood silent as the grave, her eyes never leaving Betty. She wished she'd told Eva that she loved her. Because she did. She loved her so deeply, and now she was about to die with her.

"I think it's about time I got out my tools, don't you think, boys?" Zanetti asked, getting a round of agreement from his thugs. "Yes, I think Sammy here could use a nice shave."

Betty closed her eyes. She'd heard enough about Zanetti to know why he was called the Barber. He liked to slit the throat of his victim with a straight razor, then beat them until they were through. Betty didn't have to watch, at least. Though she'd hear every moment.

She wished desperately that Leroy, or Charlie, or George would walk through the door and help them. But they had no reason to be here tonight. Not with the speakeasy closed while the drag ball was on.

"I'm trying to decide," Zanetti said, tapping his chin in faux thought. "Should I slit Sammy's throat, or should I start with these two over here? Make him watch. What do you think, boys?"

"Either way sounds good, boss," Wiley said. The suck-up. "You want them down on their knees?"

Zanetti laughed. "Sure, why not. But keep Sammy standing. I want to watch him fall."

Sammy struggled half-heartedly as Zanetti went to get the case with his razor in it, but Bianchi was far too strong. If Betty could make some sort of distraction maybe Sammy could escape.

Maybe.

But she couldn't get free. She couldn't shout with Lucky's hand over her mouth and Eva held at gunpoint. She couldn't even raise her hand to hold the nightingale necklace that Eva had given her as a last comfort.

It was hopeless. They were going to die there, on the dance floor of the Trespass Inn.

CHAPTER TWENTY-TWO

The pain in Jack's arm was nearly unbearable. He'd had this strange thought, as he was being butchered alive, that he hoped his arm wasn't too damaged for him to play piano again. As though he'd ever be able to play after they killed him today. But worse than the pain in his arm, and even the knowledge of his own impending death, was the sight of Sam, trapped and helpless and soon to die. And Betty and Eva were here too. Which meant Jack was about to lose not only his lover, but also his best friend and her love. And then himself.

And there was nothing any of them could do about it.

The man holding him shoved him hard, but Jack refused to go down onto his knees. He'd have to try a lot harder than that if he wanted to take him down.

Zanetti was grabbing his tools, whatever that meant, and Jack was sure that could only spell disaster for Sam. He just hoped that the asshole holding onto him would kill him before he could watch Sam die. Or that Zanetti started with him. He didn't intend to sit around and watch. He'd struggle, as hopeless as that struggle might be. He'd struggle until his last breath to try to keep Sam, Betty, and Eva alive.

Then, right as Zanetti bent down to pull something out of a case, something odd happened. That something was a large, high-heeled shoe flying out from the shadows, and slamming into the back of Bianchi's head.

"What the fu—" was all Bianchi managed to get out as he turned to look, rubbing the back of his head where it had hit, before Sam clocked him hard enough to send him to the ground.

"We leave you alone for one night!" Julian said, coming through the door with another heel in his hand, brandished like a weapon. "Just one night, and you almost get yourselves killed."

Francis was on Zanetti in a second, his pink skirts tucked up around his waist as he tackled him to the ground. And Julian seemed to have gone over to help Sam escape Bianchi's hold, from what Jack could tell.

Everything was such a blur that Jack could barely keep up with it.

He was reasonably certain that Betty had stomped on Lucky's foot with her chunky heel, at the same time she elbowed him *hard* in the gut. Lucky let go of her, doubling over in pain, and she took the moment of distraction to spin and knee him right in the crotch, before bashing him over the head. He tripped backward over Betty's charm bag which had slipped from her dress, and fell on his ass.

A gunshot rang out, and the man holding Eva yelped. Jack's eyes snapped toward her, and he prayed that Joey hadn't shot her in all the commotion. Instead, he found that she'd knocked his hand aside, causing him to drop his gun. It went flying across the floor, far enough away that mercifully no one could grab it. Eva turned on him in a flash and began to beat him over the head like a woman possessed. It was quite frankly more aggressive than he'd have thought she could be. She was almost as violent as Sam.

Jack took the moment of distraction from the gunshot to struggle free of Wiley's grip. The man wasn't very strong, but his knife did slice a parting cut across Jack's shoulder as he broke his hold. But what did that matter now? He'd already butchered him up. One more cut didn't matter. Jack managed to land a blow to his head, but almost as soon as he was free from Wiley's grasp, he fell to the ground. Still, it seemed he'd taken Wiley down with him. And he managed to wrestle the knife from his hands as he slammed Wiley's head onto the floor. Thank God for Sam's grappling lessons.

Jack felt rather sick, and he was suddenly so dizzy that he thought he might pass out, but he couldn't figure out why. Not until the sharp red mess of his arm reminded him. Blood loss. Right. Blood loss and shock, he assumed.

Everything went fuzzy around the edges, and his hearing seemed to dim somehow. Like he was underwater or hearing everything from a great distance away. But he kept right on slamming Wiley's head against the floor, trying his damnedest to knock him out, even as his strength began to give out. He finally let go of Wiley's hair and slumped down onto the floor.

As if from miles away, he heard Julian telling Betty, "Honey, we forgot our fans!" Jack tried to look up at him, but no one had noticed him fall in all the commotion. But that was okay. He could wait. "We couldn't possibly do a fan dance without them!" Julian continued, in a higher pitched voice, fluttering said fan as though he were a Victorian lady.

Jack laughed, a tad hysterically, and suddenly there was a warm hand cradling his head, and Sam's voice calling his name. "Jack, hey," he said, sounding somehow close and far away all at once. "Hey, stay awake. Stay with me, all right?"

"I'm tired," he complained, going to move his arm, and hissing in pain. "My arm hurts." Time moved strangely after that. One moment he was lying on the floor with Sam cradling him, and the next he was being propped up between two strong bodies over by the bar, as stinging alcohol was poured down his arm. He may have screamed, or maybe he'd just meant to, but either way Sam was there in front of him again, holding his face.

"Hey, it's all okay," Sam said. "You're gonna be fine. You're in shock I think, but you're gonna be just fine, Jack," he reassured him. He sounded more scared himself than Jack felt.

"'Course I'll be fine," he managed to slur. "I'm hard-boiled."

Sam laughed—the sound suspiciously wet. "Yeah, Jack," he said. "Yeah, you are."

And that was the last he heard before the darkness took him.

❖

Betty wasn't entirely certain she'd processed the whole fight. She knew what had happened in the most basic of ways, sure, but it felt like she'd watched it happen rather than taken part in it.

Julian had Bianchi under control after Sam had clocked him, and as soon as the fighting had started Sam had only had eyes for Zanetti. He'd jumped on him the moment he'd gotten a chance, and gotten him down to the floor, while Francis helped pin him down. The thing about Zanetti turned out to be that he talked a big game, but he was too used to his goons taking care of business for him. He might have been a tough guy at one point in time, but now it'd been easy for Sammy to take him head-on.

It hadn't been all that climactic, if she was being honest. Sammy had just pummeled the man until he was unconscious and then a little more, just to be sure. It seemed like Sammy didn't care if he killed him. Betty felt the same way. If Zanetti died, she'd sing a damn celebration song.

She'd watched him order Jack cut up like meat at a butcher. He'd ordered a man to point a gun at Eva's head. God, she'd thought for sure Eva had been shot when the gun had gone off.

Betty sat there, holding Jack's hand on his uninjured arm in one hand, and Eva's hand in the other as Sammy and the queens dealt with the nasty business of tying up the mobsters who'd attacked them. Lucky, the man who'd been holding her, had escaped somehow. Betty knew if she ever saw him again, she'd beat him within an inch of his life. But otherwise they had everyone trussed up and lined up by the bar, with gags in their mouths. Bianchi had extra rope tied around him, just in case. The guy was strong enough that Betty figured they didn't want to take the risk of him breaking out.

Zanetti looked *furious* all tied up and gagged. Good. Betty hoped he choked on his rage.

Eva glared at the men tied up at the bar. Betty felt a shiver work its way through her at the look in her eyes. A feeling like static was buzzing through the air.

"We need bandages," Sammy told Betty when he returned to Jack's side. "He's bleeding a lot."

"I have some in my apartment," Eva said, standing shakily. Betty squeezed her hand tighter, not willing to let go.

"I'll come with you," she said.

They climbed the stairs in silence, never letting each other go. Eva's hand was warm, her pulse strong. She was alive. Somehow, they were both alive. They moved like ghosts through Eva's apartment, and even when Eva needed her hand back to rummage for bandages Betty kept her hand on her arm. It was a solid reminder that Eva was okay.

Back downstairs, Eva moved forward and bent down to patch Jack up, only to have Sam stop her. "Don't worry. I'll do it. You two take care of each other."

Eva nodded and turned to Betty, opening her arms. Betty couldn't have turned down that invitation if she tried. She fell into Eva's arms, and Eva's cheek felt wet against her head. They sat then, right there on the floor, and let themselves feel.

"What do we do with them?" Betty asked eventually, her voice shaking only slightly as she stared at the impotent gangsters where they were tied up.

"Oh, don't worry, honey," Julian said. He smoothed his dress down primly. "We'll take care of them. Especially him." He nodded at Zanetti with a look on his face that spoke of a fate Betty knew she'd rather not hear the details of.

"Thanks," Sam said solemnly. "We really owe you one."

Julian waved Sam off. "You don't owe us a thing, sweet pea. We've been wanting a crack at this guy for a while. You stay by his side now," Julian said and hauled Zanetti up over his shoulders. Julian tucked a stray curl of his wig back behind his ear with his free hand. "We'll deal with taking out the trash."

Betty wasn't sure what they were going to do with Zanetti and the rest of them, but she honestly didn't want to know. It was bound to end with a long nap in a dirt bed. Whatever it was, it wasn't going to be pleasant. She doubted Zanetti would be around much longer.

"Hey, Bets," Sammy said, kneeling beside her where she sat. "How you holding up?"

She laughed and wiped at the wetness on her cheeks with the back of her hand. "Better than Jacky, I'll tell you that much."

"He'll be okay," Eva reassured her, kissing her temple.

"I know, I know. Just—" Betty broke off, pressing her face into Eva's shoulder as tears overwhelmed her. They'd given Jack some chocolate they'd found in the coat room, while they'd looked for spare clothes to cradle his head, and had managed to get him to drink some water, but he still looked so pale. They'd have to move him soon. Get him home and try to get some real food into him. But for now, they let him sleep.

"He's got it rough," Sam said. "But so do you. If you need to talk about anything—"

Betty didn't let him finish. For the first time in the evening, she detached herself from Eva in order to throw her arms around Sammy and hold him tight.

"You almost died," she said, her face buried against his neck as she cried. "We almost died."

She was shocked when Sammy didn't throw her off, and even more shocked to find that his face was wet with tears. His chest heaved with a sob, and Betty held him all the more tightly.

A few seconds in, a thin voice asked "What's everybody crying about? Did I die?" Betty couldn't help but laugh, and even if it was edged with hysteria, it still felt good.

"No, Jack," Sammy said, lifting his undamaged hand up to press a kiss against the back of it. "You're gonna be just fine."

❖

Eva refused to leave Betty's side for an instant. They'd decided to move Jack up into her apartment, unwilling to subject him to the long walk back to their house while he was so injured.

Sam had stuck by him as long as he could, before he had to go back down and help the queens with whatever horrible thing was about to happen to Zanetti and his crew. Betty was pretty sure they were packing them all into an automobile to take somewhere, but she couldn't find it in her to care. She sincerely hoped whatever happened to them was as terrible as what they'd done. Or tried to do.

They had laid Jack out on Eva's bed, where he'd immediately fallen asleep and left her alone with Eva. They sat on Eva's threadbare couch together.

"I'm so sorry," Betty said, a tad hysterically. "I was coming over to say that. To apologize for the other day."

"Hush, Nightingale," Eva said, her eyes misty with tears. "That doesn't matter now." Her hands were shaking as she took Betty's hand between them. "My sweet love, you've been through so much tonight."

Betty managed a watery laugh at that. "So have you," she said.

Eva kissed her hand, then pulled her in for a tight hug, letting her cry against her shoulder. It felt like the crying would never stop. But Eva rubbed her back through it, and eventually her tears ran out.

"I didn't see this coming," she said, so soft that Betty barely heard it.

"I don't know how to feel," Betty said, face still buried in Eva's nightgown. "I'm so relieved, but I feel so…"

Eva stroked her hair, then pressed a kiss to her head. "You're in shock, my love. Come, I'll make us some tea. Valerian root, to calm us."

Betty nodded, clinging to her as they stood and moved to the kitchen. She felt a little bit like a child, but she was still trembling, and the thought of being alone even for a moment was too much for her right now.

"I've never felt so helpless," she said, whisper soft as the tea brewed.

"Me neither," Eva admitted. "I don't know what I would have done if they'd taken you from me."

Betty hiccupped, then laughed wetly. "But we're okay. At least we're okay," she said, smiling into the kiss that Eva pressed against her lips.

"Yes, my love," she said, kissing her again and again. "You're okay. We're okay."

"My charm bag," Betty said, fishing it out of her dress. "That man stepped on it. Another one of the stones is broken."

Eva smiled, a little bit vindictively. "Did he trip on it?"

"Yes."

"Then it did its job," Eva said, sounding satisfied.

As the night wore on, Betty snuggled into the warmth of Eva's arms, slowly letting herself feel safe and warm and whole. Three things she hadn't felt in a long while. Things she hadn't thought she'd get to feel ever again when she was in the clutches of Zanetti's men.

"My sweet Nightingale," Eva said, for what seemed like the thousandth time that night. She was just as shaken as Betty had been, and wouldn't stop hugging her tight, like she was checking to make sure she was still there.

"My Eva," she said back.

"I didn't see this for you," she said again for the thousandth time. "I should have seen it."

Betty held her. "How could you have known, sweetheart?" Though she somehow thought that Eva might be talking about something other than normal foresight. So finally, she plucked up the courage to ask.

"Can you really see the future?" She asked the question that she'd been too frightened to ask before. Eva certainly acted as though she could most of the time.

"I can see a future," Eva responded, kissing the back of her head. "But I didn't see that one."

Betty, frowned. She wasn't certain that answered her question. "A future?"

Eva stroked her hair so softly and stayed silent for long enough that Betty thought she might not answer. "Yes," she finally said. "I can see a future. And right now the future I see is one I like." She squeezed Betty gently, pressing a kiss to the back of her head.

Betty giggled, then turned in her arms. "Actually though. Do you see what's in store for you and me?"

Eva traced her cheekbone with a thumb, staring at her with her wide beautiful eyes. "The future is always changing," she said, pressing a kiss to Betty's forehead. "We change it constantly by what we do and say." A kiss to her nose, her lips, her cheek. "So what's in store is always changing too."

Betty nodded. It was probably the best answer she was going to get at the moment. And that meant that the future was uncertain. But that was okay. Betty could deal with a little bit of uncertainty now. "Then how do we know if we'll be all right?" she asked after a long stretch of silently turning things over in her head.

"We have each other, don't we? That is enough. All of us here, we protect each other. We're family," Eva said. Then softer, "You're my family."

Betty moved in closer, resting her head against Eva's chest. "I love you," she said, like a prayer. And it felt like a weight off her chest. It felt like flying and falling all at once. Betty was dizzy with it.

Eva stared at her with what felt like all the love in the world held in her gaze. "And I love you too, my Nightingale."

And despite it being a mystery, for the first time in her life, Betty wasn't nervous about the future to come. It was sure to contain love, and being in love with Eva was the safest she'd ever felt.

CHAPTER TWENTY-THREE

Jack's arm was healing well. Most of the slices had been superficial, with only a few deep enough that they'd needed to be looked at by a doctor. They'd stitched him up right good, and only asked a few questions that Jack had managed to wave away. It helped that Sam had been with him, looking at the doctor like he was ready to jump him at the slightest provocation. The stitches had hurt, but Jack couldn't deny that he was lucky.

He was so very lucky.

Betty was alive. Shaken up, but not hurt at least. He wished she hadn't been there, but Betty just shook her head whenever he told her that and said, "Jack, wherever you go, I'll be there too."

And Sam. Despite the odds stacked against him, Sam was alive too. Not only alive, but mostly unharmed too, beyond some bruises on his neck and a cut-up face.

"You're a brave idiot," Sam kept telling him. "The most heroic fool I know. I can't believe you punched Lucky Lenny right in the face! In front of the Barber too." He always said it with such affection though, that Jack was only ever half offended.

Sam started spending more and more time at his house, to the point where Betty had joked that he ought to start paying rent. A joke that Sam had been surprisingly keen on. "I could, you know," he said, his arm slung around Jack's shoulder where they sat on the couch. "I could spend all my time here then."

"I'd end up killing you," Jack had told him seriously. "And then you know what I'd be? A criminal." Sam had laughed, so nice and bright and carefree that Jack had privately made plans to invite him to move in the moment he'd spoken to Betty about it. She wouldn't mind. She'd been spending more and more time over at Eva's lately.

It was one such night, when Betty went to call on Eva, that found Jack and Sam together in their pajamas, sitting together as the gramophone played a slow and sweet song. Jack half remembered dancing with Mack to this song and he didn't want any memories tied to Mack anymore. Not now, when he could make new ones with Sam. "You know I can't dance," Jack told him. "But I'd like to, with you."

Sam grinned at him. "You sure you wouldn't rather me put the boots to you? It's real romantic right now."

Jack shook his head, though if he was being honest, it *was* a tempting offer. "Dance with me."

Sam looked away, his cheeks darkening slightly. "I've got two left feet too, you know. I only dance when I'm drunk," he said, adorably flustered. "But all right. I guess I could do it for you." They both stood, moving into each other's arms like they were drawn by magnets. There was no space between the two of them, body to body, and Jack wrapped his arms snug around Sam's waist. He nuzzled his nose against Sam's hair, taking in the scent of him.

"How come I'm the doll?" Sam complained halfheartedly, before looping his arms around Jack's neck.

Jack laughed. "Because you're short like one," he said, then yelped when Sam pinched his ear. "All right, all right! You want to have your hands around my waist?"

Sam grumbled, but shook his head. "Just don't go getting fresh," he said in a way that very much implied he wouldn't mind Jack getting at least a little fresh. So Jack squeezed his butt before sliding his hands back up to a respectable spot on his waist. "Wouldn't dream of it," he said with a wink.

"Can't ever trust a man when you're dancing," Sam said, faux sadly, shaking his head.

They began to sway, awkwardly at first, before they found their rhythm. The violins played so sweetly, and the piano plunked away in a way that Jack found profoundly pleasing.

"Watch out for that hell floor of yours," Sam whispered, his voice sweet and low. "I'm sure that crack doesn't help with your left foot problem."

Jack rubbed a circle against his hip with his thumb, the fabric of the pajamas that he'd lent him soft under his fingers. "'I'll be sure to watch out," he said just as lowly as Sam.

That was, of course, the moment that he tripped over the leg of Sam's pajamas where they'd come unrolled from around his ankle. He nearly went down, with only Sam's quick reflexes saving him from falling ass over teakettle onto the floor. "Not a word," he said, his face pressed against Sam's chest where he'd caught him.

Sam, to his credit, didn't say a thing. Not so much to his credit was the way he cackled like Jack tripping was the funniest thing he'd ever had the good fortune to see. "Christ, and I thought *I* had two left feet," Sam said finally, as their dance slowed to a gentle sway.

"You're an evil little monster," Jack said. "And I'd be willing to bet you did that on purpose."

"Oh sure," Sam agreed, still laughing. "I trained these pajamas real good to trip you up."

Jack leaned forward, pressing their foreheads together as he laughed. "I knew it."

Sam stepped on Jack's foot at least three times and kept apologizing for it. "It's no problem," Jack told him after a few moments of quiet dancing. "I like your left feet."

"Well, good," Sam said. "Because I like yours just fine too. I don't need you to be no kind of good dancer, anyways. Just want you exactly like you are."

The feeling in Jack's chest was unlike anything he'd ever felt before. It was big and effervescent and so good he thought he might cry. The song began to wind down toward the end, and still they kept swaying gently, even after the gramophone ran down. The sound of scratching was the only sound they needed. Sam kissed him, slow and sweet and everything Jack would never have pegged him for before he got to know him. Everything he knew he was, now that they'd nearly died together.

God, he'd nearly die for Sam again and again if it meant he got to keep this forever.

It was the kind of kiss that wasn't headed anywhere in particular. The kind that could last mere minutes or hours long into the evening. And Jack wasn't particular about which it was.

After all, they had time. They had all the time in the world.

❖

The Trespass was hazy with leftover smoke and smelled of sweat and alcohol as the last of their nightly patrons tumbled out the door. Betty smiled watching them go. It had been a good night.

Dimitri Zanetti had mysteriously disappeared, leaving behind a power struggle, according to the papers. Betty knew that there were some drag queens with blood on their hands behind it, but she couldn't bring herself to feel bad about it. Zanetti had hurt her best friends, and had threatened the love of her life. He deserved whatever fate had befallen him.

Betty snaked her arms around Eva's neck and gave her a quick kiss. "I love you," she said, like she couldn't stop saying it. She had been such a fool holding out for so long when all it took was those three words to light Eva up like the brightest candle.

"I love you too, Nightingale," she said, her hands resting comfortably on Betty's hips.

Over by the bar Jack and Sammy were bickering as Charlie cleaned the bar's surface. Leroy and Mary had had their baby, little Helen Maria Cole, and Leroy seemed like he was itching to get out of there and get back to his family. Betty could see him inching toward the rum room, which was also the coatroom, ready to grab his jacket and flee.

"Shall we head upstairs?" Eva asked her.

"Let's have a drink first," Betty said, not willing to let the magic of the evening go yet.

"Sure, sweetheart. Let me go get us some drinks," Eva said, untangling herself from Betty's arms.

Betty settled herself at one of the tables to wait. Leroy said his good-byes and headed out, passing George on the way as he left. Betty followed him with her eyes as he walked past the bar where Eva seemed to be trying to convince Sammy to let her read his palm. And on his way over was Jack.

"Can I sit here?" Jack asked.

"Why of course, good sir," Betty replied with a wink.

Jack pulled up a chair and sat. "Eva says she'll be over in a few minutes. She's trying to tell Sam his future."

Betty laughed, looking over to where George had been roped into Eva's palm reading scheme. Poor George looked pained, while Sammy sat there with a look of pure terror, his hands held to his chest far from her grasp.

Betty leaned into Jack's side. "You know, we never did get to Tin Pan Alley," she said thoughtfully. "I know that was your dream. Do you ever regret ending up here?"

Jack looked around the room, then smiled.

"I dunno," he said softly. "I think we made it anyways, Bets."

Betty smiled, sweet and bright, and for a moment everything was right with the world.

"One Mary Pickford, and one watered down Mary Pickford for the gentleman," Eva said, placing the drinks in front of them.

"Thank you, Eva," Jack said. "Did Sam see that it was watered down?"

"No." Eva laughed. "I distracted him with a palm reading. Strong love line on that one," she said, winking at Jack who flushed bright red.

"Well, I'll go and show off to him then," Jack said, making a hasty retreat.

"You're bad," Betty said. Eva shrugged with a mischievous look and stole a sip of Betty's drink.

Betty hopped up, grabbing the drink from Eva. She took a swig, then placed it on the table. "Dance with me," she said.

Eva followed her out onto the dance floor. "We don't have any music," Eva pointed out.

"Jacky!" Betty called. "A little help with the music please."

"You got it big shot," Jack called back, grabbing Sam and rerouting toward the piano.

Jack started up a slow song, and Betty twirled Eva around, much to her delight.

"You look happy," Eva said. She tucked a strand of hair back behind Betty's ear. She looked at Betty with her beautiful brown eyes and Betty felt like she was burning up in the best way.

"Of course I'm happy," Betty said. "I have you."

And they swayed together as the piano played on.

The End.

About the Author

R.E. Ward is a lesbian living in Toronto, Ontario, Canada, with her fiancée, Elizabeth, and their three spoiled cats. She has always been enamored with 1920s style and wanted to bring a queer narrative to her favorite aesthetic decade. *Hot Keys* was written during the Covid-19 pandemic and is Rebecca's first novel.

Books Available from Bold Strokes Books

Almost Perfect by Tagan Shepard. A shared love of queer TV brings Olivia and Riley together, but can they keep their real-life love as picture perfect as their on-screen counterparts? (978-1-63679-322-1)

Corpus Calvin by David Swatling. Cloverkist Inn may be haunted, but a ghost materializes from Jason Dekker's past and Calvin's canine instinct kicks in to protect a young boy from mortal danger. (978-1-62639-428-5)

Craving Cassie by Skye Rowan. Siobhan Carney and Cassie Townsend share an instant attraction, but are they brave enough to give up everything they have ever known to be together? (978-1-63679-062-6)

Drifting by Lyn Hemphill. When Tess jumps into the ocean after Jet, she thinks she's saving her life. Of course, she can't possibly know Jet is actually a mermaid desperate to fix her mistake before she causes her clan's demise. (978-1-63679-242-2)

Enigma by Suzie Clarke. Polly has taken an oath to protect and serve her country, but when the spy she's tasked with hunting becomes the love of her life, will she be the one to betray her country? (978-1-63555-999-6)

Finding Fault by Annie McDonald. Can environmental activist Dr. Evie O'Halloran and government investigator Merritt Shepherd set aside their conflicting ideas about saving the planet and risk their hearts enough to save their love? (978-1-63679-257-6)

Hot Keys by R.E. Ward. In 1920s New York City, Betty May Dewitt and her best friend, Jack Norval, are determined to make their Tin Pan Alley dreams come true and discover they will have to fight—not only for their hearts and dreams, but for their lives. (978-1-63679-259-0)

Securing Ava by Anne Shade. Private investigator Paige Richards takes a case to locate and bring back runaway heiress Ava Prescott. But ignoring her attraction may prove impossible when their hearts and lives are at stake. (978-1-63679-297-2)

The Amaranthine Law by Gun Brooke. Tristan Kelly is being hunted for who she is and her incomprehensible past, and despite her overwhelming feelings for Olivia Bryce, she has to reject her to keep her safe. (978-1-63679-235-4)

The Forever Factor by Melissa Brayden. When Bethany and Reid confront their past, they give new meaning to letting go, forgiveness, and a future worth fighting for. (978-1-63679-357-3)

The Frenemy Zone by Yolanda Wallace. Ollie Smith-Nakamura thinks relocating from San Francisco to her dad's rural hometown is the worst idea in the world, but after she meets her new classmate Ariel Hall, she might have a change of heart. (978-1-63679-249-1)

A Cutting Deceit by Cathy Dunnell. Undercover cop Athena takes a job at Valeria's hair salon to gather evidence to prove her husband's connections to organized crime. What starts as a tentative friendship quickly turns into a dangerous affair. (978-1-63679-208-8)

As Seen on TV! by CF Frizzell. Despite their objections, TV hosts Ronnie Sharp, a laid-back chef; and paranormal investigator Peyton Stanford, have to work together. The public is watching. But joining forces is risky, contemptuous, unnerving, provocative—and ridiculously perfect. (978-1-63679-272-9)

Blood Memory by Sandra Barret. Can vampire Jade Murphy protect her friend from a human stalker and keep her dates with the gorgeous Beth Jenssen without revealing her secrets? (978-1-63679-307-8)

Foolproof by Leigh Hays. For Martine Roberts and Elliot Tillman, friends with benefits isn't a foolproof way to hide from the truth at the heart of an affair. (978-1-63679-184-5)

Glass and Stone by Renee Roman. Jordan must accept that she can't control everything that happens in life, and that includes her wayward heart. (978-1-63679-162-3)

Hard Pressed by Aurora Rey. When rivals Mira Lavigne and Dylan Miller are tapped to co-chair Finger Lakes Cider Week, competition gives way to compromise. But will their sexual chemistry lead to love? (978-1-63679-210-1)

The Laws of Magic by M. Ullrich. Nothing is ever what it seems, especially not in the small town of Bender, Massachusetts, where a witch lives to save lives and avoid love. (978-1-63679-222-4)

The Lonely Hearts Rescue by Morgan Lee Miller, Nell Stark, Missouri Vaun. In this novella collection, a hurricane hits the Gulf Coast, and the animals at the Lonely Hearts Rescue Shelter need love, and so do the humans who adopt them. (978-1-63679-231-6)

The Mage and the Monster by Barbara Ann Wright. Two powerful mages, one committed to magic and one controlled by it, strive to free each other and be together while the countries they serve descend into war. (978-1-63679-190-6)

Truly Wanted by J.J. Hale. Sam must decide if she's willing to risk losing her found family to find her happily ever after. (978-1-63679-333-7)

A Good Chance by Ali Vali. Harry, Desi, and Desi's sister Rachel are so close to getting everything they've ever wanted, but Desi's ex-husband is coming back to get his revenge and rip apart their chance at happiness. (978-1-63679-023-7)

A Perfect Fifth by Jaycie Morrison. Streetwise pianist Zara Keller and Lady Jillian Stansfield couldn't be more different; yet their connection brings a new awareness of who they are and what they truly want in their lives—including each other. (978-1-63679-132-6)

Catching Feelings by Ana Hartnett Reichardt. Andrea Foster expected to catch a lot of pitches from the Alder Lion's star pitcher, Maya, but she didn't expect to catch feelings. (978-1-63679-227-9)

Defiant Hearts by Lee Lynch. In these stories, you'll find your lovers, friends, and lesbians you wish you knew—maybe even yourself. (978-1-63679-237-8)

Love and Duty by Catherine Young. All Princess Roseli wants is to marry her three lovers, but with war looming, she must instead marry Princess Lucia to establish a military alliance between their planets. (978-1-63679-256-9)

Murder at Union Station by David S. Pederson. Private Detective Mason Adler struggles to determine who killed a woman found in a trunk without getting himself killed in the process. (978-1-63679-269-9)

Serendipity by Kris Bryant. Serendipity brings jingle writer Annie Foster and celebrity pop star Bristol Baines together, and their undeniable attraction keeps them close, but will their different paths drive them apart? (978-1-63679-224-8)

The Haunted Heart by Jane Kolven. A ghost, a ring, and a quest to find a missing psychic—it's a spell for love. (978-1-63679-245-3)

The Rules of Forever by Nan Campbell. After reconnecting at their high school reunion, Cara and Lauren agree to embark on a textbook definition friends-with-benefits relationship, but trying to keep it uncomplicated is harder than it seems. (978-1-63679-248-4)

Vision of Virtue by Brey Willows. When virtue and desire come together, be prepared for sparks in this next installment of the Memory's Muses series. (978-1-63679-118-0)

Cherry on Top by Georgia Beers. A chance meeting leaves Cherry and Ellis longing for a different life, but when Ellis's search for truth crashes into Cherry's insta-filter world, do they have any hope at all of a happily ever after? (978-1-63679-158-6)

Love and Other Rare Birds by Angie Williams. Ornithologist Dr. Jamie Martin and park ranger Rowan Fleming are searching the Alaskan wilderness for a bird thought to be extinct and they're about to discover opposites really do attract. (978-1-63679-108-1)

Parallel Paradise by Mayapee Chowdhury. When their love affair is put to the test by the homophobia of their family, community, and culture, Bindi and Rimli will need to fight for a chance at love. (978-1-63679-204-0)

Perfectly Matched by Toni Logan. A beautiful Cupid named Hannah, a runaway arrow, and just seventy-two hours to fix a mishap that could be the best mistake she has ever made. (978-1-63679-120-3)

Royal Exposé by Jenny Frame. When they're grouped together for a class assignment, Poppy's enthusiasm for life and love may just save Casey's soul, but will she ever forgive Casey for using her to expose royal secrets? (978-1-63679-165-4)

Slow Burn by Missouri Vaun. A wounded wildland firefighter from California and a struggling artist find solace and love in a small southern town. (978-1-63679-098-5)

The Artist by Sheri Lewis Wohl. Detective Casey Wilson and reclusive artist Tula Crane are drawn together in a web of passion, intrigue, and art that might just hold the key to stopping a killer. (978-1-63679-150-0)

The Inconvenient Heiress by Jane Walsh. An unlikely heiress and a spinster evade the Marriage Mart only to discover true love together. (978-1-63679-173-9)

A Champion for Tinker Creek by D.C. Robeline. Lyle James has rescued his dad's auto repair business, but when city hall condemns his neighborhood, Lyle learns only trusting will save his life and help him find love. (978-1-63679-213-2)

Closed-Door Policy by Erin Zak. Going back to college is never easy, but Caroline Stevens is prepared to work hard and change her life for the better. What she's not prepared for is Dr. Atlanta Morris, her gorgeous new professor. (978-1-63679-181-4)

Homeworld by Gun Brooke. Headed by Captain Holly Crowe, the spaceship Velocity's crew journeys towards their alien ancestors' homeworld, and what they find is completely unexpected—and they're not safe. (978-1-63679-177-7)

Outland by Kristin Keppler & Allisa Bahney. Danielle Clark and Katelyn Turner can't seem to stay away from one another even as the war for the wastelands tests their loyalty to each other and to their people. (978-1-63679-154-8)

Secret Sanctuary by Nance Sparks. US Deputy Marshal Alex Trenton specializes in protecting those awaiting trial, but when danger threatens the woman she's falling for, Alex is in for the fight of her life. (978-1-63679-148-7)

Stranded Hearts by Kris Bryant, Amanda Radley, Emily Smith. In these novellas from award winning authors, fate intervenes on behalf of love when characters are unexpectedly stuck together. With too much time and an irresistible attraction, anything could happen. (978-1-63679-182-1)

The Last Lavender Sister by Melissa Brayden. Aster Lavender sells her gourmet doughnuts and keeps a low profile; she never plans on the town's temporary veterinarian swooping in and making her feel like anything but a wallflower. (978-1-63679-130-2)

The Probability of Love by Dena Blake. As Blair and Rachel keep ending up in the same place despite the odds, can a one-night stand turn into forever? Or will the bet Blair never intended to make ruin their happily ever after? (978-1-63679-188-3)

Worth a Fortune by Sam Ledel. After placing a want ad for a personal secretary, a New York heiress is surprised when the woman who got away is the one interested in the position. (978-1-63679-175-3)